THE VINTAGE
AND THE GLEANING

JEREMY CHAMBERS

MACLEHOSE PRESS
QUERCUS · LONDON

First published in 2010 by The Text Publishing Company, Melbourne
First published in Great Britain in 2011 by

MacLehose Press
an imprint of Quercus
21 Bloomsbury Square
London WC1A 2NS

A CIP catalogue record for this book is available from the British Library

ISBN (HB) 978 0 85705 090 8
ISBN (TPB) 978 0 85705 138 7

10 9 8 7 6 5 4 3 2 1

Designed and typeset in Minion by Libanus Press, Marlborough
Printed and bound in Great Britain by Clays Ltd, St Ives plc

To my father

MONDAY WE drive to Butlers', same as where we were last week.

We're still at Butlers', aren't we? asks Roy.

We go in through town and turn down the highway into the morning sun. We go past Beaumonts', Tylers' and Crews', St Margaret's Cellars and Pulham's cherry trees. Wallace's ute is parked at the end of the rows. Roy pulls in next to it and looks at his watch. He puts on the radio and rolls a cigarette.

I get out and go over to Wallace's ute. Wallace is sitting up back of the tray, putting an edge on a shovel. I get another shovel off the tray. I sit up back with Wallace and he hands me the oilcan.

Win anything on the races? Wallace asks me.

Nope, I say.

I run my finger along the edge of the shovel. More than half the blade's been worn down and the edge isn't straight anymore. It's far from straight. It's crooked all over the place.

Win anything on the lottery? Wallace asks.

Nope, I say.

I knock the dirt off the shovel and put oil along the blade.

You win anything? I ask.

Me? says Wallace. Nah.

I show him the shovel blade.

I know, says Wallace.

Wallace finishes his shovel and sticks it into the ground. He takes another one off the tray and knocks the dirt off it.

You hear about George Alister? Wallace asks me.

No, I say.

Jeez, he says. Hasn't heard about George Alister.

I hawk and spit over the side of the tray and reach back for the water bottle and drink and spit again. Wallace hands me a stone from the toolbox and I start putting an edge on the crooked blade.

Wallace picks at a splinter.

Bloody hell, he says. Hasn't heard about George Alister. Thought someone must have told you.

Nobody told me nothing, I say.

Wallace digs around the pockets of his shorts, muttering to himself. He finds his clasp knife and snaps it open, holding onto the blade and flicking the handle out. He pares the splinter off the shaft and closes the knife with one hand. I finish my shovel and take another one off the tray. I look at the blade. It's as worn and crooked as the first one. They're all worn and crooked. All them vineyard shovels.

Wallace hands me the oilcan.

Dropped dead, he says. Middle of Main Street. Heart attack.

What, I say, George Alister?

Yep, says Wallace. Right in the middle of Main Street. Dead before he hit the ground they reckon.

Jeez, I say. George Alister.

Wallace gets an old piece of torn sandpaper from the toolbox and works it along the handle. He holds it up and looks at it, running his finger along it. Reaching back for the jerry can, he pours turps into the palm of his hand and streaks it over the shaft. It glistens in the pale sunlight.

Thought you would have heard, says Wallace. By now. Monday morning. Happened Saturday. Heart attack. Dead before he hit the ground.

I finish the shovel and stick it in the dirt. I get off the tray to stretch my knees, wandering towards the vines and looking down the finished rows. They are neat along the wire, twisting up bare from the earth and spreading out full and leafy at the top. Some are already hung with bunches of new fruit, small, hard and green. By picking time, when the women come with their secateurs and we only work mornings, the grapes will be fat and purple and heavy on the vines, the flesh sweet inside the tough, bitter skins. Some of the women eat while they pick, sucking out the insides and spitting out the rest, marking their rows with dark spittle and half-chewed skins which grow deep in colour and crisp in the sun.

Normally I like the picking, when there's the company of women, who chat away and gossip while they work and Wallace plays foreman proper but throws me a grin as he empties his bucket into the container, and Roy cheeky so the women laugh. But not this year. I'm not looking forward to it this year, not with lunchtime knockoff and empty afternoons and I wonder what I am going to do with meself.

I look down at the ragged mess of vines along the unfinished rows and I wander back.

Wallace hands me another shovel and the oilcan. I sit back up on the tray and knock the dirt off the shovel, hitting the handle against the side of the tray. It falls in a dry and silty pile, pale on the soil. Dust rises from it like smoke.

Eating an ice-cream, Wallace says. George Alister. Was eating an ice-cream when he carked it. Just come out the milk bar, taken the wrapper off and that's it.

He snaps his fingers.

Gone. Just like that. Still holding onto the bloody ice-cream when he hits the ground. Hits the deck.

Just like that, I say.

Just like that, says Wallace.

He bangs his shovel against the tray. The dirt sticks. He bangs the shovel again, hard. The metal rings. He hits it until the dirt falls off in a clump.

The noise sends the crows up from the vines. The crows go up cawing. They come back down again further along the rows.

And you know George Alister's dog, Wallace says.

Yeah, I say. I know the one.

You know what it did? What it did when George Alister has his heart attack? Has his heart attack and hits the ground?

I shake my head.

Nicked the bloody ice-cream, says Wallace. Goes up, sniffs around, sees George Alister's a goner, takes the ice-cream right out of his hand. Then dog pisses off. Does the bloody bolt. Goes and eats the ice-cream in the bushes behind the post office. And there's George Alister lying there. George Alister lying there dead, dog's nicked off with his bloody ice-cream.

Well, I say, planting my shovel in the dirt. That's dogs for you.

Too right, says Wallace, laughing. That's dogs for you. That's dogs for you all right. Bloody dogs, ay.

We finish the last of the shovels and put them in the ground.

George Alister, I say. He was Roy's mate wasn't he?

Yeah, says Wallace. He was Roy's mate.

Wallace spits on the ground and rubs the spit into the dirt

with his boot.

He was Roy's mate all right, says Wallace. But from what I heard Roy was more interested in the old lady. Nora. Nora Alister. Widow now.

That's right, I say.

Not the old lady anymore, says Wallace. Widow. George Alister's widow.

Something sends the crows up again and they go over us and come round and back into the vines. I look up at the sky.

Fair game now, George Alister's widow, says Wallace. Roy'll probably have a go at her now.

Wallace puts the oilcan and the whetstones back in the toolbox. He opens his knife again and wipes it on his shorts.

For sure Roy'll have a go at her, he says.

Well, I say. That's Roy for you.

Wallace laughs. That's Roy for you all right, he says. That's dogs for you and that's Roy for you.

He pulls himself back along the tray and takes one of his boots off, knocking it against the side of the tray. Soil and stones fall out. Wallace wears thick, filthy socks rolled over the top of the elastic siding. He does one boot and then the other.

Bloody Roy, ay, he says.

I look up at the sky. I look at the sun coming over the hill, squinting. It is coming up bright and yellow, the air fresh, a clear dawn. The old ghost gum in the next paddock catches the light and it catches it high up so that high up the foliage is rimmed with gold and it sways slightly and the leaves move all together, the branches smooth and white with swollen folds like loose skin, swaying, barely swaying, but in the light the movement seems beautiful. There is beauty there.

Wallace goes and pisses in the vines and comes back and looks at his watch and looks over at Roy's ute. He holds up his hand and points to the watch. Roy comes out slamming his door and swearing and whistling to Lucy. Lucy opens her eyes and lifts her head from between her paws. She yawns, looking around, her eyebrows twitching. She jumps to the ground and comes over and sniffs at me and Wallace. Then she goes up and down the vines with her nose to the ground, looking for snakes.

Roy comes up bare-headed, his silver hair thin and sunburnt underneath. His eyes are pale and blue. When they talk about Roy they call them baby-blue. They say it's his baby-blue eyes gets the women. When they talk about Roy that's what they always say. Roy scratches his arm and looks over at the road.

Where's Spit? Roy asks. And bloody flaming Tweedledee and flaming bloody Tweedledum?

Late, says Wallace.

You going to dock them? Roy asks Wallace. I don't mean Spit, he says to me. I mean Heckle and Jeckle. The flaming double act.

If Boss comes first, I'll dock them, says Wallace.

You expecting Boss this early? asks Roy.

No, says Wallace.

Roy goes into the vines and pisses and comes and sits up back of Wallace's ute with us. We wait for the others.

You hear about George Alister? Wallace asks Roy.

Course, says Roy. Everyone's heard about George Alister.

Smithy didn't, says Wallace. Didn't know a thing about it till I told him.

Well, says Roy, he knows now then, doesn't he?

That's right, says Wallace. I told him. Dropped dead. Middle of Main Street. Heart attack.

That's right, says Roy.

Just like that, says Wallace. Gone.

Yep, says Roy.

You heard about his dog then, did you? Wallace asks. George Alister's dog?

Roy nods.

You know what Smithy said when I told him? says Wallace. I told him, George Alister goes down, hits the deck, dog nicks bloody ice-cream. Does the bloody bolt. And you know what Smithy says? He says, that's dogs for you.

True enough, says Roy, leaning over and spitting between his knees.

That's dogs for you, says Wallace, laughing. Bloody dogs.

We sit up back of the ute. Roy leans forward and hawks and spits again. Wallace looks at his watch and swears. He pulls himself down, grunting, and walks over to the road. He stands in the middle of the road looking towards town with his hands on his hips. Lucy comes up and sniffs our boots.

You find anything, girl? Roy asks her. Find any snakes?

Lucy snorts and sits there panting. Roy rubs her side with his boot and she leans into it with her head up, licking the air.

Wallace lumbers back, hunched over with his huge shoulders and arms which seem too heavy for his body. In his shorts and singlet he is most of him bare skin, dark from the sun. He is cleaning his glasses with his terry-towelling hat.

They coming? Roy asks.

Wallace holds his glasses up and looks through them. He breathes on them and polishes them.

Yeah, they're coming, he says. They're bloody walking.

Lucy sits down, still leaning against Roy's boot. Roy leans over and strokes her head and behind her ears. Ay, girl? he says softly. Ay? Lucy half closes her eyes. Roy takes her head in his hands and rubs her jowls, showing teeth and black gums and thick spittle going all over the place. He lets her go. Lucy snorts and goes back into the vines.

Wallace stands there polishing his glasses.

George Alister, he says to Roy. He was a mate of yours, wasn't he?

That's right, says Roy.

Roy gets up and walks around in a circle, stretching his back and neck. He takes one of the shovels and sits back on the tray, looking at the blade. He swears and chucks it overarm and it lands sticking in the ground. He pulls out another one and looks at it.

You going to the funeral? Wallace asks.

I am, says Roy.

When's the funeral?

Wednesday, says Roy.

Morning or afternoon?

Morning.

You taking half-day off then or full day?

Dunno, says Roy.

May as well take full day, says Wallace. What they got after the funeral? A wake? Something like that?

Something like that, says Roy, throwing the shovel.

What, says Wallace, widow's place or down pub?

Down pub, says Roy.

Which pub? asks Wallace.

Imperial, says Roy.

Imperial, says Wallace. That where George Alister drank then, was it? Imperial?

Nah, says Roy. He spits on his fingers and runs them through his hair. He drunk at Crown or Poachers.

Well, what they going to Imperial for? asks Wallace.

Sometimes he drunk at Imperial, says Roy.

Roy pulls another shovel out of the ground and looks over the blade and slides it down next to him.

The boys are coming down the road and we watch them. They are pushing and punching each other, laughing and groaning when they get punched. Their heads are down and their long hair falls over their faces. They are trying to punch each other in the gut. Wallace swears.

Hurry up, he yells.

The boys keep shouldering each other. One of them lands a punch and the other one comes after him, feinting and then punching him hard on the arm. They tussle and lean into one another and then push each other away. They come up grinning.

You're late, says Wallace, holding out his watch. I should dock you.

Yeah, but it's miles away here, says one of the boys.

You knew where we was, says Wallace.

He stands there looking at the boys. They grin. Wallace looks hard at them.

I ought to dock you, he says. Next time I'll dock you.

Wallace stays staring at the boys. The boys grin back at him. He kicks one of them in the foot.

What'd I say Friday? Wallace says.

Dunno, says the boy. Probably some bullshit story.

Wallace holds out the back of his hand and the boy ducks, still grinning, his stringy blond hair falling over his face. The boys don't wear hats. They wear T-shirts and tight, faded jeans.

Boots, says Wallace. I told you I wanted to see you wearing boots today. Both of youse.

Didn't get them, says the boy. He is picking at the skin on his sunburnt arm.

Why not? says Wallace. I told you meself, didn't I? I told you Friday. Last thing. Friday knockoff.

Couldn't afford them, says the boy. He peels a long piece of skin off his arm and looks at it.

Whadd'ya mean you couldn't afford them? says Wallace, pushing his glasses against his face. What about your pay? I gave you pay-packet meself. Thursday.

The boy is looking at the piece of skin, holding it up to the sun. It glows.

Spent it, he says.

What? says Wallace. All of it?

Pretty much, says the boy. He tosses the skin and it flutters to the ground. He takes a shovel and stands both feet on it, twisting it into the dirt.

Wallace is standing there hunched over, his scarred and callused hands held palms up. He watches the boy. Wallace's hat is pulled down tight, the brim touching his big, thick glasses, his oversized jaw jutting out. Wallace's jaw is too big for any man and with his hat on Wallace's face is nothing but glasses and jaw.

What on? says Wallace. What you spend it on? Whole bloody pay.

Dunno, says the boy, trying to balance on the shovel as he churns it into the soil. Booze. Tea. Had tea from the shops Friday night. Chicken and chips. Fried pineapple. Coke.

Well, says Wallace. Booze. Tea. What else you spend it on?

Mostly booze, says the boy.

He falls off the shovel.

Wallace looks at his watch and swears, peering over at the road. He watches the boy, looking at his sneakers. The boy is back on the shovel and he is trying to jump it out of the ground.

Well, don't you come crying to me, says Wallace. Don't come crying to me when you cut your toes off.

I'm not gunna, says the boy, jerking about on the shovel.

That's what you say now, says Wallace.

He looks at his watch again.

Where's Spit? he says to me.

Don't ask me, I say.

You reckon he's going to show?

I shrug.

I'd say it's a no-show, Wallace, Roy says.

Wallace swears. The boy comes off the shovel again. He pulls it out of the ground and grips the handle like a cricket bat and swings it at a dry clod. He makes a whooshing sound as he swings. The clod explodes into a cloud of dust which thins and hangs and is gone.

Well, says Wallace, looks like Spit's not showing then.

Wallace goes over to the ute, wiping his hands on his shorts. He puts his mattock over one shoulder and a shovel over the other.

Righteo, says Wallace and he goes into the vines.

We take our shovels and we follow him.

Somewhere in the distance the sound of a motorbike starting. The engine idles and then the bike goes across paddocks and away. We work our rows, knocking the shoots off the vines, going vine to vine and row to row. The sun has come up behind the trees on the hill and they are fiercely gilded. Light slides along the long threads of spiders' webs strung across the rows and it comes dappled through the vines and onto the soil and there is the shadow of vines on the ground, twisted and quivering, leaves fluttering in the breeze, and where it hits the earth the earth is red.

In the paddock behind us, the wheat is bare and bleached under the sky and it tosses and whispers. Lucy comes past me, nose to the ground and she stops to sniff at my boots and at the fallen leaves and shoots and is off down the row. And there is nothing but the sound of shovels scraping against the vines, the metal ringing on the wood, the rustle of falling foliage. And the caws of the crows, the smell of soil. And as we work I can feel the sun coming up hot on my back and I start working faster, vine to vine and row to row.

Wallace finishes a vine and stands there, mopping his brow with his hat. He leans on his shovel and watches the boy over the rows.

You must've been drinking like a fish, he says to the boy.

What? says the boy.

You must've been drinking like a fish, says Wallace. Spend your whole pay. Must've been drinking all weekend.

Nah, says the boy. Just Saturday. Saturday night.

Where were you drinking? asks Roy.

Wasn't at the pub, says the boy. Went down to the river. Got take-away.

Everyone's stopped working now except me. They're all leaning on their shovels, talking over the rows. The other boy is grinning. I keep knocking off shoots.

Well, what you buy then? asks Wallace. What you spend your whole pay on? Whole bloody lot?

Dunno, says the boy. Slab, lemonade, bottle of Blue Curacao.

Jesus, says Wallace. That's top-shelf isn't it, Roy?

It's top-shelf all right, says Roy.

What'd you want to go drinking that stuff for? asks Wallace. What's the point of wasting your money on that? Whole pay-packet?

Wasn't for me, says the boy. Was for my girlfriend. She won't drink anything else.

I hope you got a root out of it, says Roy, leaning forward on his shovel.

The boy doesn't say anything. He takes hold of a tendril and starts twisting it around his finger.

He did, the dirty devil, says Roy.

The boy is smirking. He keeps twisting the shoot around his finger. The other boy starts working again. Roy and Wallace watch the first boy, leaning on their shovels.

What, says Wallace, she drink the whole bottle? She drink the lot?

Nah, says the boy.

I was going to say, says Wallace. She'd be sick.

She was sick, says the boy.

I hope you got a root out of it first, says Roy.

Wallace shakes his head. He pulls his shovel out of the ground and turns around muttering, going back to his vine. Roy spits and whistles to Lucy. The boy pulls at the shoot, pulling hard until it comes off, tearing it green near the base. He throws it away and looks at his hand. The other boy keeps working, chopping hard, puffing and sweating and red in the face. Wallace finishes his vine and turns back to look at the boy, letting his shovel fall against the wires.

So where's the rest of it then? he asks the boy. This Blue bloody Curacao.

I drunk it, says the boy. I was sick too.

Wallace takes his hat and glasses off and polishes his glasses with his hat and stands there swearing. Roy lifts up his legs to slap the ants around his ankles. He scratches his legs and whistles to Lucy and she comes down the row and he bends down and strokes her all over. Wallace looks at the other boy.

And what's your story, he asks him. How come you got no boots?

Bought a model aeroplane, says the other boy, puffing away.

Wallace stands and swears. His shoulders hang out front of him, making him stoop forward, his arms low and his neck bent out and up like a tortoise, jagged bile-coloured teeth a mess in a mouth that doesn't know which way it's turned. When I look at Wallace, with those big arms and shoulders and that jaw, his squat body and long legs thinner than mine, he looks like someone's made him up from bits and pieces which don't fit right. He puts his hat and glasses on and goes back to work, still swearing.

Roy's still leaning on his shovel.

You hear that, Smithy? he calls over to me. One of them spends his pay getting a root and the other one buys a model aeroplane.

Yeah, I heard, I say, knocking off a shoot.

Can't root a model aeroplane, says Roy.

I just keep working, keep knocking off shoots, working fast, moving up the row. I keep moving up the row until I can't hear them no more.

Boss comes down after smoko. He takes a deep breath and looks up at the sky and then he looks at us.

Well, he says, and how are you all going here?

Fine, says Wallace, hacking away at a vine.

Well, says Boss. That's good. Good to hear.

We are working hard with our heads down, pretending not to listen to Boss and Wallace. Boss crosses his arms and nods over at the boys.

And how are these two coming along? he asks.

Fine, says Wallace, pushing back a heavy vine. Yeah, not too bad.

He looks over at the boys.

All right, he says.

Wallace finishes his vine. He pulls a leaf off and hands it to Boss.

14

Boss looks at the leaf.

Well, he says, we'll have to spray then, won't we?

Looks like it, says Wallace.

Yeah, says Boss. Well then. He looks at the leaf some more.

What do you think? he asks Wallace.

I say spray, says Wallace.

Certainly looks that way, doesn't it, says Boss.

Wallace keeps working and we all keep working and there is the sound of shovels going at it hard and fast. Boss stands there with his arms folded over his gut. He wears an old jumper full of holes and stained with wine. He smells of wine, of the cellar. He wears army shorts and he wears the same jumper and the same shorts all year round. He picks a few shoots off a vine.

We seem to be one short today, he says.

That's right, says Wallace. Spit.

Yeah, Spit's not here is he, says Boss. He picks off a few more shoots. He folds his arms back over his gut and leans back on his heels. Lucy comes and sniffs around him. Boss squats down and scratches her behind the ears.

And what's Spit doing with himself today then? he asks, stroking Lucy's flank.

Nobody says anything. We keep our heads down, working.

Probably crook, says Roy, not looking up from his vine.

Crook is he? says Boss. Well. That's no good, is it? He gives Lucy a slap on the backside and she trots away. Boss stands up and looks at the sky.

Spit's crook then is he, Smithy?

Could be, I say.

Hard to tell at this point, is it? says Boss, looking at me. Hard to say?

He is looking at me smiling. Smiling and squinting. He shades his eyes with his hand.

What is it? he asks. One of those one-day things?

I keep working on my vine, picking off tendrils with my fingers.

I wouldn't know, I say.

No, says Boss, pulling the top of a vine towards him and examining it. No, well you never can tell, can you?

He picks another leaf off the vine and holds it in both hands. He pulls the vine back again, pushing it up with one hand and looking at the underside. He lets it drop and looks back at the leaf and turns it around and he looks up at the sky and looks at the leaf again and tosses it onto the ground. Lucy comes over and sniffs at it. Boss rubs her side with his boot.

Well, I'm sorry to hear about Spit, he says. That's no good, is it? No good at all. No good being crook, he says. Poor Spit. Poor old Spit.

He has another look at the leaves and he leans over and strokes Lucy's nose.

I think we'll spray, Wallace, he says.

Righteo, says Wallace.

Best to spray, says Boss.

He pats Lucy on the head and he stands up and stretches and he looks at the vines and looks at the sky and he turns around and goes.

We watch Boss go. We watch his ute leave and we watch it all the way down the road.

Roy stops working and leans on his shovel.

Spit was down Imperial Saturday night, wasn't he? he says. I'm sure I saw Spit down Imperial Saturday night.

He yawns.

You weren't down Imperial Saturday night, were you, Wallace? he asks.

Nope, says Wallace.

Well, I'm pretty sure Spit was there, says Roy. I'm pretty sure I talked to him.

He pulls his shovel out of the ground.

I think he said he was going fishing, says Roy.

Boss comes to spray lunchtime. I'm sitting with Roy in his ute and Wallace's got the boys in his. The windows are wound up and I am drinking sarsaparilla. Roy is smoking and the smoke rises from his cigarette and fills the cabin.

Boss brings in the tractor, spluttering and heaving with the sprayer behind, bouncing over the uneven earth. It has five pipes at the end of its chassis and they are bent. Boss is wearing an old oilskin with the collar turned up and buttoned to his nose. His hat is pulled down over his forehead. He stops the tractor next to Wallace's ute and undoes the top of the oilskin and yells something to Wallace. Wallace winds down his window and yells back. They are yelling over the growl and the thud of the tractor engine. The diesel exhaust hazes upwards. Boss yells again. Wallace waves and winds the window back up.

Boss does up his oilskin again and pulls at his hat. He wheels the tractor into the front row and turns on the sprayer. The spray comes out of the pipes in a strong fine jet and the tractor kicks up dust, and a cloud of dust and spray blooms behind the tractor like a slow explosion. Roy is studying the form guide.

I watch the tractor through the dirty cloud as it ends the first row. The sprayer goes off and the pipes drip and the tractor makes a tight circle and comes down the next row towards us. It ends the row and the sprayer turns off. Boss takes the tractor round and the cloud billows behind and into us and when it hits it is all dust and spray through the windows and you can't see a thing outside. You can't see anything at all.

After knockoff, Roy drives us into town and parks outside Poachers. Men are standing on the footpath underneath the pub balcony, smoking and spitting in the shade. Kids ride up and down Main Street on bikes, dinking their friends and pulling wheelies. Some of them are still in their school uniforms and others wear jeans and T-shirts. They gather in groups outside the bank and the post office, sitting on the steps and sprawled across the footpath, eating chips out of butcher's paper. Dogs lie under parked cars, tongues hanging out.

Lucy jumps down onto the road and Roy grabs her and chains her to a pole. He gets her bowl from the back of the ute and sets it beside her. He fills it and she drinks.

I'm off, I say.

Still sulking are you? Roy says.

I'm not sulking, I say.

Yes you are, says Roy.

A cat prowls about under one of the cars, watching the dogs and sniffing the ground. It darts across the street and down a concrete lane mottled with the rainbow tint of oil stains. The cat is sleek and black, its bones jutting from under its coat, looking hard as a carved thing.

You been sulking ever since you been to the doctor's, says Roy.

I look for the cat, but it is gone.

I'm not sulking, I say. I'm just not drinking. Sulking's got nothing to do with it.

Roy takes Lucy's bowl and throws the rest of the water out onto the road. He flings it back into the tray and takes out his tobacco pouch and papers and rolls a cigarette, lighting it with a match. He shakes out the match and flicks it away.

It's not just about the drink, he says. It's about being sociable. I don't see why you can't come in while I have a drink. I'm your mate, aren't I?

He drags on the cigarette and lets the smoke float from the side of his mouth. One of the men on the footpath calls out to him and Roy points his thumb at the pub. The man nods.

Yeah, I say. Yeah, I spose so.

We go into Poachers.

The pub is cool and dark and hung with mounted Murray cods, fat and pink and silver on their undersides. Each board has an engraving saying when the fish was caught and who caught it. Liz is tending the bar.

Roy flicks his cigarette butt into the trough which runs the length of the bar. Embers scatter and fade. The trough is piled high with ash and cigarette butts and rubbish, all of it sodden with spilt beer. Roy takes off his hat, smoothing down his hair. He puts the hat on the counter and sits on a barstool, looking at his bare legs. He scratches his legs and winks at Liz.

How are you Roy? Liz asks, stacking pots. Keeping out of trouble?

I'm doing my very best, Liz, says Roy. Yourself?

Aw, yeah, she says. She sounds tired. The pots knock against each other as she stacks them. She picks up another crate. Liz is big and dressed in black.

Down the end of the bar, old Ted Matthews is watching the television, a glass sitting on the bar towel next to him.

Any lady wrastlers today, Ted? Roy asks him.

Ted Matthews doesn't say anything. His eyes stay fixed on the television screen.

Liz is straining to hold a crate with one hand, pressing it against her ribs. It is full of trembling pots and the sound of glass on glass.

Ted missed out on the lady wrestlers today, she says. I had the greyhounds on.

That's a shame, says Roy. Greyhounds aren't lady wrastlers, are they, Ted?

Ted Matthews doesn't say a word. He just keeps staring up at the television. It's the harness racing now, afternoon races. On the screen a buggy overturns. Ted Matthews sits there, not moving one bit.

I pull up a barstool and sit next to Roy.

Come and work your charms on Smithy here, Liz, Roy says.

What's that, Roy? Liz says, giving him a funny look.

Cheer him up, says Roy. He's sulking. He's sulking because he's off the piss. Off the grog. Doctor's orders.

Liz finishes stacking the pots and takes the empty crates outside. She comes back brushing off her hands and holds up a pot, looking at Roy. Roy nods and she fills it from the tap.

Off the grog? she says. Why's that, Smithy?

Because, I say. Because I've buggered up me insides. Buggered them with the drink.

Liz puts Roy's beer down on the bar towel. Roy leans back, feeling in his pockets for coins. He piles them on the bar towel and raps the club soda sign on the tap, pointing at me. Liz pours me a glass of lemon squash and begins sorting through the coins.

He given you something for it? Liz asks me. The doctor?

Yeah, I say. Pills. Pills they make from pigs.

Roy skols his beer and hands the pot back to Liz.

How they make pills out of pigs? he asks me. What good's that going to do you?

Don't ask me, I say. That's just what he tells me. Because pigs got something I don't have. I don't have it no more on account I've buggered up me insides. With the drink. The grog.

Liz hands Roy his pot back full and keeps sorting through the money on the counter. Roy blows the froth off the top.

Well, can you drink after that then? he asks. Once you take these pills?

Roy's pot is beaded with liquid and the froth runs down the sides. He puts the beer down and wipes his hand on the bar towel.

Pills aren't for the drink, I say. They're for the digestion. For my stomach. Because I've stuffed that too. With the drink. I can't keep anything down.

Liz is counting coins.

You not eating, Smithy? she says. Off your tucker? She opens the cash register and slides the coins in, one at a time.

Roy leans back again and squirms to pull his tobacco out of his pocket. He slaps the pouch down on the counter.

I can't keep a thing down, I say. I take one bite and I feel sick. I can't even look at the stuff without feeling sick.

Liz closes the register and it rings.

That's no good, Smithy, she says. You should be taking better care of yourself.

Roy holds up his empty pot to her, dripping with suds. Liz puts it upside down on the pile of empties and gets him a clean one. Roy takes his papers and peels one off, putting it between his lips. He opens the pouch and takes out a pinch of tobacco.

Well I am looking after meself, I say. That's why I'm off the drink. I haven't touched the stuff. Not once.

Roy rolls the cigarette and puts it in his mouth. He gestures to Liz and she gets a lighter from under the counter. She lights the cigarette for him and hands him his beer, sorting through the coins on the counter again. Roy turns to me, holding his pot against his knee.

But one drink's not going to do you any harm, surely, he says. Just one glass.

I shake my head.

Doctor said if I started drinking again I'd end up in hospital, I say. I'm not going to hospital.

Roy blows smoke into the air. He takes a long drink from his pot and puts it back on the counter. He rests his arm on his leg, knocking ash between his knees.

Hospital wouldn't be so bad, says Roy.

He drags on his cigarette and sits sipping his beer, flicking ash into the trough, looking at me with his pale eyes, his baby-blue eyes.

Hospital, he says. It's just lying there, isn't it? Everything brought to you. Good-looking nurses caring for you.

He leans his elbow on the counter, turning back towards the bar.

Not as good-looking as you though Liz, he says.

Yeah, thanks Roy, says Liz.

I look at Ted Matthews sitting down the end of the bar. He still hasn't moved, not one inch, just sits there staring up at that television. He's got a face like stone, Ted Matthews does.

No, I say. I'm not going to hospital. You haven't got nothing left once you're in hospital. All you've got is just yourself and your own thoughts. No, I say, I'm not going to hospital. I'd rather be out on the vines.

I walk home along the disused railway track, past the abandoned wheat silos. It's all crows now on the silos. The tops are black with them. There must be hundreds of crows on those old silos.

YOU'D BE surprised, the dreams I've been having. I've been dreaming of people I haven't seen in years, people I haven't even thought about since I last saw the back of them, people I hardly even knew. Men I worked with, one season, one station even. Girls I used to know, met in towns between jobs, girls I saw one year to the next and then never saw again. Girls I only ever been with once, met outside town hall dances, girls whose faces I only ever saw in the flame of a struck match, the light from a passing car. They're coming up, coming back, clear as day now, in my dreams, clear as though I saw them yesterday, as though they were still young as they were then, as though I were still young, still the young man I was.

I've even been dreaming of the sisters and the orphanage kids, the mission school kids, little kids I can't remember the names of anymore, long faded in my memory to ragged short pants and shrill voices, dirty faces. The piccanins we called niggers and coons and left beat up and crying behind the wilgas and the desert oaks. I see them too, in my dreams.

But most of all I dream of Florrie. And I have this dream and I have the same dream every night, always the same, almost always the same. And I dream it is Main Street, night-time, but the street is all lit up, not just street lights, but lit everywhere, white like under

23

fluorescent tubes, strong, savage, blinding light, and the streets and pubs lit the same, because in my dream the pubs have no front to them and no end and you don't know street from pub, the two flowing onto each other, into each other, and there is nothing but street and pub and light everywhere for as far as you go and you keep going through both. And there are no shadows cast by the light and all around in the streets and in the pubs there are men, the whole place teeming with men, men everywhere, more men than the town has ever seen, and they are massed together and you don't know where you are, only shoulder to shoulder with the men, pressed up against them, suffocated by the men. And the men are drinking and their noise is all around, a roar, all talking and yelling and arguing and shouting, smoking, spitting, laughing and fighting, whistling and cheering and pushing, their faces coming out of the brilliant night, red with drink, charged with drink, eyes glazed and bulging, wet-lipped, grimacing, gawping, faces warped and monstrous, deformed with the drink and strange, barely the faces of men anymore, dead drunk and hard, all of them hard, all of them the faces of working men, and they are everywhere and their noise is everywhere and there are no places of darkness or quiet or solitude, only the thundering, jostling crowd, and I can do nothing but keep on moving through it all, through the riot of men and the pubs big as open spaces and Main Street lit brighter than day and wide as a stockyard.

And Florrie is there.

Florrie is there and she is walking through the crowd of men with her back to me, walking away from me. And I am following her, calling to her through the men and their noise, through all the shoving drunkenness, but she keeps walking, never stopping, never turning around and she is always moving, always moving away, going further and further ahead of me until I lose her somewhere in that lit-up roaring night.

And in those dreams she is young. She is as young as when I first met her.

And once, one night, one dream, I dreamt I finally caught up to her, finally talked to her. And she looked back at me, smiling, but she was still walking, still walking away from me. And I was trying to keep up with her, speaking to her, speaking desperately as she went. I've got to talk to you, Florrie, I said. I've been dreaming about you, Florrie. I dream about you every night. I've got to talk to you. I've got something to say to you. But she just smiled, glancing back, the way women do. And she never said a thing.

And in that dream I lost her like I always lose her, among drinking men and bars that go on forever.

When I woke from that dream I still wanted to talk to her, still had something to say to her. Even when I was awake enough to remember that she wasn't there anymore, wasn't there to say anything to, even then I still had something to tell her. And I knew what it was as well. In the dream and in real life it was the same. I wanted to say I was sorry. I wanted to say I was sorry for the life I gave her.

TUESDAY, SPIT doesn't show.

I hope it's nothing serious, says Boss.

Boss is standing looking at a muscatel vine. One of the boys has put his shovel through it. We are all standing looking at the vine.

Boss squats down to look at the break. He pushes the upper part of the trunk and it swings free on the wires.

Well you certainly did a proper job of it, Boss says to the boy.

The boy is standing there puffing and red in the face. He doesn't say anything. He looks like he is going to cry.

Boss stands up, his hands against his back.

Has he seen the doctor yet? he asks me.

What's that? I say.

Spit, he says. Has he been to the doctor's.

I wouldn't know, I say.

Boss squats down again and rubs his thumb against the inner wood. He picks at the rough and scabby bark around it.

I mean, I know accidents are going to happen, he says to the boy. But try and be careful with the old vines.

He looks up at the boy, smiling. He smiles but not in his eyes. His eyes are not smiling.

The boy looks down at the ground. He looks like he's going to cry any second now.

26

Boss stands up.

They knew this was one of the old rows, didn't they? he asks Wallace. You told them, didn't you?

Yeah, I told them, says Wallace.

That vine's older than you boy, he says. That vine's older than any of us.

The boy keeps looking at the ground, his jaw clenched.

Boss is still looking down at the vine. He looks at me and he looks at me for a while without saying anything, his eyes looking out pale from his face like leather, dark and tough and creased like leather, his eyes looking right through me, his mind somewhere else.

He really should see a doctor, he says to me. If he's still feeling crook. You can never be too careful.

True, I say.

Well, you tell him I said that, says Boss, smiling. Tell him he should take himself down to the doctor's. Tell him that's what I said.

He smiles, showing his gums and his gaps and his gold teeth.

For his own good, he says.

I take my shovel out of the dirt and stick it back in. I lean on the shovel.

I'll tell him, I say.

Boss goes to the next vine along and starts digging about the base with his fingers.

He stands up, grunting.

Anything? asks Wallace.

No, says Boss.

He walks around to the vine on the other side and digs about. He stands up, flicking the dirt from his fingers and goes back to the broken vine, looking at it.

Lucy comes past with her nose to the ground. She stops and sits with us for a bit, panting and snorting, and then she's off again.

Who planted them? Wallace asks. Your grandfather?

Probably, says Boss. Him or his father.

You hear that? Wallace says to the boy. His great-grandfather planted that vine. His great-grandfather planted it, you put your shovel through it. You've got to think. You got a brain, don't you?

The boy looks at Wallace with his cheeks blowing out and his eyes glittering.

What do you want me to do? Wallace asks Boss. Tie it up?

Boss keeps looking down at the vine.

Yeah, he says. Yeah, well that's all we can really do with it at this stage.

He squats down again to look at the break, running his finger along it.

Wallace goes off to the ute to get twine.

Boss stands looking at the broken vine. He pushes it with his boot and it swings on the wire.

Just try and be careful with the old vines, he says.

After knockoff I go down Poachers with Roy and then set off home.

Broken glass glitters on the railway track, scattered across the stones and sleepers, catching the light as I walk. Along the sides, the thick and spongy mass of winter clover has thinned. It is frayed and spindly now, yellowing, delicate and dying. The ditch of quartz-flecked clay is festooned with debris. Grease-mottled paper bags, cardboard takeaway boxes, cans and beer bottles, a brassiere. Plastic bags fill and rise and hover, ghostlike in the breeze. Dog turds turned to chalk. The embankment rises in thick swathes of long grass, meeting hardwood fences, cracked and worn, scrawled with profanities, roofs looming behind them, patches of lichen turned to

28

dust on the terracotta tiles. Here and there sprays of colour, the jacaranda in blossom. I pass a sunk and rotten fence. Inside the yard a gutted car body sits choked with onion weeds, rusted engine parts scattered around it. I smell the onion smell. There are kids down the line.

They are standing huddled together in the grass at the foot of the embankment, their backs to me. A collie is pacing back and forth behind them, growling and barking and whimpering. The kids push the dog away with their feet. They are looking down at something.

When I come up, one of the kids, a girl, turns around.

We caught a rabbit, she says to me. We caught a rabbit.

Some of the other kids turn to look at me and then turn back. The girl watches me, looking up at my face. She is breathless and flushed, excited.

In the middle of the group of kids, a boy is down on his knees. He is holding onto a small grey rabbit with both hands.

I just grabbed it, he says. I saw it sitting there and I just grabbed it.

The dog is frantic, trying to break through the circle of kids, yelping and growling. They keep pushing it away. It goes from one side to the other, sniffing and pawing the ground, pushing its head against their legs.

I look at the rabbit. It is shivering and its eyes are popping. It is breathing fast, its chest pumping in and out. It is only a little rabbit and it is scared half to death.

Best put it out of its misery, I say.

I take the rabbit by the hind legs and smash its head against a rail. The dog comes up sniffing and begins to lick the blood and brains off the metal and the stones and the sleepers.

I see the girl watching with a frozen smile and she looks up at me and the smile breaks and tears well and flow. She wipes her face with the backs of her hands, trying to stop, but the tears keep coming, her face dirty where she has wiped it. She lets out a sob and the sob becomes a wail. Then she is running away from us bawling, running through the long grass and along the ditch, her dress billowing as she runs. She slips over in the ditch and gets up again and keeps on running. She keeps running and slipping and crying.

I've upset her, I say, watching her go.

It's all right, says the boy who caught the rabbit. She's just my sister. She cries about everything.

I didn't mean to upset her, I say.

She's just my sister, says the boy. She's always crying.

Blood is dripping from the ruined head of the rabbit and the dog comes over, sniffing and licking the blood on the ground. It sits down and looks up at the rabbit in my hand, pawing the grass and growling from its throat, trying to catch the drops of blood with its tongue, licking them out of the air as they fall. Blood drips onto the dog's nose and face and into its eyes. It blinks and shakes its head and sniffs around for the blood.

Get out of it, I say, kicking the dog away. The dog skitters backwards and then creeps towards us whining, watching the blood splatter.

I take my knife from my belt and show the boys how to skin a rabbit.

See how easy it comes off, I say, rolling away the pelt.

I gut it and throw the pelt and the offal into the long grass. The dog goes after them.

When I hand the carcass to the boy he steps away from it.

Go on, I say.

He takes it with one hand and holds it out at arm's length,

looking at it like he doesn't know what to do with it.

You take that home to your mum, I say. She can cook it up for your tea.

The boy gives the carcass a funny sort of look.

You mean eat it? he says.

What else are you going to do with it? I say. That's fresh meat. Better than anything you'll get at the butcher's. Just take it home to your mum. Give it to your mum.

When I leave, the boy is still holding the carcass at arm's length. Looking at it funny. Looking like he doesn't know what to do with it.

WEDNESDAY SPIT doesn't show.

It is the day of George Alister's funeral. Me and Wallace and the boys stand in our rows, watching the distant line of slow-moving cars going through the outskirts of town. They turn onto the highway and head towards the cemetery, taking George Alister's body to put it in the ground.

Once and for all, says Wallace. Once and for all.

Far off the cars shimmer in the heat, the space of vision like liquid. There is the flash of chrome and glass, quick and gone and flashing again, the bursts of light moving along the motorcade as the motorcade moves.

Can you see Roy's car? Wallace asks the boys.

Wallace has his glasses up on his forehead and he is squinting into the distance. His glasses keep slipping down onto his nose and he keeps pushing them back up again. Wallace's glasses are as thick as the bottom of a bottle and behind them his eyes are huge and seem a long way off. Without his glasses, Wallace looks like a different man.

Which car? asks the boy. The flash car or the ute?

Flash car of course, says Wallace. You don't take a ute to a funeral.

The boys keep looking, shading their eyes. Wallace's glasses fall onto his nose and he pushes them back up and they come down again, falling right off and Wallace tries to catch them, fumbling the catch and catching them again as they spin in the air. Wallace's glasses have been broke more times than I can remember.

Wallace sees me watching him and grins, holding up his glasses. He puts them in the pocket of his shorts. Without his glasses Wallace looks like he's younger or smaller or something. Without his glasses he could be a different man altogether.

Can't see it, says the boy.

It'll come, says Wallace.

We all of us look into the distance, through the rippling heat and the cars swimming in petrol fumes, distorting them to the eye, and they seem as though molten. The bright vaporous haze thrashes about like a live thing. We keep looking into the distance until all the cars have gone.

Maybe he didn't go, says the boy. Took a sickie.

Wallace is still looking out at the empty highway.

Course he went, he says. You don't take a sickie from a funeral. Funeral is a sickie.

Nah, Wallace says, pulling his shovel out of the dirt. He's there all right. Probably riding with someone else. He's probably riding with the widow. Up front with the widow. Probably comforting her. Being her shoulder to cry on.

Wallace leers at me, the skin around his naked eyes soft and crinkled.

In her hour of need.

We go back to work. Wallace knocks off a shoot and then remembers his glasses, taking them out of his pocket and putting them back on. He picks up his shovel and drops it again, turning to look at the boys.

33

Who ever heard of taking a ute to a funeral? says Wallace.

Boss comes straight up and asks if Roy is crook too.

Nah, says Wallace, hacking at a vine. Gone to a funeral.

Boss stands shading his eyes with his hand.

Well what about Spit? he asks. He still crook or has he gone to a funeral as well?

Spit's crook, says Wallace, Roy's gone to a funeral. He slashes hard at the vine as he talks. Mourning, he says. Roy's mourning. Spit's off crook and Roy's off mourning.

Wallace stops working to mop his brow with his hat. He takes off his glasses and spits on them, wiping them on his singlet and holding them up to the light. Boss stands there watching him.

Well, righteo, says Boss. Spit's crook, Roy's at a funeral, nothing we can do about that.

Nope, says Wallace, studying his glasses.

I mean, we're a bit short-handed today, says Boss. But if Spit's crook and Roy's at a funeral, then that's just the way it is.

Roy'll be back tomorrow, says Wallace. Might be back this afternoon. Depends how long all this mourning goes on for.

All right then, says Boss. Fair enough.

He walks off with his hands in his pockets. Then he turns around and comes back.

So I take it someone's died then, he says.

Wallace is polishing his glasses with his hat.

I mean, if Roy's gone to a funeral I assume someone's died, says Boss. I mean is that a reasonable enough assumption to make? Seems reasonable to me.

Now he is smiling that smile of his.

Wallace finishes polishing his glasses and puts them back on.

George Alister, he says.

He pulls his shovel out of the dirt.

George Alister, says Boss. George Alister, ay? He toes the dirt with his boot, looking down at the ground.

Wallace starts working again.

So George Alister's dead, says Boss.

That's right, says Wallace, knocking off shoots.

Does anyone know how it happened? asks Boss, looking up and squinting.

Something like a heart attack or something, says Wallace. Something like that.

Wallace moves around the vine, chopping at it with his shovel, pushing the foliage back with his elbow and shoulder as he works.

You knew him did you? Wallace asks Boss. George Alister.

Yeah I used to, says Boss. I was at school with him.

I thought you went to school in the city, says Wallace. City school.

Wallace is working hard, sweating and red in the face. He is trying to make up for Spit and Roy.

Before that, says Boss. When we were just little tackers. Up in the old country school. The little one-room school.

You was mates was you? Wallace asks, wiping his brow with his arm.

Oh, I don't know about that, says Boss, folding his arms and looking up at the sky. We used to knock around a bit. Don't know you would have called us mates though.

Wallace finishes the vine and inspects it, picking off small shoots with his fingers.

Well, he's dead now, he says.

After knockoff me and Wallace go down to The Imperial to join

George Alister's wake. Wallace leans over the bar to talk to Les.

Where's all the mourners? he asks Les. I thought they were supposed to be mourning here.

Les is sitting on his stool. He belches and blows out his cheeks. He does not move from the stool.

They were here, says Les. He is looking at the counter, waiting for Wallace to put money down.

Don't tell me they've gone already, says Wallace. How can they have gone already? George Alister dead, where's all the mourning?

They were here, says Les, but now they've gone.

He nods his head towards the counter.

Wallace pulls some coins out of his pocket, grumbling. He slaps them down on the bar towel. Les looks at the coins and slides off his stool with a grunt. He pours Wallace a pot and keeps his hand on the lever, looking over at me.

On the wagon, Les, I say.

Les snorts and shakes his head. He drags himself back up onto his stool and the stool creaks. Les sits on that stool all day long. He's a fat little man with a fat little gut and a puffed-up face and he sits there belching and when he belches his cheeks blow out. Everyone says Les looks like a toad up on that stool of his.

Wallace drains his beer and leaves the pot on the counter. He comes back to the table and sits down.

Bloody mourners bloody gone home, he says to me. Not very sentimental is it? Not much chop George Alister's mates.

You want to go into the ladies' lounge, Smithy? Les calls over to me. I'll get my wife to make you a nice cup of tea. We've got Devonshire too, if that takes your fancy. Does a nice scone, my wife.

Piss off Les, I say.

Les looks at someone down the bar, grinning. The man says something and Les laughs.

Wallace looks at his watch and shows it to me.

Gone home already, he says shaking his head. What happened to paying your respects?

He stands up and goes into the lounge.

Hey Les, he says coming out, was the widow here?

What widow might that be Wallace? Les asks. He throws a grin at the man down the bar.

Wallace stands there pushing his glasses against his face.

George Alister's widow, he says. Nora. Nora Alister.

I believe she was, says Les.

Wallace comes back to the table swearing.

What bloody widow he think I was talking about? he says to me. Bloody George Alister's bloody mourners, who else's widow he think I was talking about?

He's just having you on, Wallace, I say.

Wallace swears and turns in his chair.

Well, how about Roy Thompson then? he yells over to Les. He here?

Roy Thompson? says Les. Was Roy Thompson here? he asks down the bar. He shifts on his stool, listening, and turns to Wallace and nods.

Wallace winks at me.

You see him go, Les? he asks.

Les belches, shaking his head.

Wallace looks at me again.

What about the widow? he asks Les. You see her go?

I wasn't keeping a book on it, Wallace, Les says.

Wallace turns back in his chair and leans over the table.

Roy's gone, widow's gone, he says quietly.

He gives me a look.

The man down the bar says something to Les and Les grins.

Hey Smithy, he shouts. How about an apple juice? We can water it down if it's too strong for you.

Piss off Les, I say.

Les is laughing. He is a fat little man with a fat little gut and he sits on that stool all day long. Even when Les is laughing he looks like a toad.

Spit's car isn't at his house and his boots aren't on the mat. Belle answers the door, holding the baby in one arm. She is red in the face and her eyes are bulging and staring. She wipes her hair back with her spare hand. She looks like she's been screaming all day long.

So where the bloody hell's Spit? she asks.

I was going to ask you the same question, Belle, I say.

I follow her into the house.

In the living room the television blasts away and the older boy is sitting in his highchair. He is eating chocolate muck out of a plastic container.

Say hello to your grandpa, Belle says to him.

The boy just looks at me and then starts banging his spoon against the container, smiling and then laughing. His face and bib and all of him is covered in chocolate.

The carpet is stained and scattered with infants' things. Blankets, a baby bouncer, dummies and chewing toys. The room smells of milk and talcum powder, dirty nappies.

Belle puts the baby down on one of the blankets.

There's soft drink in the fridge, she says.

I go into the kitchen and pour myself a glass of lemonade and drink it standing at the sink. Out the window the sun falls across the fence at an angle, making a line with the shade below. The older boy's plastic tricycle is sitting overturned on the grass and the grass is long. Faint swirls of cloud move across the sky. I put the bottle back in the fridge and rinse my glass, placing it upside down on the dish rack.

Back in the living room Belle is trying to get the baby to drink from a bottle, talking to it in baby talk. The older one is still banging his spoon on the highchair, squealing nonsense.

Roy Thompson reckons he's gone fishing, I say.

Belle snorts, cooing to the baby.

Trust Roy Thompson to know, she says.

The baby is laughing and kicking its plump and powdered legs, pushing them together like a frog in water. It swings the bottle in one hand and the bottle rolls across the floor.

Well, he'll be back soon enough, I say.

Belle snorts again.

He'll be back all right, she says. I know he'll be back. That's the least of my worries.

She fetches the bottle and gives it back to the baby and stands up. She is wearing a singlet and tracksuit pants, bulging out of both. Her arms are large and puckered.

He'll be back, she says, but that's not the problem, is it?

No, I say. No, it's not.

Trust Roy Thompson to know, she says. Sleazy old bugger.

She goes over to the older child who is still banging away with his spoon. She takes the spoon and starts trying to feed him. He smiles coyly, turning away every time she tries to put the spoon into his mouth. The muck smears all over his face. It is slick with gelatine like oil on water.

39

So they going to dock him? Belle asks. Spit. They going to dock him?

They're not going to dock him, but they're not going to pay him either, I say. You don't get paid if you don't work.

Belle takes the boy's jaw and tries to force it open, pushing the spoon into his mouth. It knocks against his teeth and he shakes his head, howling. The muck goes everywhere and Belle swears, wiping a spot on her singlet. It smears.

Well what about holiday pay? she asks. What about sick leave? Suppose he got sick? They'd have to pay him then, wouldn't they? If he got sick?

I shake my head.

Not if you're on seasonal, I say. You only get paid for what you work on seasonal.

Belle stops trying to feed the boy, who is still screaming over the noise of the television. She puts the spoon in the container and takes off his bib, sitting him on the floor against the couch. He is filthy with chocolate. The glow of the television flickers over the boy, quick with changing colours. He goes quiet, staring at the screen. Belle picks up the baby and puts it in the highchair. She hands him the bottle and he chucks it and she goes and picks it up and gives it back to him. Her hair hangs limp.

So how come Spit's on seasonal? she asks me.

We're all on seasonal, I say. Apart from Wallace. Wallace's on full.

The baby has chucked the bottle again and Belle goes and gets it. She puts both his hands on the bottle and tries to get him to take the teat in his mouth. He won't take it. Same as the other one he won't take it. He turns his face away, flapping his arms and letting out little angry groans.

So how come you're not all on full? Belle asks. You all work full time. You should be on full.

Seasonal pays better, I say.

The older boy is sitting propped up against the couch, looking at his hands. He looks at them like he's never seen them before. When he sees me watching he stares at me and then he looks back at his hands and claps once. He looks up at me again with wide eyes. He seems surprised, like he's surprised he can clap his hands. Like it's the first time he's ever done it. He claps again and he keeps clapping and he is smiling and laughing and the stuff on his hands goes flying all over the place. Belle leaves the room and comes back with a damp tea towel and wipes his face and hands. She picks him up and takes him out of the room and I hear a tap being turned on in the kitchen.

The baby has chucked its bottle and I go and get it off the carpet and hand it to him and he chucks it again, holding onto the teat and swinging it. It rolls under the couch. I get down on my hands and knees and feel around for the bottle. On the television they are singing.

I find a toy fire engine under the couch and I roll it out and keep feeling around for the bottle, lying on my side. When I get it I stand up and give it to the baby. He chucks it and I leave it.

Belle comes back in with the older one. He is cleaned up and his clothes have been changed. She sits him against the couch again. I hand him the fire engine and he holds it close to his face, turning it around. Belle goes looking for the bottle and takes it back to the baby. Outside it is beginning to haze and glare.

So they're going to dock him then, she says to me.

It's not a matter of them docking him or not, Belle, I say. It's about not getting paid for not working. He's not showing up to work so he's not getting paid.

Belle takes the fire engine away from the boy, who is trying to chew on it. The boy starts bawling and Belle tickles him under his ribs. He cries out and pushes her hand away.

Still, she says, the bastards never give you a chance.

The baby chucks the bottle and it rolls across the floor.

Going home along the railway track I see the crows in the long grass. They are bunched close together in a frantic quivering mass, squabbling and pecking at each other. Their heads go up and down.

Other crows circle the air above the glistening mob, coming and going and cawing. They swoop down from the silos, passing low over my head, flaring out their wings and wheeling over the huddle, slowing and flapping about and landing among the crows on the ground and there is squawking and fighting and the mob goes back to its busy, jerking movement. Now and then commotion as a crow leaves in a flurry and streaks off into the air, a few others chasing it, calling angrily.

They do not seem to notice me coming until I am close and then only glance at me before putting their heads down again, going at it even faster than before, not moving until I kick at the whole dirty lot of them. They flap up in the air and drop down behind me onto the tracks, making threatening noises.

I squat down in the long grass to see what they were getting into. It is the rabbit I skinned for the boy yesterday. The top half is stripped to the bone, the eye pecked out, entrails left untouched and perfectly intact.

Flies crawl among the carcass and I wave them away and look back at the birds. They are standing around with their heads tilted, each of them watching me with one flashing eye. I pick up a handful of railway stones and fling them. The crows go up in the air and come down again, same as where they were before.

I take a large stone and get down on my knees in the ditch and start breaking the hard baked crust of yellow clay. I chuck away the stone and dig with my hands, pulling out lumps of clay and pieces of rusty-veined quartz. I scoop the clay from around a rock and pull it out and hurl it at the crows. They just sidle away and sidle back, watching me with their heads cocked. I keep working, pulling out the clay and heaping it on one side, piffing the rocks out at the birds. I dig deep, as deep as I can into clay which is hard as clay can be, and the deeper I go the harder it gets. I keep digging until my hat and shirt are soaked through with sweat and my knees are aching and I thought I had dug it deep but when I stand up and look at it, it doesn't seem anything, it doesn't seem much more than a hollow in the ditch. I wipe the clay from my jeans and I look at the crows.

They aren't looking at me anymore. They are looking at the carcass in the long grass. I walk onto the line shooing them away, but they don't even fly up, they just hop away from me, keeping their eyes on the carcass. I go round at them from the other side and they hop back in the opposite direction, not fearing me, just moving away like I was nothing.

I go over to the hole and look at it and I suppose it is deep enough. I go and pick up the rabbit and put it in. It fits, but it sits barely deeper than the surface of the ditch.

Now the crows are watching me again and they are starting to fidget, coming closer, not hopping now, but walking with their necks stretched out, their heads low to the ground. When I turn around they step back, but soon they are close, surrounding me. One of them flies up towards the silos, cawing, and I hear them all cawing from the silos but the ones around me are silent, watching me, and I can tell I've got them worried now. I know I've got them worried.

I take the lumps of clay I piled next to the hole and crumble them over the carcass and when it is covered I push down on the clay with my boot and I can feel the carcass underneath. I pack down the clay as hard as I can and put more on and pack that down and I keep packing down clay but the clay feels loose and I can still feel the give of the carcass and I think the crows would have no trouble getting through clay as soft as that.

The crows stay silent and still, watching. They barely move when I turn to face them. I start taking handfuls of railway stones and piling them over the top, pushing them into the clay. I take handful after handful until there is a great mound of stones over the buried carcass.

I look at the crows and they don't seem worried anymore, they are just looking at the pile of stones. They know what I have done and now they are waiting to see whether they can get under those stones. And knowing how smart crows are, they probably will and that is why they are standing calm now, waiting. But that's crows for you and it is still a big pile of stones and I packed them down tight and I couldn't have done more without a shovel and a mattock and it was only a rabbit, only a little rabbit after all.

It is dusk and the crows are scuttling shadows. I take one last look at the mound of stones and start walking home. I wipe my hands on my jeans and when I look at my hands I see that they are bleeding.

THURSDAY, SPIT doesn't show.

One of the boys drops in the heat. It is the quiet one and we hear him go down, his shovel falling against the wire, scraping against the wire as it falls and the whole line sounding and the thud of his body on the dirt.

In the next row the other boy goes to jump the vines.

Don't be stupid, says Wallace. He's not going anywhere, is he?

We go and look at the boy.

Anything broken? Wallace asks him.

The boy has come to and he is trying to sit up but he can't. His eyes are dazed. Wallace picks him up and carries him to the ute. He lays the boy on the tray and pours water over his head. The boy looks around wildly and keeps trying to raise his head but he can't.

You just lie there, says Wallace. It'll pass.

He hands the boy the water bottle and the boy takes it and tries to drink, the water spilling everywhere, the boy finding it hard to hold the bottle to his mouth. He turns his head and vomits and the puke runs down the tray.

He needs something stronger than that, says Roy.

The boy closes his eyes, shivering, his face gone white.

Take him down Poachers, says Roy. Be nice and cool in there. Get him out of this heat.

Yeah, give him a minute, says Wallace.

We stand watching the boy until he opens his eyes. He stares at us and closes them again. Wallace takes him by the shoulders and hauls him up, leaning him against the back of the cabin. The boy wavers, trying to steady himself.

You still dizzy? Wallace asks him.

The boy nods weakly and Wallace hands him the water bottle and he drinks again.

He's all right, says Wallace. He slides the boy down the tray and helps him stand up. The boy staggers, Wallace holding onto him. He eases the boy into the ute.

If you're going to throw up again do it out the window, Wallace says to him.

The boy sits slumped against the door.

Brandy, says Roy, as Wallace walks around to the driver's side. That'll set him right.

We watch them leave and go back to our rows.

After a while Wallace's ute passes us on the road, then comes back.

Told Boss, did you? asks Roy.

Wallace nods.

I am finishing Wallace's row. Wallace gets his shovel and works the row with me. Roy has stopped and is standing looking out at the road, waiting for us to catch up. The other boy is still going.

What'd Boss say? asks Roy.

He's worried isn't he, says Wallace. Going up to the house later. Talk to the mother.

Roy hawks and spits.

Reckon he'll come back?

Wallace reaches into some tangled vines, mumbling.

Roy spits again and rubs the spit into the dirt.

I don't reckon he'll come back, he says.

Wallace shrugs, pulling at the vines with both hands.

He was a good worker, I say.

Yeah, says Wallace, yanking hard. Good worker but he worked too hard, didn't he? We got one of them works too hard, other one doesn't work at all.

He tilts his head at the other boy.

Yeah but so what, says the boy. At least I don't faint.

Wallace is trying to tear the vines apart but they won't budge. He swears and takes out his knife.

Course you don't, says Wallace. Take it too bloody easy, don't you. At least your mate gave it a go.

Wallace cuts the vines and pulls out foliage, throwing it into the row. He takes off his hat and wipes his brow and his glasses and his knife.

Yeah, but I never fainted, says the boy. Fainting's for women.

Wallace puts his hat and glasses back on and looks at his knife. He folds it and puts it back in his pocket. He looks over at the boy, pushing his glasses against his face.

That's what you reckon is it? he says. Shows how much you've seen of life, boy.

I stick my shovel into the ground and lean against it. It is a hot day, still hot.

It's a pity about the boy, I say.

Yeah, says Wallace, picking up his shovel. I know.

It is hot all day long and nobody asks about the funeral.

After knockoff Roy parks the ute outside The Imperial.

What you parking here for? I ask.

Having a drink, says Roy, pulling up the handbrake. What'd you think I'm doing?

Yeah, I say. But here?

Roy takes off his hat and tilts the rear-view mirror to look at himself. He licks his fingers and combs his hair back with both hands.

It's a pub, isn't it? says Roy, looking at himself. It's a pub, serves drinks. He feels his stubble with his thumb.

Yeah, I say. But Imperial? I don't mind Imperial nights. Friday night. Saturday night. But afternoons?

Roy is looking at his fingernails.

Afternoons Imperial, I say. Mob of ratbags.

Roy is studying his face in the mirror, turning it this way and that. I watch men going into the pub.

Well nobody's forcing you, says Roy.

When I get out of the ute, Roy is still sitting looking at himself.

I walk down to the river and along the bank out to Spit's fishing spot. Twigs and leaves crackle under my boots. Skinks dart before me and butterflies dance. I pick up a stick and pound it against the ground as I walk.

I find the spot all right, but no sign of Spit. The ashes of a dead campfire sit in a shallow hole, rocks set around them. I scoop some up and rub them between my fingers. They are still warm and smell of urine. I cooee but nobody comes and nobody calls back.

Across the river cormorants line a dead branch fallen across the shallows. They are unmoving, their black wings outstretched, drying in the fading sun. I pick up a stone and shy it across the river. It skims the surface, jumping six times in a curve, water beading and flashing from out of the brown murk. The cormorants watch without interest.

Squatting down on my heels, I rummage through the brittle groundcover, the bark warped, the leaves bleached and pitted. There are hooks and lengths of line, the hooks bent out of shape, some new, some tarnished, some rusted through. I pick one out and snap it between my fingers. It is Spit's spot and has been for some time.

I go and sit on the roots of an old rivergum, leaning down to wash the ash off my hand. Resting my back between the buttresses of the trunk, I stretch out my legs, waiting.

A pelican comes down and hits the water in front of me, its wake rippling and churning. It holds its beak up and flaps its wings and rises from the water, shaking itself. It glides away up the river.

By the time I leave, the sun is setting red behind the rivergums. It looks as though the sky is burning up. And in the water the water is burning too.

Going back through town I see Spit's ute parked outside Poachers. Inside it is empty except for Ted Matthews sitting watching the television and Spit at the bar talking to Liz.

I thought you was fishing, I say to Spit.

I was, says Spit.

Liz pours me a lemon squash.

Roy Thompson said you was fishing, I say. I just been down the river looking for you.

Yeah? says Spit.

Spit hands Liz his empty pot and lights a cigarette. He is leaning with his elbow on the bar.

I'm in the doghouse at home, he says.

Liz hands him the pot back full and he drains it and slides it back to her.

It'll blow over, won't it? I say.

Yeah, I suppose, says Spit.

Noise comes from the television. The greyhounds are on. Light flickers over Ted Matthews' face. Liz puts another pot down on the counter.

It always blows over, doesn't it? I say.

Yeah, says Spit. Eventually.

Spit fiddles around in the pocket of his jeans and takes out his wallet. He hands Liz a note and she opens the cash register and puts change on the bar towel. Spit grinds his cigarette into an ashtray and lights another one. He picks up his glass and turns around, leaning his back against the counter.

How was the fishing? I ask him.

Piss-poor, says Spit.

FRIDAY, SPIT doesn't show but the boys do, both of them.

Wallace is pleased. He is trying not to let on but you can tell Wallace is pleased.

Whaddya doing coming in today for, he says to the one who'd dropped. You should have taken the day off. Take it easy. Build your model airplane.

I'm all right, says the boy.

Yeah, well, don't work yourself too hard today, says Wallace. Just take it slow, all right. Smithy'll pick up the slack.

Wallace gets the jerry can from the back of the ute. He tells the boys to hold out their hands.

Not like that, says Wallace. Like this.

He shows them, cupping his hands.

Wallace pours turps onto the boys' hands.

Rub it in, he says.

The boys rub their hands together.

That'll toughen them up, he says. Put some calluses on them.

He shows the boys his hands.

What about the old-fashioned way, says Roy.

Wallace laughs.

I still reckon the old-fashioned way's better, says Roy.

They want to do that it's their business, says Wallace, pushing his glasses against his face. Nothing to do with me.

He watches the boys rubbing the turps into their hands and gives each of them a shovel. They run their hands up and down the shafts, making them shine.

When you got some calluses there, I'll give you a go with the mattock, says Wallace. Put some muscle on you.

He looks at the boys for a moment.

Righteo, he says and goes into the vines.

Boss comes up to see how the boy is going.

Glutton for punishment, isn't he, Wallace, he says.

I'll keep an eye on him, says Wallace.

Boss leans over the vines.

You're a glutton for punishment, aren't you, he says to the boy.

I'm all right, says the boy.

Boss folds his arms and rests his chest against the tops of the vines, looking at the boy.

You were pushing yourself too hard, he says. No point in that.

He smiles at the boy and stands up straight, wiping off his jumper.

No point pushing yourself, is there Wallace? he says. Not if you're going to knock yourself around.

That's right, says Wallace.

He is chopping at a knot. Wood chips fly about and he grunts as he works.

I mean, these vines aren't going anywhere, are they? Boss says to the boy. It's not a competition. Not a race.

He picks at his jumper.

You make sure he takes it easy today, he says to Wallace.

Yeah, I got my eye on him, says Wallace.

He brings his shovel down hard and the knot splits off, scudding across the ground.

Best put some tar on that, says Boss.

Righteo, says Wallace.

Boss heads off down the row and then turns and comes back.

You mind if Iris borrows someone for the afternoon? he asks Wallace.

Yeah, no worries, says Wallace.

Boss looks up at the sky.

Just a bit of garden work I think today, he says.

Wallace squats down to look at the vine. He rubs the raw white gash with his fingers.

I'll send someone up, he says.

Good-o, says Boss.

Boss leaves.

Wallace stands up and points at the boy, the other one.

That's you, Yap-yap, he says.

Roy laughs.

Wallace is grinning. He looks at the boy.

He's going to love working for Iris, says Roy.

What'd you mean? asks the boy, stopping his work and looking up.

Roy and Wallace look at each other over the rows and then they both look at the boy.

By gee boy, you're in for it today, says Wallace. There's no fooling Iris. No getting away with things like you do down here. Not with Iris.

The boy says something.

You'll see, says Wallace.

He's going to love Iris, says Roy.

Wallace laughs and goes back to work. Roy spits and pulls up his shovel.

I'll go, I say. Makes no difference to me.

After lunch I walk to the cellar through paddocks and lanes. The sun is strong and high and the land suffers. Paddocks are littered with the bones of livestock, the grass grazed short, scorched or gone to clay. Solitary eucalypts stand dead, dry and enormous, their fallen branches split and hollowed. Flocks of filthy, daggy sheep press together underneath the scrapes of shade, their fleece gone the colour of the earth. I feel their heat and there is the stench of damp, dirty lanolin. Rams jostle through the mob, dipping their horns at me, giving deep-throated warnings.

Flies find me. They swarm and I walk with one hand waving, slapping my neck. I catch one and look at it dead between my fingers, its body bloated and tinted blue in the sunlight. I flick it away. Rabbits bolt before me. My shadow bobs.

Lanes rough with rock, glutted with long grass, soft and loamy beneath their crusts, bearing the deep indents of tractor tyres, crumbling beneath my feet. Vineyards back onto them, the vines crawling wild over the fences and webbing the lanes in a crazed tangle, leaves tiered to the ground.

Brief canopies of trees cast a scattered shade, sunlight glancing through the still shadows. Their bark is thick and scarred and they creak in the heat. The deafening screech of cicadas. I break a branch from a stringy-bark and peel it to its pale wood, pummelling the bald stick against the ground as I go.

Dogs bark as I pass. Quartz juts from the earth and sparkles. A single birdcall sounds across dead open spaces. A motorcycle comes towards me down a rolling paddock, lined by a high deer fence. The farmer, Dan Patterson, waves as he recognises me and turns back to the doe pen. The stags graze in the open. One of them raises its head to look at me, chewing its cud. It is young, bay-pointed, strips of velvet hanging from its hard naked antlers.

Farmhouses in the distance. Crops of blanched wheat and barley. Orchards of towering cherry trees, glossy-leaved citrus, walnuts, olives, vines, always the vines, some disbudded in neat rows, others still wild with summer growth.

A flock of sulphur-crested cockatoos line the bare branches of an ancient gum. They call their harsh call and flare their crests and take off with a sound of wings and the flock dazzles against the shifting vapours of the sky. I spot a half-dead tortoise struggling through the grass and I pick it up, turning it in the direction of the river.

In one paddock a horse trots cautiously towards me, a big Irish hunter. It dodges and feints as it approaches, sniffing and snorting. Coming close, it rests its head on my shoulder, its great weight against me. I stroke the nose and mane.

You're a big fella, aren't you, I say.

The horse half closes its eyes, occasionally flicking its nose at the flies crawling over it, making gruff sounds. Its nostrils flare and sigh and I feel its hot breath. Muscles twitch under the sheen of the coat and its back legs shuffle from side to side. Sweat prickles against my cheek and neck. I push its head away with both hands. The horse leans back heavy against me.

All right big fella, I say.

I twist away and it follows me to the fence, stopping to graze and making quick retreats, looking back with large, liquid eyes and then trotting after me again. It pushes its flank against me as I climb the gate. When I come down the other side I stroke the chestnut nose again. The fence creaks under the horse's chest and it snorts and whinnies as I leave, before turning and galloping away.

I cut through Boss's old farmyard with its empty dam and broken barley silo, littered with derelict equipment from Boss's father's day and his grandfather's and all the way back. Old winepresses of cast-iron and cracked wood, ploughs and yokes and rusted rims, machines with forgotten purpose. It is overgrown with cactus now, a great sprawling mass of pale leaves spreading out toothed and thick and taller than a man, drooping under their own weight.

Past Boss's father's stables, full of saddles turning to powder, mice nesting in the blankets and uniforms, his dress-sword rusted fast to the scabbard, the old .303 gone to pieces and nothing left of the medals but the medals themselves, scattered among the rodent droppings, tarnished green and black and beyond recognition.

In the paddock behind, the descendants of his thoroughbreds have gone brumby, ribs showing through their mangy coats. They turn and flee as I pass.

I cross the road to the cellar and go looking for Boss in the tasting shed and the cooling shed and among the vats and in the stockroom. I stop to chat with the women but they don't know where he is.

Outside I go around the back to the slumping shanty of the old cellar. It is dim and cool inside, the air heavy with wine and fermentation. I walk through the maze of barrels. Tangled hoses run along the dirt floor. One of the barrels has a ladder against it and I climb it. There is hardly enough light to see inside but I can make out Boss well enough, sitting inside the barrel with his legs stretched out and propped up against the rounded wall, half sunk in the residue and covered in it, his bare arms and legs shiny with the dried sludge, Boss purple all over. He is eating a pie.

Boss looks up at me and scowls.

What the bloody hell are you playing at? he asks.

There is another pie sitting on his lap in a paper bag and a bottle of tomato sauce.

You said Iris needed a hand this arvo, I say.

So what did you come down here for then? he says. Iris is up at the house, isn't she?

Boss takes an angry breath.

I mean, where's your common sense?

He takes a bite of the pie and chews it.

Come poking around here, he says. Poking around the bloody place. I mean, what were you thinking? You expect Iris to be down a barrel? Now come on.

He swallows and grins, his eyes white in the wine-soaked darkness.

I was just looking for Iris, I say.

Well, can you see her here?

He picks up the sauce bottle and shakes it.

For Christ's sake, he says.

I climb down the ladder and start to walk off when Boss calls me back. I cup my hands against the barrel wall and yell into them.

Yeah?

Boss's voice comes out echoing.

No need to tell Iris about the pies, he says.

Righteo, I say and I leave.

Boss's house is in the middle of what we call the house vineyard. Before Iris came along the vines crawled the sides of the house and matted the sunken verandah, climbing the chamfered wood supports and running along the guttering. In late summer bunches of dark ripe grapes would hang from the eaves.

But Iris wanted her garden and it was me and Wallace cleared the rows from out the front and a few acres round the sides. We pull up more of them every winter when the ground is frozen solid and us splitting our fair share of mattocks, Boss standing there watching us

57

with a look on his face like we was pulling teeth, as Wallace says. And Iris got her garden all right and now she grows roses that win prizes at local shows.

I walk along the garden paths. The lines of silver birches planted at the sides of the garden are tall now and gleaming. Underneath the hardwood bower, shaded with new-leaved wisteria, purple blossoms bloom. Soon they will bend their stalks, hanging in bell-shaped masses and they will bloom and die and bloom again all summer long. The jasmine flowers have withered and fallen now, the leaves grown thick over a long trellis bordering the front lawn and pruned like a hedge. In spring the breeze wafts the smell of the jasmine into town. And when those first warm and fragrant nights break through the long chill I know the season has come.

Iris is on her knees, tending roses with secateurs. She is wearing long filthy gloves and a straw hat. She stands up when she sees me coming.

Smithy, she says. I thought they would send up one of the boys.

Well, they sent me, I say.

Iris brushes dirt off her gloves.

It's just weeding the paths today, she says. Nothing exciting.

Makes no difference to me, I say.

Iris looks at me from under her hat.

But what about your knees, Smithy, she says. What about your poor old knees?

My old knees will be fine, I say.

Iris clucks her tongue.

Rubbish, she says. No point playing the tough man with me.

Iris pulls off her gloves and throws them into the wheelbarrow. She takes off her hat with one hand and pats down her hair with the other.

No point trying to impress me, she says.

Iris goes into the house through the sunroom. She comes back with a cushion and hands it to me.

The cushion is corduroy, a burgundy colour and embroidered with a picture of two birds on a branch. The birds are blue with coloured wings and the wings are patterned with gold thread. The branch spreads across the cushion. One of the birds is beginning to fly, but the wind is blowing it back.

You don't want to use this Iris, I say, looking at the cushion.

Iris laughs.

It's old, she says. It's the cat's cushion. The cat sleeps on it. See?

She brushes short hairs from the cushion and hits it with her palm. Dust billows out. Iris laughs.

She gets me a bucket and a trowel. I place the cushion on the gravel and kneel on the birds and the branch and the wind.

Rosebushes run along the fence line fronting the lawn and free-standing roses flank the paths behind box hedging. They are red, white and yellow. The yellow roses are like buds, small and closed, even in the blasting sun. The white roses lay their petals right out, rippled and limp, long stamens sticking out and heavy with pollen. The red roses are the same as red roses always are. The garden smells of roses and I like the yellow ones best of all.

I begin to work. The day moves slowly with the noise of insects.

Iris's niece comes out the front door letting the flyscreen swing free. It slams shut and Iris's voice comes raised from inside. The niece is wrapped in a towel, wearing sunglasses and carrying maga-zines, a bottle of sunscreen and a walkman. She goes down to the lawn without seeing me and I am about to say hello but she takes off the towel and spreads it out on the lawn and she is hardly wearing a thing underneath. After that I keep my head down.

The sunscreen bottle spurts and whistles and the niece slaps it on. I can smell it. The tinny sound of the walkman starts up and the niece lies unmoving in the sun.

Iris comes out of the door carrying a tray. She hooks the flyscreen door with one foot and lets it close slowly, putting the tray down on an old wrought-iron table sitting on the verandah, topped with fractured whitewashed slats.

Teatime Smithy, she yells out into the garden.

I sit up on my knees and stretch my back.

She'll be right, Iris, I say. We work through the afternoons. Just morning smoko.

Iris looks for me from the verandah, shading her eyes. She comes down the steps and prods the niece with her toe.

The niece takes one of her headphones out.

What? she says.

Iris looks for me again.

I don't care what you lot do out there, she says. At this house we have afternoon tea.

She prods the niece again and the niece looks up through her sunglasses.

Come inside and wash up, Iris says to me.

It's all right, I say. I'm fine with the hose.

Suit yourself, says Iris.

I go and wash my hands at the garden tap and go past the niece to the verandah. The niece stays sprawled out in the sun. The heat brings a faint chemical smell from the verandah, the thick stain sticky under my boots.

Iris has put out a pot of tea and a plate with slices of fruitcake arranged around it, cups, saucers, a sugar bowl and milk jug. It is good china, patterned with blue flowers and all of the china matches. She pours me a cup of tea and puts a slice of cake onto a plate. I put three spoonfuls of sugar into the tea and stir it in. Iris clucks her tongue and offers me the milk jug. I shake my head.

We sit drinking tea. Iris has her chair facing out onto the lawn. She has slipped off her house shoes and is swinging her bare feet. There is something about Iris that reminds me of a little girl. Sometimes there is, anyway. She is wearing a sun frock.

Iris nods out at the niece.

She's in disgrace, Iris says. Her father sent her up here as a punishment.

The niece is lying on her front with her bikini straps undone. She is all brown body out on that lawn.

Oh yeah, I say.

Running with the fast crowd, Iris says. Up till all hours. Getting up to God-knows-what. Her father thought it was about time she saw how real people live.

She shouts out to the niece.

Didn't he? she shouts.

The niece doesn't hear her.

Iris walks down from the verandah onto the lawn and pokes the niece with her toe.

Oi! shouts Iris.

What? says the niece, turning, holding onto her bikini top.

Sent up in disgrace, weren't you? says Iris.

The niece puts her head down between folded arms.

Iris comes back and sits down.

Just you look at her, she says, taking a sip of tea. Getting herself all primped up for the boys.

Oh well, I say. There's worse things in the world.

Still, says Iris. More to life than sunbaking and boys.

Iris pours more tea. I spoon in sugar.

Aren't you going to eat my fruit-cake? she asks me.

Sorry Iris, I say. It's just I'm not used to eating during work hours.

I pick up the cake and bite some of the icing off, letting it dissolve in my mouth before I swallow it. Iris watches.

You don't look like you eat much anytime, says Iris with a snort.

That's just age, I say.

Iris snorts again.

I know what you men do, she says in a singsong voice. I'm nobody's fool. I know where you go after work. You might not eat but you certainly have no problems with the beer.

I try to eat as much of the icing as I can. I take a bite of the cake but it hurts to swallow and it sits like a brick in my stomach. I put it back on the plate.

Suit yourself, says Iris, swinging her feet.

Iris yawns and leans back in her chair, looking at the niece again.

I made her fold sheets with me this morning and now she's sulking, she says. Apparently madam is too good for that. Won't even help with the dishes.

We both look at the niece. She has turned over onto her back and put her sunglasses back on. The headphone wires curl across the grass.

I've never said no to anyone staying with us, says Iris. You know that, you've seen it. And I'm always very pleased to oblige. I enjoy having guests. But I do expect them to pull their weight.

The afternoon sun is starting to come around the side of the house, the wood supports casting shadows across the jarrah boards. A light breeze stirs. I am reminded of other summers.

Iris is still talking about the niece.

Well, you're only young once, I say.

Friday night Roy and Wallace are taking the boys down to The Imperial to teach them how to drink. They say I'm coming even if they have to drag me kicking and screaming.

I walk into town along the railway line. A voice calls my name. I look up and see Charlotte Clayton coming out her back gate. She waves and starts walking carefully down the embankment, tripping in the ditch. I catch her.

Sorry Smithy, she says. It's these heels.

We walk down the line together, me holding onto her shoulder as she stumbles on the railway stones. She is a slim girl with long hair and she is all done up.

So where are you off to tonight? I ask her.

I'm meeting up with some friends at The Imperial, she says. Then we're going clubbing in Albury.

Yeah? I say. They got some good clubs there?

Charlotte laughs.

Not bloody likely, she says. I just had to get out of the house, take my mind off things. You know, with my husband getting out and everything.

That's right, I say. When's that happen?

Monday, she says. This Monday.

Charlotte slips on the stones and swears. She grabs onto me.

I just don't know what I'm going to do, she says. I'll see when the time comes, I suppose.

We walk along the line, Charlotte tripping and swearing and apologising all the way.

You usually come into town along here? I ask her.

Always, she says. And I love going back this way. You can see the whole sky in front of you.

Yeah, well you ought to be careful, I say. There's some nasty characters in this town.

Charlotte laughs.

I know, she says. But they're all my husband's mates, aren't they?

I shake my head.

There's whole other generations, I say.

The Imperial has not started to fill yet. A few teenagers are playing pool and the usual ratbags are drinking at the bar. Les is sitting fat and puffing on his stool. Friday nights every working man goes down Imperial.

I look at Les as I pass him, waiting for a comment. Friday nights Les drinks too, heavily, with a pot and a brandy under the counter. I nod to some men I know.

Roy and the boys have a table with a half-empty jug of beer sitting on it. I sit down with them. Roy is rolling a cigarette.

Where's bloody Wallace? he asks me. Still having his tea? Playing happy families? He shakes his head and lights his cigarette, pouring beer into the boys' glasses.

Boys are matching me glasses for pots, he says.

What about Smithy? asks one of the boys.

Smithy's not drinking, says Roy, dragging on his cigarette.

How come? asks the boy.

Because I drunk enough, I say.

What, already?

No, I say. I mean I drunk enough for good.

Don't worry about Smithy, Roy says to the boys. And don't worry about Wallace neither.

Why not? asks the boy.

Because you can't match him, says Roy. Can't match Wallace.

I reckon I could, says the boy. Give it a go.

You reckon do you? says Roy.

Why not? says the boy.

Because no one can match Wallace.

Roy finishes his pot and looks over at the boys' glasses.

I thought you was here to drink tonight, he says to them.

The boys start gulping down their beers, Roy watching them.

I watch the slow traffic up and down the staircase above the bar, going to the residents' floor where seasonal workers rent rooms and old men live. The railing is worn smooth and shiny. There are balusters missing and broken, leaning outwards over the wainscotting, its whitewash dirty from the hands of men standing against it and cracked dents in the boards where heads and bodies have slammed and fists gone near through them in pub brawls and friendly drunken melees.

Wallace comes into the pub carrying his bicycle with one hand and Roys says speak of the devil. Wallace makes like he's going to throw the bike over the counter to Les, right over the two pool tables. Les doesn't move from his stool but he watches Wallace as he lifts the bike so that it's pointing upwards, the back tyre high in the air. Holding it in one hand, he hooks it over the pool table light. The long green shade rocks on its brass chain and the front tyre spins just above the felt. Wallace walks off.

The teenage boys playing pool have stopped their game and are looking over at Les. Wallace sits at the bar and Les doesn't say nothing. The ratbags are laughing at the teenagers. Les pours Wallace a pot and Wallace skols it and then goes and unhooks the bike and carries it to the end of the bar. He leans it against the back wall and comes over.

Boys matching me glasses for pots, Roy says to him.

Wallace tops up the boys' glasses and takes the empty jug to the bar. He comes back with a new one, fills his pot and skols it and fills it again.

They sit and drink and we watch as the pub fills up. Roy squashes the butt of his cigarette between his fingers to get the last puffs out. The butt is wet and tan, Roy's fingers gone the same colour a long time ago.

I get up and go to the counter. Les doesn't move, because Fridays Les's wife does all the work. Les just sits there on his creaking stool. He licks his thin toad lips and makes a crack about me. The men down the counter laugh.

His wife comes over and pours me a lemon squash.

Now don't you worry about those jokers, Smithy, she says. She puts the glass down on the counter and waves back the coins I offer her.

I hear you've given it up, she says.

I nod.

That's right, I say.

You given up for good? She asks.

That's right, I say. For good.

Well, good for you, Smithy, she says. And don't you worry about that lot.

They don't worry me, I say.

Les's wife is a thin woman with a hard face and short permed hair. She is wearing a patterned cardigan and is strong from heavy work.

And I seen you at church too, she says. I never seen you at church before. You raised a Catholic, were you? she asks.

I nod.

So you coming to church now? she asks. A regular church-goer?

I'm planning on it, I say.

Well, good for you, Smithy, she says. Good for you.

At the table, the boys are already flushed with drink. Wallace skols.

It is the time of arrival and men arrive. It is the quiet time and men have few words for one another. A nod here and there, men stand together with glasses in hand and the silences are long and the talk is talk between closed lips. The men gather and wait. They are at the counter coming away with pots, glasses and jugs, the empties stacked high, carried in one hand. They drink in the pauses of quiet conversation and they still have the pride of the day and the work about them. Wrists tip and glasses empty and men go back to the bar and I know what they are waiting for. More men arrive.

Nah, this is slack work, easy work, Wallace is saying to one of the boys.

It's hard work though, says the boy.

Boy says it's hard work, Wallace says to me.

What's that? I say.

On the vines.

It's a holiday, I say. I'm retired from hard work. Vines is a holiday.

It's only the sun gets you, Wallace's telling the boy. The other day, day you dropped, that's the sun, the heat. We knock off if it gets too hot.

How often do you do that? asks the boy.

Wallace shrugs.

Not often, he says. Hardly ever.

More men, more voices, noise rising, low and dull, but growing loud all the same. They stand at the bar, sit on stools, flicking glowing cigarette butts into the trough at the bottom of the bar, the trough smouldering, resting their elbows against the brass pole that runs flush with the bar, the plating scratched and gouged through to the steel by the knives of men bored or angry or just drunk and the many silver cuts flash along the pole and the men lean against it, pots in their hands, pots on the bar towel, pots on cardboard coasters with the emblems of breweries going sodden from running suds and they take off their hats, weary from the day.

Roy, Wallace is saying. Oi, Roy.

Roy is smoking, holding his cigarette overhand, watching a group of girls at one of the pool tables. Wallace reaches over and pokes him in the shoulder.

Yeah, what's that? says Roy, watching the girls.

You remember that day? says Wallace.

How's that? asks Roy, still looking at the girls.

They are young girls, local girls in blue jeans and blue denim jackets. The jackets have studs and stars and gold sequins on them and patterns sewn in shiny coloured thread, fine and gleaming in the light. Some wear necklaces of cowrie shells and their faces are made up, heavy black lines around their eyes and their eyelids painted green, make-up thick and uneven over their faces, caked and cracking at the sides of their mouths and their foreheads, showing up their unpainted necks white and freckly. One girl has taken off her jacket and wrapped it around her waist with only a singlet underneath and that is the girl Roy is watching. She leans down to take a shot and Roy looks back at us, grinning.

Real scorcher, says Wallace. You and me went for a counter meal.

Oh yeah, says Roy.

So me and Roy are driving back to the cellar, to tell Boss we knocked off and there's Smithy still out on the vines. Out there on his own, still working. It was that hot wasn't it Roy.

Yeah, it was, says Roy.

Bloody hot, says Wallace.

It was hot all right, says Roy. He is watching the girls.

And Smithy didn't knock off at all, says Wallace. Worked the full day.

Vines is a holiday, I say. For me it's a holiday.

Older men wear their work clothes and the young ones come showered and changed and there is cream in their hair. The older men make fun of them. A lot of sheilas here tonight, they say. The men are fat in singlets and shorts, stained and dirty, bloody from the abattoir, gaunt in flannel shirts and workpants, all wearing elastic-sided boots, thick socks rolled over the tops, filthy and bristling with sawdust and burrs. And there are hats, all styles, most of them too old and worn to be any style at all, some with feathers in the hatband, cockatoo, galah, whole budgerigar's wings of all colours, others pinned with metal and enamel badges. The older men mess up the young men's hair and sniff them under the armpits.

Jesus Christ, they say.

Roy belches and picks up the jug. He empties it into the boys' glasses.

Drink up, he says. You're holding me back.

The boys drink.

Roy gets up and stretches his legs. He is wearing his pub shorts which are white, tight and obscene. Roy wears those shorts to attract the women though he's never said it straight out and everybody jokes about Roy's pub shorts behind his back. He takes the jug and goes into the crowd and the noise.

You'll get used to it, says Wallace. Few years.

Not me, says the other boy. Not once I got enough for a car.

Roy has gone over to the pool table where the girls are playing. He is trying to talk to them, leaning against the table with his beer in his hand and the empty jug in the other. The girls keep playing around him as though he is not there and Roy keeps on talking.

Wallace turns around to look.

Christ, he says.

I am looking at the back of one of the girls' jackets where a butterfly has been sewn in electric colours. I watch as the butterfly disappears when the girl turns from the hanging lamp and then the dazzle of the thread as she bends to take a shot, the light flowing and settling as she walks around the table, the brightest points following the swirl of the pattern until the girl turns away again and the butterfly is gone. I wonder whether she sewed it herself.

Once I get a car I'm going to Sydney, says the boy. Bondi beach. Go on the dole. Learn how to surf. Get a girlfriend. Surfer chick.

He grins.

Surfer chick, he says grinning. No tan lines.

Wallace is looking hard at the boy over his tilted pot. He drains the suds. He looks over at Roy, who has moved in close to one of the girls, talking to her while she smokes a cigarette, watching another girl take her shot. Wallace looks back at the boy.

Where's your self-respect? Wallace says.

Better than working, says the boy. Making the rich man richer.

Wallace swears and looks back at Roy. The girl is bent over the felt, her cigarette smouldering in the ashtray at the edge of the table. Our empty jug is sitting next to it and Roy is trying to show the girl how to work the cue, pressing himself against her. He has his hand on her arm. She shrugs him off and moves away around the table.

Well, you're not going to hold onto a woman bludging, Wallace says to the boy. Not once you're hitched. Soon as you're hitched your old lady's going to be sending you out to work. That's a lesson in life, boy. Once a man gets married it's the woman calls the shots. That's true as I'm sitting here.

Why buy the book when you can borrow from the library? says the boy, grinning.

The other boy guffaws. He's got the smile of an idiot.

That's easy enough said at your age, says Wallace. But you want to end up like Roy Thompson over there?

He points his thumb behind him where Roy is following the girl around the table, leaning against her every time she tries to line up the cue, talking, pretending he's trying to teach her how to play pool. He is holding his beer in one hand and has a cigarette in his mouth. The girl keeps pushing him away.

You know what Roy Thompson is? says Wallace. He's a small-town Casanova.

He says it again.

A small-town Casanova.

He's said it before, plenty of times.

He's a grown man, says Wallace. But he never growed up.

Wallace holds out a scarred and callused hand, dirt tracing the deep creases and round the nails. He counts off fingers.

Still lives with his parents, grown man. Still chasing women. Still scared of the dark.

Bull, says the boy.

No bull, says Wallace. Grown man, still afraid of the dark. Scared of spiders too.

He looks over at Roy and the girl. He thumbs behind him again.

Look at him will you, he says. Still running around like a bloody teenager. Nearly sixty years old, thinks he's sixteen. Bloody Roy.

Roy's all right, says the boy.

Wallace drops his hands onto the table.

Roy's my mate, he says to the boy. And I'd never say a word

against him. But he never growed up and that's a fact. That's truth.

Wallace leans back into the vinyl cushioning. The cushioning wheezes from holes burnt through by cigarettes, showing grubby tar-stained foam inside. It squeaks with the movement of Wallace's sweating back. He puts his elbows on the table and his arms are brown and hairy. Muscles tighten and disappear.

Now you look at me, says Wallace. I got my own house, a wife, kids. I got responsibilities. I got a family to take care of. But that's leaving a legacy, right? Because my family's going to keep on going long after I'm dead. Makes me a part of history. A part of human civilisation.

He leans back against the wheezing, squeaking vinyl and tilts his pot, draining the last trickle. He puts it down on the table.

Yeah, but Roy's got a better car than you, says the boy.

Wallace sits there with his hand wrapped around the empty pot and swears.

Over at the pool table, the girl has gone after Roy with her cue, trying to pummel him in the crotch. Roy is backing off fast, spilling his beer, his cigarette falling from his mouth. She has him against the wainscotting and he shies away from her into the cue rack, the cues falling as he backs into it, one of them hitting the side of his head. Roy holds one hand above him, the other splayed between his thighs. The men at the bar laugh. The other girls move in on Roy, hurling abuse. The back pockets of their jeans have flowers stitched into them, each petal perfectly traced. They surround him, yelling and swearing, and then leave him cowering against the rack.

Roy just about lost his balls, says one of the boys, who has turned to watch the whole thing. He turns back, grinning.

The men at the bar and the other pool table are all laughing at Roy as he sidles away from the girls. Even Les is laughing and he blinks his eyes as slow tears squeeze out. Les's wife comes from behind the counter, her face red and angry. She tells the girls that they're barred if they pull a stunt like that again and that she has never seen such unladylike behaviour in all her days.

And if you're going to act like an animal, then you can go and sit outside with the dogs, Roy Thompson, she says.

What'd I do? Roy whines, still hunched over.

Wallace turns back around to us, shaking his head.

Well, it wouldn't be the first time, he says to the boy. And I mean for real. On that very same pool table with a pair of bull knackers. Nearly had them cut right off.

That's bullshit Wallace, says the boy. You talk so much bullshit.

No. No bullshit, says Wallace. Why'd I bullshit you about a thing like that. That's truth, isn't it Smithy?

I wasn't there, Wallace.

Yeah, but you heard about it, didn't you? And you was there that day, wasn't you? Day Roy didn't have his hat.

Yeah, that's true, I say.

Roy is sidestepping around the girls to the bar. The men are cheering him on and calling out to him.

Wasn't a fair fight was it, Roy boy? they say. Outnumbered, weren't you Roy?

So one day Roy comes to work without his hat, says Wallace. And he's whingeing about it, come late because he couldn't find his hat.

At the bar the men are patting Roy on the back and making fun of him, holding their fists up.

And you know Bob Carter?

No, says the boy.

Course you do. Big bloke. Works at the abattoir.

Oh, yeah.

73

One of the men at the bar buys Roy a brandy.

Dutch courage, he says.

Well, Roy was having it off with his wife. So day before, Bob Carter comes home and finds Roy's hat hanging on the bedpost.

Roy is sitting at the bar and rolling a cigarette. His hands are trembling. He is whining in a high voice.

Unprovoked, we hear him saying. That was unprovoked assault.

So Bob Carter gets a pair of bull knackers, takes Roy's hat and comes looking for him, finds him drinking here. Now he's a big bloke, Bob Carter, and I kid you not, he picks up Roy with one hand, just like that.

Wallace shows them, lifting up his hand, making a tight fist. His muscles bulge.

I kid you not, says Wallace. Has him pinned down on the pool table, pair of bull knackers in the other hand. And he would have used them too and that's truth. If it wasn't for me and Mick-the-Pom grabbed him, he would have used them. Ask any man here. He's a big bloke, Bob Carter.

Roy slides back onto his seat.

You see that? he says. Bloody feminist brigade we got here. He drinks down the brandy.

Tell the boys, says Wallace. Didn't Bob Carter nearly knacker you? Cut off your balls?

Bob Carter? says Roy. Nah, that was just a joke

He found you out having it off with his old lady didn't he? says Wallace. Found your hat on his bedpost.

True, says Roy. But we're mates, me and Bob Carter.

What happened to your hat? asks the boy.

What do you think happened to my hat? says Roy. I'm wearing it, aren't I.

Roy starts rolling a cigarette and looks down at the table and the empty glasses.

I thought we was drinking tonight, he says. Whose shout is it?

Yours, says Wallace. Only you went to the birds and not the bar.

Wallace likes that.

The birds and not the bar, he says. Send Roy to the bar and he goes to the birds instead.

Roy grumbles and licks his cigarette and smooths it over and puts it behind his ear. He slides back off his chair.

The birds and not the bar, says Wallace, his eyes playful behind his glasses. That's Roy for you.

I feel a hand on my back and a kiss on my forehead.

Sorry Smithy, says Charlotte Clayton, licking her finger and wiping the lipstick off my head. There are two girls with her. They have come in from the lounge and the men are all looking at them, the girls uneasy from wolf-whistles and men's comments. They are all done up flash, their hair curled and their faces made up, black-lined eyes large and liquid, skirts short over dark stockings and tops hardly there, one trimmed with lace, the other riveted with a swath of black sequins, its shape like the turning of birds in flight. They wear high heels and clutch tiny leather handbags to their chests.

We're off, says Charlotte.

Take care, I say.

The boys watch them go. They watch them until they are out the door, then turn back grinning. One of them whistles.

Who's your girlfriend, Smithy? the boy asks me, grinning.

I'd watch who you look at like that, says Wallace in a low voice.

You mean, don't look at what you can't afford, says the boy.

Wallace is serious.

No, I mean, watch how you look at her, he says quietly. You could

75

get yourself into trouble there, boy.

No harm in looking, says the boy.

You reckon, do you? says Wallace, looking at him.

Wallace pushes his glasses against his face and sits back, watching a drunk stumble past with a glass of whisky in one hand and a beer in the other. The drunk steadies himself, stands straight, downs the whisky and then the chaser, his head back and his Adam's apple working fast. He stoops and turns back to the bar.

A wise man knows when to keep his head down and his mouth shut, says Wallace. Hear no evil, speak no evil.

What do you mean? asks the boy.

I mean, some women are more trouble than they're worth, says Wallace. That's Brett Clayton's old lady.

The smell of beer is everywhere and it brings memories to me, shapeless, formless memories, all soaked in the smell and the smoke and the noise around me and they are the forgotten memories of an entire lifetime.

Who's Brett Clayton? asks the boy.

Who's Brett Clayton? says Wallace. Boy doesn't know who Brett Clayton is, he says to me.

He turns back to the boy.

You know John Gibson, he says.

No, says the boy.

Course you do, says Wallace. Bloke they found down the river-bank, .22 in the back of his head.

Oh, yeah.

Was Brett Clayton done it, says Wallace. Drugs. All over drugs.

The boy looks around the pub.

Which one's Brett Clayton, he asks.

Wallace snorts. He's not here is he? He's inside.

Oh. Yeah, right.

Nah, not for shooting John Gibson, says Wallace. Copper never got him for that. Incompetent is what he is. Incompetent copper. Everyone knows Brett Clayton did it, but we got an incompetent copper in this town.

So how come he's in jail? asks the boy.

Wife-bashing, says Wallace.

Who'd he bash? asks the boy.

Wallace swears with his knuckles on his glasses. Who'd you think he bashed? Put away for wife-bashing.

What, her? says the boy, nodding towards the door.

Well that's his wife, isn't it, says Wallace.

Jeez, says the boy, leaning back against his chair and sipping his beer.

Ask Smithy, says Wallace. Smithy knows all about it. Even went to the trial, didn't you?

I nod.

Pleaded guilty, I say.

Wallace looks over at the bar for Roy, who is talking to a bloke sitting on a barstool, balancing on it with his boot against the trough. Wallace leans forward and puts his elbows on the table.

Was Smithy found her, he says. Beaten black-and-blue, wasn't she Smithy?

That's right, I say. Black-and-blue.

Down the old railway line, says Wallace. That's where you found her wasn't it, Smithy. Going home from pub. Pub after closing. Found her down the tracks, didn't you? Beaten black-and-blue.

That's right, I say.

Wallace stretches his shoulders back and his singlet pulls tight around his chest. He slumps back over the table again.

Neked, says Wallace.

Cor, says the boy, the talker. He looks towards the door again. I wouldn't mind seeing that.

I look at the boy and he looks down. He reaches for his beer.

Roy comes back with the jug and new glasses and pots. He sets out the glasses and fills them. He takes a drink standing and then looks at me.

You've got lipstick on your head, he says.

I know, I say.

They all drink.

They all drink and all the men are drinking and their faces shine with the drink and their eyes and lips are with drink, drunk and dead drunk and talking loudly. Voices slur and stools scrape. They hawk and spit into the trough, their noise like dull constant thunder. Men sprawl out around the bar and the tables, sitting and standing and leaning, some men red-faced and angry, others cheerful, content with the faces of children. They lope and stagger and stride towards the bar.

No way, says one of the boys to Wallace. Not going to catch me going to that.

Course you are, says Wallace. It's tradition. Isn't it Smithy?

What's that? I ask.

Iris's Christmas party, Wallace says.

I suppose it is, I say.

Who's going to be there? asks the boy.

Boss. Iris. Girls from the cellar.

They're not girls. They're old ladies, says the boy.

They're not so old.

The boy shakes his head.

Not catching me there.

You got no choice in the matter, says Wallace. It's a tradition.

They got beer? asks the quiet one, holding up his glass.

Yeah, but not enough, says Wallace. Boss doesn't approve of beer. So we bring our own.

What's the point though, says the other one. We can't get pissed.

Course we get pissed, says Wallace. No way I'm going to Iris's Christmas party without getting pissed first. We get pissed before we get there.

Wallace picks up his pot and drains it.

Really?

Course. It's a tradition, says Wallace, putting his pot down. The table is wet with spilt beer and mired with streaks of ash, the coasters sodden.

We start drinking down Crown morning, ten o'clock, says Wallace. Drink until the party starts, and then we keep drinking once we get there. Take down Roy's big esky. Longnecks, whatever Boss gives us. I never been so pissed as I get at Iris's Christmas party.

Wallace fills his pot and downs it.

Last year Smithy got so pissed he fell into Iris's fish pond.

I thought Smithy didn't drink, says the boy.

Last year he did.

I wasn't that pissed, I say. I just didn't see the pond.

How can you miss Iris's fish pond? says Wallace. It's huge. Biggest fish pond I ever saw.

Yeah, I say. But it's all lily pads and duckweed on the top, isn't it. You can't tell it from the rest of the garden. That's how come I went in.

Well what was you doing wandering round Iris's garden in the first place? asks Wallace.

Going for a slash, I say. I went round the side of the house. To be discreet, go behind a tree. So I cut through the garden. Didn't know there was going to be a fish pond there.

Well you should of, says Wallace. Was you and me built the thing.

Yeah, well, I say.

And so we're off round the other side of the house, says Wallace, pointing behind him with his thumb. At the barbecue. And we hear this big bloody splash and then Smithy yelling his lungs out. So we go round and there's Smithy, Smithy right in the drink, splashing round like he's drowning in it, hat's come off, and he's all caught up in the lily pads, all mud and duckweed over his face, yelling blue murder. Couldn't get out. Too pissed to get out of the thing.

Wallace fills his glass and puts it to his lips.

You was in a panic all right, he says. Thought you was drowning. Only in a bloody fish pond.

Wallace laughs and drinks and the drink goes down wrong and he coughs and laughs until he is red in the face. The boys laugh too, looking at me.

Wouldn't have missed that for the world, ay Roy?

It was quite a show, says Roy, looking up from his cigarette.

And afterwards, says Wallace, pushing his glasses against his face. Afterwards, you know what Iris calls him?

What? asks the boy.

You remember, don't you Smithy? says Wallace, staring at me

I look at him, look into those huge eyes watching me from behind their thick walls of glass, the eyes twinkling, dancing, wrinkled at the corners with amusement, Wallace's turned-up mouth grinning.

Yeah, I remember, I say.

An old fool, says Wallace. He chuckles and takes a drink. That's what she called him. That's what Iris says. An old fool.

All around is the noise of men.

I look out the window. The sun has set in mute tones and weary, the sky low and still, its heavy cover illuminated, a dirty blush across rolling surfaces and shadow. The gloomy, flickering light of the street lamps comes misted through the glass, moist and beaded from the hot damp bodies of the men inside. It illuminates a single strand of spider's silk, hung with the tiny husks of insects, gutted and mummified, the shells quivering in fast and minute vibrations. The base of the pane is littered with them, with dead and decaying flies and moths, nested in the thick mass of web, splayed and funnelled at the corners. The ulcers in my throat and mouth and on my tongue are stinging and I bite my tongue to feel the sharp pain. The quiet boy finishes his glass and smacks his lips and lets out a sound of contentment. His face is flushed and his eyes are lazy. He looks at me without focus and sways slightly.

I'm not pissed yet, he says, pouring himself another glass from the jug.

Yes you are, I say.

I get up and go to the bar.

Walking past the swarming mass of ruddy faces and loud talk and laughter I hear my name called but I go down to the far end of the bar where the lights are dimmed and a man sits alone at a dark table in the corner. Les's wife brings me another lemon squash and I drink it, the sour liquid harsh on my mouth and throat. I become lost in my own thoughts.

Les's wife comes back down the bar, carrying crates of empties.

How you going there, Smithy? she asks me. All right?

I watch her carry more crates over. She puts them down with a clatter and wipes off her hands, smiling over at me. I start saying something to her.

What's that love? she asks.

You asked me before, I say. You asked if I was raised a Catholic. It was the sisters raised me. Up north. Aborigine orphanage, mission school, somewhere up north. Course there was plenty of us weren't Aborigine. Plenty weren't orphans neither.

Les's wife is counting the glasses and she stands up and presses her hands against her back and leans against them, rolling back her shoulders.

Now that's something I always forget about you Smithy, she says. I always think you're from round here, but you're not, are you?

No, I say. Up north. I'm from up north.

But Florrie was from round here, wasn't she?

Yeah, Florrie was, I say. That's how I come here. But I'm from up north originally. Aborigine orphanage. Mission school.

Cheering comes from down the other end of the pub. A kelpie has slipped its leash and run inside. It sniffs about the place, panting. Men turn their ruby faces and crane their necks to watch the dog.

Give him a drink, say the men.

Down the bar, Les doesn't move from his stool. He watches the dog as the owner grabs it and hauls it into his arms like a baby, letting the dog lick his face.

Give him a beer, yell the men.

The owner carries the dog over to the bar and lets the dog lap at his beer, its head twisting around to reach the pot, whimpering and squirming in the man's arms as its tongue darts in and out of the liquid, the dog blinking as it splashes him in the eyes. The man throws the dog about in his arms and the dog shoves its muzzle into the pot, pulling it out covered in froth. Whimpering still, the dog struggles to lick up the dregs.

All right, that's enough, says Les.

The owner carries the dog out and the men hold up their drinks as it goes past. The kelpie twists and squirms, its tongue stuck out, trying to reach the glasses. The man chains the dog outside with the others and the excitement dies.

The sisters were all right, I say to Les's wife. I never learned to read or write, but that was my own fault. I used to slide down the banister for fun and one day I come off and cracked my head open. Doctor come to look at me and said I'd grow up an idjit. Said there weren't no point teaching me nothing because I'd grow up an idjit.

Les's wife is looking down the other end of the bar where men are milling about the taps.

But it wasn't so bad, I say. Growing up there. I just spent me time knocking around the place, looked after the chooks and the cow, did the milking every morning, collected the eggs. Then I went shearing forty-seven years.

Les's wife looks over at me.

Well, good for you Smithy, she says. Now I'm going to have to look after that lot down there, if you'll excuse me.

Fair enough, I say.

Come down if you want to have a chat, she says. Only if I don't keep the taps running they'll be baying for blood.

I go down the bar and stand by the tap. Men are holding their empty jugs and pots and glasses. Les's wife takes a jug and puts it under the tap. I am close up against the men and I can feel their heat. They smell of sweat, beer and tobacco. I look up at Les, who is watching me from his stool.

What? I say. You got a comment, Les? You got something to say?

What me, Smithy? he says. I would never say a bad word against you. Les looks down the bar. You ever hear me say a bad word against Smithy here? he says. Les is drunk.

Les's wife is handing out jugs and pots and glasses and taking empty ones. Men put money on the bar towel. I push through them to get to the counter. A man slaps me on the back and says something. I lean against the bar and talk to Les's wife over the taps.

But there was this one sister, I say. Sister Bernard. She taught music and she said even if I was touched in the head there wasn't any reason I couldn't learn music.

Les's wife hands out a jug and takes another.

What's that, Smithy? she says. You'll have to speak up.

One of the sisters, I yell. Sister Bernard. She discovered I had a talent. I could sing. Said I had a natural talent.

I feel a hand on my shoulder and someone grabs my hat. I look around and a young bloke has lifted it off my head, showing my white hair. Everyone around is laughing. Down both sides of the bar and at the tables they are all laughing.

You look like an old man, Smithy, one of the boys shouts from our table. Wallace is sitting next to him, grinning.

I am an old man, I say. I grab back the hat. The young fellow slaps me on the shoulder and goes away.

Les's wife is shaking her head.

Well I think it's dignified, she says to me. They got no reason to be laughing, Smithy. Old age is a blessing now, isn't it. Makes you wiser and all those things, doesn't it?

She smiles at me.

I suppose, I say.

She goes back to the taps and the money.

I could really sing, I say to her, yelling again. Like a proper little choir boy, I was.

Well isn't that nice, she says. That's just lovely. That's a lovely story, Smithy.

84

I shake my head.

What it was, I say, it was I had a talent. I had a talent but I lost it. I went shearing instead. It was me own choice. All me own choice. But sometimes I wonder whether I could have done something with it. Gone somewhere, you know.

A man takes his pot without paying and Les's wife leans over the bar and grabs him by the shirt as he turns to go.

Oi, Les's wife says. You think this is tastings at the cellars?

Sorry, says the man. He is drunk and sweating and he fumbles with the money, dropping coins and bending over to pick them up. Sorry, he says, handing over notes and coins all bunched together.

Les's wife laughs.

Not to worry, pet, she says. It was an honest mistake.

The man stands there and keeps apologising. He is sweating a great deal and when he leaves he forgets his pot. Les's wife shakes her head at me, smiling.

Aren't you glad you gave it up? she says to me.

Yeah, I suppose I am, I say.

Because it wasn't long ago I seen you in a state like that yourself, she says.

She nods, her eyebrows raised.

I seen you worse than that, she says. I seen you much worse.

I know, I say.

So you just make sure you keep off it now, she says. It's very easy to fall back into bad habits.

No, I'm off it for good, I say. There's no going back for me.

Well, good for you, Smithy, says Les's wife.

I go and sit back down the end of the bar.

Now the pub is drowned in the full roar of drunkenness. Men knock against one another. Stools tip and slide and strike the boards. There is the clatter of glasses as Les's wife puts down crate after crate. The ring of the cash register, the floor thumping with the steps of men heavy with drink, Les's wife's voice raised in outrage as some drunk overturns a table and an unsteady hand lets a glass drop, shattering on the tiles to hilarious uproar. A man slumps his head against a wall and vomits up beer and bile and the stench of both. Lips, once loosened, pour, and the voices continue raised, men spewing forth what they have kept inside themselves for days or weeks or for a lifetime and they see only the blur of faces and they speak not to men but to something greater than men and they do not know that it is empty and uncaring. And there are men who talk and there are men who are silent and those who talk do not know what they are saying and those who are silent do not listen, but drink for the very silence, for the silence of their souls. And I was such a man.

Wallace comes over from the table. He slams his pot down on the counter, the beer spilling, and flops against the bar.

I just thought up names for those two, he says, pointing to the boys.

Oh yeah, I say.

That one's Aspro, he says. Because he's a slow-working dope. And that one's Cocaine, because he's an even slower-working dope.

I thought you were going to call that one Yap-yap, I say.

We can call him both, says Wallace.

Wallace starts talking and he is half-drunk now and I find it hard to follow what he is saying. Wallace's wife sent him to a speech therapist once, but the speech therapist said it was his underbite that was the problem. Then he went to a city doctor who said he could break Wallace's jaw and reset it, but Wallace would have to wear a wire mask for two years and even then he couldn't make any promises. So Wallace talks the same as he always has, the words coming out pitched all over the place in gruff bursts and high whines. Most people don't understand a word he says and when he drinks even we can't make much sense of it. I know what he is saying when he sees the schoolteacher though.

Aw, Christ, he says. The bloody schoolteacher.

The schoolteacher is dead drunk and he comes up slowly, unsteady on his feet, putting them down carefully, one at a time. He has a glass of port in his hand and he is trying not to spill it but it swills in the glass and over the sides. His jumper is stained with the port and he sweats all over, his hair plastered to his forehead and his eyes glazed. Saliva has dribbled down his beard and it sticks there slimy and white with bubbles. He looks like he could topple over at any moment. He nearly goes past us when he sees Wallace. He leans in to look at Wallace's face, spilling half his drink.

Wallace! says the schoolteacher.

Wallace swears under his breath, ignoring the schoolteacher, facing away from him.

Wallace! says the schoolteacher again. He looks into his lapping glass, mumbling something, and then starts talking loudly again, slurring his words.

Wallace! he says. How are you Wallace?

Fine, says Wallace, not looking round.

The schoolteacher looks back into his glass, swilling the remains about and he moves towards Wallace.

Wallace, he says. He leans slowly forward and takes hold of Wallace's hand. Wallace pulls it back in a fist, swearing, his mess of teeth a snarl.

No, no, says the schoolteacher. It's all right Wallace.

He takes Wallace's hand again and gently prises open the fist with shaking hands. He holds Wallace's open hand and studies it, squeezing the fingers and the palm.

Wallace, he says quietly, fascinated. Look at that Wallace, he says.

He holds out his own palm to Wallace.

And look at that, he says. Look at that.

Wallace shies away from the schoolteacher's hand, swearing.

No, no, says the schoolteacher. Look at that Wallace.

He lets go of Wallace's hand and stands up straight, wavering, his eyes half closing.

You, Wallace, he says. This. He taps Wallace's palm. Me, he says. He holds out his trembling hand. He looks at it with unfocused eyes.

Me, he says, tapping his head hard with his finger. I'm a hypocrite.

Me, he says. He holds his finger to his head with his thumb raised. He flattens the thumb and makes a noise like a gun going off.

He stands there with his eyes wet and staring, swaying on his feet, looking at nobody. He stands like that for some time and his eyes close and he rocks dangerously. Wallace looks away, swearing under his breath and he drinks with his head down.

The schoolteacher opens his eyes and looks around.

Good on you Wallace! he shouts.

He slowly turns to look at me, squinting as though I were a long way off.

Good on you mate! he says.

The schoolteacher stands there, his mouth moving but saying nothing and then he lurches off.

Wallace watches him go.

Bloody schoolteacher, says Wallace. You know what that man is? He's what you call an educated idiot.

That's what Wallace always says about the schoolteacher.

He drains his pot and stands up.

Bloody schoolteachers, ay Smithy, he says to me, slapping my shoulder and leaving.

Les's wife starts putting out food in wooden bowls along the bar. The men at the tables stand up and stretch their legs and wander over. Les's wife comes down the bar and puts a bowl of dim sims in front of me. The smell turns my stomach.

The men crowd the bar, eating with one hand and drinking with the other, still talking, they never stop talking. Les's wife puts plastic squeeze bottles of tomato sauce and soy sauce and vinegar next to the bowls. I look over at Wallace and Roy and the boys. Wallace is talking, waving his arms about, his gabbling like a howl. The quiet boy's head is sagging.

Oi! I yell over to them. I whistle. Oi!

Wallace looks up in mid-speech, his arms spread out. I point to the quiet boy and motion for him to come over. Wallace shoves him off the chair with a rough sweep of his arm. He turns back to Roy, still talking. The boy stumbles forward and sidesteps in my direction. I go and take him by the arm and help him over. I sit him down.

The boy turns slowly to look up at me. His eyes are bloodshot and the lids heavy. There is a sly look on his face.

Smithy, he says, like it is something funny. He pats me on the back and hugs me with one arm.

Smithy, he says, grinning.

Yeah, well, I say.

I slide the bowl of dim sims over to him.

You'd best get stuck into that, I say. Otherwise you're not going to last the night.

You should drink, Smithy, says the boy, holding his glass up as though he's making a toast. It's good.

It's all right to have a few drinks after knockoff, I say. And there's no real harm getting pissed Friday nights, even Sundays. But I spent half me life pissed.

Good on you, says the boy, toasting me again.

No, I say. You don't understand. When I was drinking it used to be I had to drink myself sober. Mornings I had to drink to get sober, you understand?

What'd you mean? says the boy. You mean you couldn't get drunk.

If I drunk enough I'd get drunk, I say. But you're not getting my point. Here, I say, pushing the dim sims closer to the boy.

The boy takes a dim sim and eats it. He licks his fingers and looks at the bowl.

Go on, I say.

He takes another one.

Well it's been my ruin, hasn't it, I say. I been drunk half me life and now I can't hardly remember nothing. All them years, hardly nothing. Can't hardly remember me own life. Because I drank it all away, you understand. And it's ruined me inside too, done my health in. Doctors say the only way to keep me alive now is to put me in hospital, feed me from a tube. And it's the grog done it.

Half your life, says the boy thoughtfully, slurring his words. He grins, struggling to look at me, his eyes rolling.

He takes the dim sim and holds it above him, dropping it into his mouth.

Yeah, I say. Half me life drinking, other half working. Because you only worked the season. You did a station, hit a town, and then it was on to the next station. But outside of the season you didn't work. No need to. The pay was good, providing you was a hard worker, good enough for back then, anyway. Enough to provide for your family, buy a house, all that. So outside of the season there was nothing to do but go down pub. I used to be down pub from the time it opened to the time it shut. Get pissed every day, go home, have me tea, go to bed. Never spent time with me wife. Never saw me kid grow up. And now I look back at me life and I wasted it, didn't I? You only got one chance in life and I already used mine up. And I stuffed it. Stuffed it good and proper.

The boy nods, wolfing down dim sims.

I mean, when you're young you work, you get pissed, you go with women, you do this and that, but you never think about the consequences. Everything's moving, everything's going along and you don't stop to think. But it goes fast. It goes so fast you barely notice it. Notice it going. And then it's over. It's over before you even know it. All of it. One day it all just stops. Because it's stopped now. For me it has, anyway. Everything's stopped.

I rest my elbow on the bar towel and it is wet. I look at the damp patch on my sleeve.

Nowadays I'm doing all the thinking I should have done when I was young, I say. When I could have done things right. But all I got now is memories and regrets. And there's not a thing in the world I can do about it. That's it. That's me life. Gone. Can't change a thing. Can't go back. Can't put it right. You understand what I'm saying?

The boy's eyelids are half closed and his head is beginning to nod. His hair has fallen over his face and into his beer.

Yeah, he slurs, you gotta look before you leap.

But that wasn't what I meant. That wasn't what I meant at all.

I look down the bar at the men. One of them is smoking a large-bowled billiard pipe, clenched between his teeth as he talks, striking matches in brief bursts of flame before they disappear into the bowl. He puffs at it hard and smoke rises in jets and then disperses. He is talking to Bob Martin, who busted his kneecap when a jack slipped from under his truck. He is not the only cripple in the pub. There are men with metal claws for hands, plastic forearms, hobbling about on prosthetic legs. They most of them got injured on the job and paid out and some of them not so old either. Bob Martin grows orchids now.

I look at the boy slumped over his beer.

I reckon you've had enough, I say to him.

Me? says the boy. He raises his head and brushes his hair back. He takes a drink. Nah, he says. I'm only just getting started.

I see John Langtree coming towards us, heavy on his feet, his big gut shaking from side to side as he lumbers along. He stoops and sticks his face up close to the boy's, his face like a slab of meat, his gut pushing against both barstools.

Who's your girlfriend, Smithy? he yells, spitting the words right into the boy's face.

Lay off it, John, I say.

Oi! he yells, staring the boy in the eye. He pokes the boy in the chest and the boy's eyes open up wide.

You think you can take him on? he shouts, pointing at me.

The boy is blinking as though he has been suddenly woken up. He grins nervously and looks around at me.

You think you can take him on? John Langtree shouts again, wheeling his huge, quivering body to turn to me, shaking his finger at my face.

That old man! he shouts. He look like a weak old man to you? You think you can take him on, do you? Ay? Young bloke like you? You think you got muscle?

John Langtree stands up and his gut flops below his belt. He puts a hand on my shoulder. He's got big hands and arms, his bloated face bursting scarlet across the cheeks. He's a big man all round and he is not a good man, drunk or sober.

That's an old shearer, that is, he says, slapping me on the shoulder. There's nothing tougher than an old shearer. You think you can take him on? Bullshit!

He takes his hand off my shoulder and pushes the boy hard in the forehead with one finger. The boy's head reels back and he grabs hold of the rail.

You think boxers is tough? roars John Langtree, holding his finger up to the boy's face. You think wrastlers is tough? He drains his beer and slams it down on the bar towel. Pissweak!

He wipes his mouth with the back of his hand.

There's nothing tougher than an old shearer, he says.

He dumps himself against the bar, his elbow hitting the counter. He leans over the boy.

You think you can take him on? he growls. Yeah? He stays there bent over, steadying himself against the rail, his angry face with its firework cheeks right up to the boy's. He moves his head about, glaring at the boy.

Just let him be, John, I say.

John Langtree keeps staring. The boy grins. John Langtree mumbles and stands up. I am not looking at him but the boy is. I look straight ahead.

John Langtree stands there with his finger pointing nowhere and there is a long silence. He drops his arm and looks into space, muttering and swearing and then he turns, pitching against the bar, next to me.

You was gun shearer, wasn't you, Smithy? he says.

I can feel his hot sour breath on the side of my face but I do not turn around.

That's right, I say.

He takes his hand off the bar and rests it on my shoulder again.

You was ringer, wasn't you? he says.

That's right, I say.

John Langtree stays there with his hand on my shoulder. I shrug it off and he mumbles and looks around for his pot.

He leans towards me against the bar, the wood squeaking against his bare arm, his face close to mine.

How long was you ringer? John Langtree asks me.

I went shearing forty-seven years and then I quit, I say.

John Langtree looks at me. He drops his elbow onto the counter and his body thumps against the wood.

Yeah, but how long was you ringer? he asks.

That's when I quit, I say. When I wasn't ringer no more.

John Langtree stays there, his eyes searching my face. I look in the other direction. He belches and wipes his mouth with his arm, looking over at the boy, swearing under his breath. He reaches across the bar from behind me and tries to grab the boy's hair. He misses and grunts and slides along the bar until his body presses into me, hot, damp and stinking. I stand up and John Langtree slips forward into the barstool, its feet scraping across the tiles. He blinks and reaches out and snatches at the boy's hair, pulling the hair and the boy's head with it, twisting it to the side. The boy makes a sound of pain and his hands flail. His stool starts to topple. I put out my boot and steady the stool and I look at John Langtree.

John Langtree gives the boy's hair a yank and the boy is in pain again, holding his hand to the tight strands in John Langtree's fist.

What's this? John Langtree scowls. What the bloody hell you call this?

Even with the hard grip tearing at his hair and his face forced downwards, the boy is grinning.

It's just the fashion, John, I say.

John Langtree gives it one last yank and lets go. The boy straightens his neck and takes his hair in his hand and looks it over, drawing out thin blond strands and running his hand over his scalp. He brushes it back, still grinning. He takes a drink from his pot.

John Langtree pushes himself up from the barstool, swearing as it slides under him. He heaves his chest to the railing with a grunt, rolls of pink flesh naked through the back of his drenched singlet. Finding his footing, he staggers over to me.

What's say we do him like the old days, he says to me in a low voice. Take him down the sheds. Give him a run over with the clippers.

I walk past him and sit back on the barstool.

John Langtree turns, looking for the boy. He goes over and grabs a full fist of the boy's hair, jerking the boy's head back and looking him in the eye. John Langtree's face is raw and mean.

That's what we would have done in the old days, he yells. Take you down the shearing sheds give you a haircut.

He's just a boy, John, I say. For Christ's sake just bloody well leave it will you.

John Langtree mumbles and lets go of the boy's hair. He stands there looking at us and I do not look at him and he leaves.

You'd be well advised to stay away from that bloke, I tell the boy.

Nah, he was all right, says the boy, grinning. Just joking around.

No, I say. He's been inside. Stay away from him.

The boy brushes his hair back again, running his fingers through it. He is sweating. He rubs his eyes with his palms and looks at me, more sober than he was, but his eyes still tired and full of drink. He reaches for his pot.

So were you a shearer, Smithy? he asks me, drinking.

Of course I was, I say. Wasn't I just telling you about it? About the season?

Oh, he says lazily, I thought you meant season like grape picking season or something.

No, nothing like that, I say. I never went out on the vines till I got old. I been a shearer all my life. Forty-seven years. I was gun shearer at your age and I was ringer not much older.

The boy fixes his sleepy eyes on me.

I wasn't much older than you at all, first time I made ringer, I say. I remember it, remember the station. Saltbush country. Ever been to Saltbush country?

The boy shakes his head.

There's nothing hotter than a shearing shed in Saltbush country, I say. And that's not just my opinion. Everyone used to say that, back in the old days. Common knowledge. Hotter than hell, Saltbush shed. You been in a shearing shed before? Working shed?

The boy shakes his head again, his head drooping and his hair brushing the counter.

Well, you got to be there to know what it's like, I say. Stinks. Stinks of men and stinks of sheep. You get a mob of dirty, sweating sheep. Nothing like the stink of that. Lanolin. You know what lanolin is? I ask the boy.

The boy shakes his head.

It gets all over you, I say. When you're hauling sheep all day. Lanolin, daggy fleece, sheep shit. Iodine, ammonia, diesel. That was how we run the plants in the old days. Diesel. Nothing like the stink of a shearing shed.

It is Mick-the-Pom's birthday and Wallace and Tony Malone are trying to wrestle him down but Mick-the-Pom keeps dodging them. They are all three of them big men and they belt up and down the

96

pub and around the pool tables. Wallace and Tony Malone lope low to the ground as they go for the tackle, Mick-the-Pom swears as he runs, glancing behind him as he goes. Les watches them, looking nervous.

I remember the station, I say. Remember the day itself. Saltbush country. Hot, stinking shed. But I was young then. And I was strong and I knew it too. And proud of it, that's for sure. I had me pride, back then. Plenty of it. You know how it is, when you're young. Everything ahead of you. Arrogant. I was proud and I was arrogant. I was as young as you are now.

I go to take a drink but realise I don't have one.

I suppose you have to make the most of it while you can, I say.

Wallace and Tony Malone have Mick-the-Pom trapped against the side of one of the pool tables. Mick-the-Pom feints this way and that, but the two men stay steady. They rush him and the three of them sprawl against the pool table. The pool table tips up onto two legs and the balls clatter together and spill over the side, rolling across the floor. The players complain. Les's eyes pop.

So I'd tallied one ton by the afternoon, I say to the boy. And I've got the others watching me, the old men saying you'll never last boy, working like that, and they're shaking their heads, but it only spurred me on. And I'm hauling sheep like buggery and I'm aching all over, but it didn't feel so bad. Felt good far as I was concerned. Dripping in sweat and I'm shearing quick, but I'm shearing steady too, barely a nick. Shear them, chuck them down the chute, haul them up. One after another I keep going. So that's shearing for you. When you're serious about it. When you got pride in it. And I just keep on going. Every muscle in me body aching, but I just keep going. And so I made ringer that day.

Wallace and Tony Malone and Mick-the-Pom scuffle underneath

the pool table and it lifts up and down and nearly topples with the players trying to hold it steady. Mick-the-Pom breaks free and runs past the bar and out into the beer garden. The other two charge after him. Stools and chairs overturn and then they come hurtling back in and pass us, thundering like horses at the track. Wallace tackles Mick-the-Pom and all three of them hit the floor and Tony Malone sits on Mick-the-Pom's chest. Wallace gets up, picking his glasses off the floor and putting them back on. He takes a jug of beer from the counter and pours it slowly over Mick-the-Pom's head. Men laugh and cheer. Tony Malone holds out his hand to Mick-the-Pom and pulls him to his feet.

You bastards, says Mick-the-Pom, shaking his wet head. You right bloody bastards.

So there was about ten thousand head still to go and we sheared them, I say. And afterwards we all went off in the contractor's lorry, sitting around the plant, downtubes swinging all around us. And we go to the nearest grog shanty and there's another team there who were finished for the season and with all the men the grog shop smelt same as the sheds. And me team were buying me brandy and I remember looking in the bar mirror at meself, standing there with a brandy in me hand. Looking strong, all that. And the men were calling me gun shearer and speed merchant and they said I had a thing or two to learn yet. And they talked about gun shearers they had known and women they had known and the big cities and cockies and unions and their homes and they sent me outside with a boy from the other team and I knocked him down and I came back in and I looked at meself in the mirror again. And the publican calls last drinks and I remember one man drinking down a whole bottle of gin. Whole bottle, just like that. Pinching his nose while he did it. So we leave the pub and go back to the lorry. But there was this one old shearer, Percy Olsen was his name, and Percy Olsen sits down on the ground outside the grog shop and there's men standing around smoking and drinking from bottles, but the old fella's just sitting there. And the men are calling to him but he's just sitting there and he wouldn't come over, so they go and try to pull him up but he wouldn't get up and they had to drag him over to the lorry and I remember his boots coming off as they dragged him and him not saying a thing and one man hauls him up into the back of the lorry, up over his knee like a sheep, and they sit him opposite me and then they go and get his boots and throw them in after him and we drive off. And the other men are still talking and drinking and I remember Percy Olsen sitting there across from me, not looking at anything. He wasn't looking at anything at all.

I go to take a drink and remember again that I don't have one and I look at the boy and the boy leans over and vomits onto the carpet and he retches and spits and wipes his mouth and vomits again and he keeps vomiting until there is nothing left. I look over at Les, who is watching, and I grin.

Walking home along the railway tracks I remember that night.

It was a night not unlike this one. The air warm, the breeze in the long grass, its rustling movement regular and all around, swaying to and fro like the ebb and flow of the sea. And I was moving with its tide.

And the dry, dull fragrance of the grass and the far-off crops, the air fresh, the dark outlines of fences and houses and backyard trees above me, staining the glassy sky. The silhouettes of owls, still as fixtures on the branches, and then falling and soaring before me, their wings beating the air, throbbing with deep vibrations. Frogs chirping in the undergrowth, the nocturnal hum of insects, the twitter and rasp of possums and mosquitoes all around me. The rustle of leaves.

So it was, I remember. A night like this.

I was drunk that night, nicely drunk. Just nice enough so I didn't feel the stones under my boots or the gnawing in my guts. Just nice enough to be moving without effort and feeling without thought. Moving with the hot gusts pleasant on my back, driving me along, carrying me, and I felt as though I were drifting. Just drunk enough to forget who I was or what I was except a man walking, walking towards that great star-clouded dome at the horizon, and in the darkness I felt that I myself was walking among the heavens. Just nice enough to forget everything.

And it was the sound I heard first, the wailing. And the drink had slowed my senses so there was the wailing coming from far off and then it was all around before I heard it for what it was, and it was the same for the misty shape down the track, that dun glowing blur coming closer and the strange high noise had pierced me before I understood, and it turned my guts to ice, the white naked woman emerging from the darkness and the blood flowing from her, from her eyes and from her head and it flowed black down her pale moonlit body and her mouth was open and her cry was loud and dreadful and she kept coming towards me and her arms reached out and grasped at me. And I thought my time had come.

SATURDAY I do some work in the garden and help my neighbour change a tyre. We talk about the locust plague and what the government's going to do about it.

Sounds like they're going to poison half the country, he says.

Saturdays I try to keep meself busy.

SUNDAY I go to church.

After service the congregation gathers outside. There are farmers and shopkeepers and their wives. Italian widows in black. Working men stand uneasy while women talk. The priest moves from group to group with his soft, smiling face, his high-pitched laugh sounding over the general hubbub. Kids are playing noisy games on the lawn, running about and chasing each other. Teenagers flirt among the cypress trees.

I am standing by the wall of the church in the shade of a buttress. A boy hurtles past me, nearly knocking himself against the bricks. I catch him.

Careful there, I say.

The boy looks up at me, stepping back, looking at me like I'm something strange, something he is trying to figure out but can't. Then he turns and runs off again, piping even louder than before.

I am not wearing my hat and my hands keep going to my hair, smoothing it down. I slouch and squint in the sun. I am waiting for the priest.

The congregation does not move and after a time I go back into the church. It is cool and empty, shafts of sunlight falling from the high windows, catching the play of dust motes, printing light and shadow in stark angles across the pews and the hardwood floor. The floor is rough and nude in the light.

I sit but I do not kneel. I look for the words but the words do not come.

It is late and I am standing at the sink drinking a glass of water, about to turn in for the night. The doorbell rings and Charlotte Clayton is standing there, her eyes like a child's.

I'm sorry Smithy, she says. I've been walking and walking. And I saw your house.

She looks away.

It's tomorrow, isn't it? I say.

She nods and looks at me.

I don't think I can do this, she says. I don't think I can face him.

Charlotte goes home to get some things and I start fixing up Spit's old room. It hasn't been much touched since the day me and Spit had our blue. Roy's slept there often enough, times he was too pissed to go home. But I never bothered to make any effort for Roy. I look around the room.

Over the bed there is a large poster of a naked woman lying on the bonnet of a sports car. I take that down first and then all the other naked women tacked to the walls and doors, pages torn from magazines.

There is a girl coming out of water, her beaded wet breasts showing, another in a pleated white skirt, bent over, nothing under the skirt, a woman sitting naked with her legs spread, holding a red rose between them. It is all tits and arses and cars and motorcycles and the women looking right at you and every one with the same expression. I take them all down and throw them in a pile on the floor.

The mirror on the old rosewood dresser is covered in pictures as well. There's the naked girls again and underneath them long strips of photos, taken in a booth. Spit and his mates, making faces, flexing their arms, showing their bare arses. Spit and Belle kissing, hugging, touching their tongues together, row after row of them. There is Spit with other girls too, Spit at different ages with his long hair and earring, tight T-shirts showing off his tatts, a cigarette packet tucked under the sleeve, holding one lit while he kisses the girls, girls I don't remember. I take the photos down and put them on the dresser.

Underneath there are more things on the mirror. A swimming certificate with Spit's name printed on it and a bronze stamp. A green ribbon with Third Place written in faded gold letters. I try to think but I can't remember Spit being in any sort of competition and I can't remember him learning how to swim neither. A photo falls to the floor and I pick it up and look at it and then I sit on Spit's bed and look at it some more.

It is a family photo, a proper portrait, one we had done in a studio just before Florrie went into hospital. And I remember now about those photos, remember getting them in the mail during my bender and opening the envelope and chucking them in the bin soon as I saw the first one. And it wasn't because I was angry or grieving or anything like that, but because I wasn't feeling anything, because I didn't care about nothing no more. And I didn't know that Spit had got hold of one of them. And I didn't know he had kept it all those years.

We all three of us had driven into the city, decided to make a day of it, and I had asked Florrie beforehand if she wanted to do something special while we were there. And I had meant whether she wanted to go to a restaurant or do some shopping in a department store, something like that. And Florrie said that what she'd really like would be to get a family photo taken, a proper one, because we'd never had one done before. And she must have rung up a photographer and booked it and she set out clothes for us that morning.

So we got the photos taken in the studio and we wandered around town for a bit and I bought Spit an ice-cream from a van and then we took Florrie to the hospital. I didn't know she wouldn't be coming out.

I sit down on the bed and look at the photo. There's Florrie sitting on a chair in her Sunday best, her hat with plastic flowers on it. Spit in front of her, just a boy in his school uniform, cross-legged on the floor, his legs brown and gangly, smiling for the camera. Both of them smiling for the camera. And there's me standing behind them, standing dead straight in a short-sleeved shirt and a tie, my hair in tight steely waves and my hard shearer's face and my jaw clenched because I am not smiling for the camera, I am the only one not smiling.

I look at the photo for a long while and I feel my heart go tight and I throw the photo onto the dresser with Spit's other stuff.

I change the sheets that have not been changed for a long time and open the window to air the room. Then I gather up the poster and all the other naked pictures and throw them into the outside bin. I put the photos and the other things from the dresser into a plastic bag which I leave on the hall table and I suppose I will give it to Spit when I see him.

There is still a bottle of brandy in the kitchen cupboard and I pour myself a full glass and sit down at the table. The brandy burns the ulcers in my mouth and throat and all the way down to my stomach and guts. I double over in pain. Drinking again I taste blood and bile. I tip the rest of the glass down the sink and drink some cold lemonade, but my insides still burn. The pain comes in waves and I go and sit hunched over on the toilet until I pass blood and mucus and start to feel all right.

Charlotte hasn't come back yet and it's getting so late I wonder if she will come back at all. I go into Spit's room again. The musty smell is leaving with the warm night air. I check that Spit's things are all out and notice the dust on the dresser and the bedhead. I wipe it off with my sleeve. I open the wardrobe doors and more dust billows out with fluttering dead moths, powder spilling from their wings. The cupboard is empty except for wire hangers and a studded khaki jacket. I take the jacket and turn it inside out, using it to wipe out the cupboard and the drawers, the floor runners and the windowsill.

I pass the hall table and stand looking at the plastic bag. Sitting back down on the bed I watch the clock for a while and then go back into the hall and take out the photo. I place it on the mantelpiece in the living room, standing it up against Florrie's crystal cakestand. I look at it until the doorbell rings.

Charlotte has been crying. I take her suitcase into Spit's room.

It's not much, I say.

Charlotte grasps my arm and puts her head against my chest.

Try to get some sleep, I say.

She looks around the room, sniffing.

I can't, she says.

Try anyway, I say.

She nods, turning away from me.

MONDAY, SPIT doesn't show. Charlotte is still in bed when I leave.

Wallace is giving the boys a hard time.

Call that drinking? he says. Sniff of the barmaid's apron, the both of you.

Yeah, but I didn't spew, says the talker.

At least he was trying, says Wallace.

After knockoff Wallace drives me home and we see Roy's ute parked outside Imperial.

Roy's drinking down Imperial now, I tell Wallace. Afternoons and all.

Wallace grins and pulls over to the kerb.

Roy isn't in the bar. Les thumbs in the direction of the lounge.

Wallace grins at me again.

Here we go, he says.

Wallace goes to the door and tries to look through the lettering on the frosted glass. His glasses knock against the pane and he swears, pushing them up. He squints and closes one eye, looking with the other, then turning away. He pushes his foot against the door, carefully, opening it a fraction and wincing when the hinges squeak. He looks in through the open crack and lets it close carefully.

He comes back shaking his head and goes over to the bar.

Nora Alister been here? he asks Les.

Les shakes his head.

She usually come down? Wallace asks. Afternoons? Mondays?

Les slides off his stool, hitches up his shorts and goes to the tap.

What are you having Wallace? he asks.

Wallace pulls some coins out of his pocket and chucks them on the bar towel. Les pours him a glass and Wallace points over at me. I come over and Les gives me a lemon squash and a dirty look.

Have a look at this, will you, says Wallace.

We take our drinks and go and look through the door of the lounge.

Roy is sitting drinking from a glass. He is alone at his table and alone in the lounge. His hat is hanging from the back of a chair and his hair is slicked back with Brylcreem. The cream shines on the skin underneath his thinning hair and over his bald patch. Wallace nudges me and points and I see that Roy has his pub shorts on. He sits looking out the window.

Wallace grins at me and we go back to the bar.

You should put some oil on them hinges, Les, Wallace says.

He looks about the pub.

You don't do much round the place, do you, he says to Les. Look at it. Going to pot.

Les shifts on the cushion of his stool and the stool creaks.

Come and criticise me when you got your own place, Wallace, he says.

He looks at the both of us through his bulging yellow eyes.

Don't teach them to hold their drink down there, do you? he says.

There is a sneer in his voice and on his face and he stares at me, waiting for an answer.

He sits back on his stool and folds his arms.

But then you can't hold it yourself, can you? he says, sneering even more.

Wallace nudges me.

Probably wearing aftershave too, he says.

We are about to leave when Wallace says, well look what the cat dragged in. He says it quietly, under his breath.

Brett Clayton has come into the pub with a group of men. He is thinner than I remember, his hair longer. His face is gaunt and long-jawed, unshaven. He looks around the place before he sits down. His eyes are pale, almost without colour at all. Spit is with them. They take a table near the front window. A few of them go to the bar and get jugs and pots.

Wonder when he got out, Wallace says. He turns his glass in his hand, watching the group.

Wallace talks quietly.

He's supposed to be barred, he says.

He looks over at Les.

Spit wanders over and leans against the bar next to us, putting his pot on the counter and shaking a cigarette out of a soft pack.

Since when you been mates with Brett Clayton? I ask him.

Brett's all right, says Spit, shrugging his shoulders. He taps the butt of the cigarette against the back of his hand and lights up.

Les is watching the group too. The puffing and blowing and belching has stopped and his face is frozen, his popped eyes popping even more than usual. The burst vessels which run like crazy maps across his face have gone scarlet and lavender. He is waiting and we are watching him wait.

Spit drains his pot and goes back to the table. The men are getting rowdy. Me and Wallace keep watching Les.

Eventually Brett Clayton comes up to the bar. He lets a handful of change drop through his fist onto the bar towel. Les sits there staring at the money. He can't take his eyes off of it. There is a moment. Then he slides off his stool and pours Brett Clayton a pot.

Looks like he's not barred anymore, Wallace mumbles into his glass.

Brett Clayton takes his pot and walks down to where me and Wallace are sitting. He stands next to me and drinks. He is standing dead straight. He drinks slowly.

You know where my old lady is, Smithy? he asks, not looking at me, not for a moment. He looks straight ahead to the back of the bar.

Yeah, I say.

She staying with you?

That's right, I say.

I thought as much, he says. He drains his pot, leaves it on the counter and walks back to his mates.

When I turn to Wallace he is sitting there looking at me, just looking at me, not saying a word, not saying nothing, staring at me through those thick lenses with huge faraway eyes.

When I get home, Charlotte is curled up on the couch in Florrie's old bathrobe, her feet tucked up underneath her. She is looking off nowhere. The gas fire is going despite the heat. It doesn't look like she's moved from that spot since she got up.

The family photo is sitting in front of her on the coffee table.

She gives me a faded smile as I come in. It goes quickly. There are twitching lines at the corner of her mouth and on her brow.

Well I saw him, I say. Down Imperial.

She looks up, barely interested. Her eyes are tired.

Drinking, I say.

She nods slightly.

You had anything to eat today? I ask her.

Charlotte shakes her head.

You want me to go and get you something? I ask. Put some colour in you.

I couldn't eat, she says.

I sit next to her on the couch. She picks up the photo and looks at it.

Is that your family? she asks me.

Yeah, I say. Taken some time back.

Charlotte points at Spit in the photo.

How old is he now? she asks.

What, Spit? I say.

Oh, that's Spit is it? she says, looking closer at the picture. Belle's Spit?

That's right, I say.

She looks at the little bare-legged boy in the photo.

I can see that now, she says. I didn't realise he was your son.

Well he's his own man now, I say. Got his own family.

I stretch, craning my neck.

He was down Imperial too, I say. With your husband. I didn't realise they was mates.

I don't think they are, really, she says. I mean, we know Spit and Belle, we see them around. But I never really thought they were mates.

Spit, I say. I look down at my hands. Spit's not perfect. He's got his own faults like everyone else. But he knows what Brett done. I would of thought, you know, after what happened.

Well, the boys stick together, don't they, Charlotte says.

Yeah, I suppose so.

Charlotte pulls her feet under herself some more.

I like Belle, she says.

Yeah, I say. Belle doesn't have it easy. I suppose most women don't. Working men's wives anyway.

Charlotte turns her worn eyes on me.

Brett's never worked a day in his life, she says. I don't know where he gets his money. He doesn't say and I don't ask.

She looks at the photo again.

But I know the rumours, same as everyone else.

She is pointing at the picture of Florrie.

My wife, I say. I lost her. Cancer.

Charlotte keeps looking at the portrait, tracing it over with her finger.

Florrie, I say. Florence. But I always known her as Florrie.

Charlotte puts the photo down on the coffee table.

Florence, she says. Was she named after the city?

I'd doubt it, I say. It was a common name in my day. Florence, Florrie, Flo.

Charlotte's head is down, her face sad. She is chipping at the polish on her fingernails.

When I was at school, my Italian teacher used to say that Florence was the most beautiful city in the world.

Well, I wouldn't know about that sort of thing, I say.

I could have gone there, she says. To Florence.

You should of, I say. Broaden your horizons.

Charlotte nods weakly.

I know. I should have. But I didn't.

She leans over and looks at the photo again and then curls back up on the couch. She stares off. Outside the light is fading.

TUESDAY, SPIT doesn't show and Lucy catches a snake.

We can hear her snarling from down the rows. Roy drops his shovel and runs, losing his hat as he goes. We follow him. He stands at the end of the row, watching.

Jesus, he says. She's got the wrong end.

Lucy's lips are drawn back showing her teeth with the snake's tail clamped between them. She is making frantic noises, growling and barking and whining all at once. She shakes her head violently and swings the snake across the dirt, the snake trying to arch itself back, its fangs drawn.

Roy steps forwards with his shovel raised. The snake sweeps towards him. He leaps back, swearing.

I go and lop the snake's head off.

The snake's body writhes and Lucy keeps shaking it. Roy goes and pulls the tail from her mouth and Lucy growls, circling the twitching body. She sits down panting, her tongue out, and she looks up at Roy, whimpering.

Aw, Christ, he says. I think she's been bit.

He picks up Lucy in his arms and she snaps half-heartedly at him. He strokes her head, looking into her eyes.

Aw Christ girl, he says. Oh Jesus.

He starts carrying her down the row and towards his ute.

You drive Wallace, he calls over his shoulder.

Where to? asks Wallace.

Animal hospital, says Roy. Come on, will you.

We walk after Roy. He is putting Lucy gently into the back of the ute, stroking her head and talking softly to her. She half closes her eyes.

That was a brown snake, Roy, I say. If she got bit she'll be dead before you get there.

Roy climbs onto the back of the tray and sits next to Lucy, sliding over and putting her head on his lap.

He's not wrong, Roy, says Wallace.

Roy looks up at us. There are tears in his eyes.

Just bloody drive, will you, he says to Wallace.

Wallace swears under his breath and chucks his shovel. He takes the keys from Roy and we watch them drive off.

I go back to where the dead snake is lying and dig a hole in the dirt, rolling in the head and burying it. I pick up the long body and look at it, feeling the scales with my fingers. I fling it towards the back of the vineyard. It goes wheeling in an arc and lands on the wire fence, hanging there for a moment and then slipping to the ground, light running off the scales in a quick flashing stream. The crows go after it.

Well get back to work, I say to the boys.

We walk back to our rows.

You reckon she's gunna die? asks one of the boys.

If she got bit, I say. If she got bit, she'll die.

Boss comes up not long after.

He walks towards us scowling and stands there with his arms

folded, watching us work. He watches for some time.

So what's this? he says finally. Everyone off crook or we had some more funerals?

Roy's dog got bit by a snake, I say, pushing back a vine.

What? he says. The little blue heeler?

Yeah, I say, sticking my shovel in the dirt. Roy's dog.

I get my knife out.

Him and Wallace have taken her into Corowa, I say. Up to the animal hospital.

Well that's a shame, says Boss, pushing his hat back and scratching his forehead. Hope it pulls through. Fingers crossed.

He goes and looks at some leaves, turning them over. I bend over and cut off some shoots at the base of the vine.

You see the snake? Boss asks me, looking at leaves.

Yeah, I say, standing up and closing my knife. Brown snake.

I put my knife back into its pouch and pull my shovel out of the dirt.

Boss stops sorting through the leaves and looks at me.

Brown snake? he says. It'll be dead before they get there.

That's what I said.

So what's the point of taking it all the way out there then? Boss asks. Bitten by a brown snake. You would have been better off shooting it. You should have come and got the shotgun from the cellar. I mean, that's the humane thing to do, isn't it?

I start on the next vine.

I mean, poor bloody thing, says Boss. It's a hell of a way to die.

Well they weren't sure whether it got bit or not, I say, chopping into a thick shoot.

You would have known soon enough, says Boss. I mean, where's the logic in that? There's no point taking it in if it did get bitten and no point taking it in if it wasn't.

Well, that's Roy for you, I say, gripping the shovel above the blade and pounding hard.

Boss folds his hands over his gut again.

I mean, what do they think they're playing at? The afternoon's wasted now, isn't it? Spit still crook. These two still learning.

He watches the boys work.

It's just a waste of time, isn't it? Wasting all our time.

Boss shakes his head and walks off. Then he turns around and comes back again.

I look up and he is smiling at me.

Sounds like the end of days, doesn't it Smithy? he says.

What's that? I say, moving around a vine.

The end of days, he says, smiling, his mouth open. Now come on, Smithy, you're a church-goer, aren't you?

I stop my work and face him.

End of days? I say.

Well, yeah, says Boss, looking up at the sky. The signs.

He holds out his palm and counts off fingers.

Well, there's pestilence for one, he says. Spit crook. And I don't know, what do you reckon? Snakes count as pestilence?

I shrug my shoulders.

Could be a double meaning there, says Boss. Something like that.

I wouldn't know, I say.

Well, there's this locust plague, isn't there, he says. Can't get more biblical than that now, can you?

The sun is coming in behind him and I shade my eyes.

So after that there's war, says Boss, counting off another finger. Always a war going on in some part of the world.

And then, well, he says smiling, putting his hands in his pockets and rocking back and forth, well I always think the next one's drought, but it isn't is it?

He smiles his gummy smile at me.

I always feel we got a bit short-changed there, he says, chuckling. I mean a good few years of drought now. Certainly feels like the end of things sometimes. Crops going to ruin. Bad vintages. But it's death, isn't it? Am I right there? Can't forget old death, now, can we?

No we can't, I say.

I pick up my shovel.

Well, we've got Roy's little dog if that brown snake got it.

He stands there.

And there was George Alister, wasn't there.

Boss looks up at the sky, scratching his chin.

Now what's the other one? he says.

I stick my shovel in the ground and churn the dirt, watching it. Down by the fence the crows are squabbling, flying up and stretching out their wings and circling back down to where the snake carcass is, hidden behind the vines. More crows come. I look up at Boss.

Famine, I say.

Wallace and Roy come back just before knockoff. Lucy jumps off the tray and runs over to us, excited. She sniffs our boots, snorting and panting, looking up at us. Then she turns and races along the rows.

Roy wanders up, smoking a cigarette.

False alarm, he says.

When I come home Charlotte is same as she was yesterday, rolled up on the couch, pale and listless.

How you holding up? I ask.

All right, she says in a tiny voice.

117

She starts to cry silently, tears running down her face, gathering on her nose and chin and dripping onto the bathrobe.

I take my handkerchief from my pocket but it is dirty and slick with oil. I get a tea towel from the kitchen drawer and give it to her. She holds it loosely in her hands. The tea towel was given us by Florrie's sister after she went to Scotland and the pictures of castles and stags and mountains have faded. Charlotte's tears fall onto a large purple thistle.

The black make-up around her eyes has spread with the tears and runs in lines down her face. And those black eyes remind me of that night.

I feel like it's all over for me, she says.

How do you mean? I ask.

She sniffs and shudders.

Like I'm at the end of things, she says. Like there's nothing out there for me anymore.

I sit down opposite her and go to put a hand on her shoulder but she flinches and I take my hand away.

It's not about whether I leave Brett or not, she says.

She sobs and breathes.

I look at her face and her eyes, the pupils large, her brow tight and lined.

How are you sleeping? I ask.

Not good, she says. Everything seems worse at night. I keep waking up and looking at the clock. All night long. Sometimes I think I've slept but when I look at the clock it's only been ten minutes, twenty minutes. I just lie and wait until morning.

I hate the nights, she says.

You should try and get some decent sleep, I say. A good night's sleep can do wonders.

When I do sleep I dream, she says. Last night I dreamt I was walking around the city, looking for my shoes. I'd lost my shoes and it was freezing. I found a whole pile in the city square and I started looking for my shoes but they were all boots, men's boots. I never found my shoes. I can't seem to sleep without dreaming.

The gas fire pops. The afternoon sun streams through the back window. Charlotte's face is downcast and I look at that face and at those black running eyes and I keep thinking about that night.

Why don't you try to eat something, I say to Charlotte. You'd sleep better with some food in you.

Besides, I say, you need to keep your strength up.

Charlotte isn't listening. She is looking at her fingernails.

My parents are never going to forgive me, she says. They'll never trust me again, not after what I did to them. I just threw it all back in their faces. I've failed them. I've ruined my life.

I shift my legs away from the fire. Outside, the tortured day is fading. Birds call. They go in flocks, the sky growing pale behind them, a weak light falling high in the canopies of trees. The slight movement of leaves suggests the cool of evening.

You haven't had a life yet, I say. You're just starting out. There's nothing you can't do, put your mind to it.

She shakes her head and wipes her face with the back of both hands and sighs, looking up at me.

You remember how I told you I could have gone to Florence? she says.

Yeah, you were saying.

I feel like that was my big mistake. I feel like if I'd gone to Florence my life would be different. Everything would be different.

She wipes her nose and looks away.

I'm only just realising that now, she says. But it was so long ago. I don't even feel like I'm the same person anymore.

Her face is red and swollen from the crying.

I can't make a new start, she says. I just can't. I don't have it in me anymore. I feel like everything's over, like it's already ended. It's like I died and just kept on going. Like I'm a ghost.

Charlotte looks out the window at the breeze in the trees, wringing the tea towel in her hands, and I don't say a thing. Because that night I thought she was death itself.

WEDNESDAY MORNING I am sitting on my bed in my work clothes, waiting for Roy to come pick me up. Charlotte is awake. I stay in my room while she gets herself together, listening to the shower running and the hairdryer and Charlotte moving about. Then I hear her scream.

She is standing in the living room, staring out the back window.

I saw him, she says. Behind the fence.

I go outside and out the back gate onto the railway line.

The day is overcast and windy. Trees toss. The grass flattens and rises with an angry noise. The rubbish along the ditch shifts and scatters. Across the fences Hills Hoists turn slowly with the rasp of metal on metal, hung clothes blowing violently about.

I look down the track but there is nobody there.

Back inside, Charlotte is standing same as she was.

I shake my head.

No one, I say.

Charlotte sits down.

Well, he was there, she says.

I turn on the gas fire and get a blanket and go to put it over her.

No, I'm all right, Charlotte says. There's no need for that. I just got a fright, that's all.

She takes the blanket anyway and puts it over herself, pulling it up to her chin.

Just my bloody husband acting like a child, she says. It just took me by surprise.

In the kitchen I pour out a glass of brandy.

Get that down you, I say, putting it in her hands.

She takes a drink from the glass and gags.

God, that's awful, Smithy, Charlotte says. What did you give me that for?

Drink it all, I say. It'll calm your nerves.

My nerves are fine, Charlotte says. I'm fine. I told you, he just gave me a fright. I wasn't expecting it. Of course I wasn't expecting it, first thing in the morning. I mean, of all the idiotic things to do.

I hear Roy's ute turn into the drive, the engine running. The horn sounds twice and I go out.

Roy has the driver's window open, one arm hanging out.

The wind is warm now, strong and squalling. It is moody weather.

I'm not coming, I say.

Roy leans his head out the window and looks at the day.

Why not? he asks.

That's my business, I say.

Roy looks at me, his hair flying about. I scrape the gravel with the toe of my boot. Roy turns off the engine. It is grey all around.

So what you want me to tell Boss? he asks.

No need to tell him anything, I say.

Well, he's going to want to know, says Roy. Not like you to miss a day.

He stretches his neck and rubs it and looks at me again.

You want me to tell him you're crook? he asks.

Nope, I say.

Yeah, but you are crook though, aren't you? he says. I mean, with your digestion. That's a medical condition isn't it? You got a medical condition fair enough.

Yeah, well that's why I don't want you to tell him, isn't it, I say. Just don't tell him nothing.

Jesus, says Roy. I'm just trying to help you out.

Roy raises himself from his seat and takes his tobacco pouch out of his shorts. He rolls the tobacco slowly in the paper, pulling out strands with his fingernails and putting them back into the pouch. Trees rip from side to side.

It's not your problem, he says quietly as he rolls. He bobs his head down to lick the paper and smooths it over, looking at it.

Well I made it my problem, I say.

Roy strikes a match and lights the cigarette, turning away from the window and cupping it in his hands. He puffs heavily on it, shaking out the match. He glances at me and holds the tip of the cigarette to his lips, blowing off the fluttering embers.

The wind gusts around us, picking up dust from the gravel and blowing it over the ground. The dust spins and scatters.

Roy takes the cigarette out of his mouth.

Aren't you too old to be playing the hero? he says.

I turn and walk back to the house. As I reach the front door I hear Roy starting up the engine.

Inside, the gas fire splutters. I sit down opposite Charlotte and watch the blue and orange flames licking at the honeycombed ceramic. The day stays overcast, the sun a dirty bright disc behind the clouds. The morning traffic starts up, a dull roar in the distance. The wind howls.

*

Charlotte has another shower. I clear up the coffee table and sit in the armchair. The gas fire is hot through my jeans and I shift away from it. I watch the day.

Charlotte comes out in her bathrobe with a towel around her head. The steam of the shower follows her in. Her face is flushed and shiny. She crouches down by the fire.

Bloody Brett, she says, drying her hair with the towel. You know I could call the police about that, get him put back inside. For that.

Well, why don't you? I say.

Because, she says. She is squeezing her hair with the towel, one part and then another.

Well, it's complicated, she says. The whole thing is complicated. I mean, it's not like Brett hits me and, yes, I know he did that one time, but there was a reason.

There's no reason for that, Charlotte, I say. Come on now.

But there was, says Charlotte. John Gibson. It was all because of John Gibson and what Brett did to him. And because I knew. I mean Brett did do it, he killed John Gibson and I'm well aware that everyone says he did, but I know it for sure. I'm the only one who actually knows.

What, did he tell you? I ask.

No, she says, looking at the flames. But I know. I saw.

I probably shouldn't be telling you this, she says.

I pat down my jeans. Charlotte finishes with the towel and puts it over the back of the couch.

I don't mean I saw him shoot John Gibson, but it's the things I saw the night it happened, after Brett got back. I was asleep and I got woken up by this smell of burning. Petrol burning. And when I opened my eyes the whole room was lit up. I thought the house was on fire. But when I looked out of the window, I could see Brett standing over the incinerator, stoking it with a lead pipe. And the weird thing was that he wasn't wearing any clothes. He was standing there in his underwear.

So that was strange, but I never said anything to him about it. He didn't ever know that I saw him. I just shut the window and went back to sleep.

It did seem strange, she says. But when Brett gets pissed.

Charlotte's hair, damp and dark with the damp, falls down over her face and shoulders. She takes strands and holds them in front of her, looking at them.

But it was the next day, she says. He was wearing an old pair of Dunlop Volleys. And as long as I've known him I've never seen Brett wear anything but boots. So when I heard about John Gibson I knew. I knew Brett had done it, just like everyone says. I just knew.

Charlotte takes the towel off the couch and flings it out and starts to fold it.

And when the police came I lied. I just lied. And it was so easy.

She finishes folding the towel and runs her hand over it, smoothing it out. She sits down with her glowing skin and long damp hair.

I'm no better than him, she says.

I start to say something.

No, she says. It's true. You can't tell me it's not true.

It's a difficult thing, Charlotte, I say. I've known plenty of men's wives lied for them, would have said anything to keep their husbands out of trouble. Wouldn't give it a second thought.

But this, she says.

I known wives lied about worse, I say.

Charlotte gives me a sour glance.

How could anything be worse?

There's worse, I say.

It's just, I never told you, Smithy. I couldn't have told you. Not back then, that night you found me on the railway line. Because that's why he did it. Because I threatened to tell. I said I was going to go to the police and tell them how I'd lied and that I was going to tell them everything. We were having some argument. I can't even remember what it was about. But I told him. About the incinerator, how I'd seen him. And his boots. I said I was going to tell the police everything and it scared him. And I'd never seen Brett scared before. And somehow I felt, I don't know, it was like I had some sort of power over him. But Smithy, I really frightened him. And that's when he started hitting me.

Charlotte sits with her head and shoulders slumped.

And he wouldn't stop, she says. I thought he was going to kill me too.

Leaves and twigs fall on the roof like a light rain. Magpies and wattlebirds swoop and gather and fight among the trees. Willie wagtails twitch and click. The fire burns.

Brett should have gone away for what he did to John Gibson, Charlotte says. But instead they put him away for what he did to me. And I was as guilty as him. I deserved it. I deserve much worse.

Now come on Charlotte, I say.

She shakes her head.

No, Charlotte says. I was glad of it. When he was hitting me I was glad of it. Somehow it was a relief. Because it was eating me up inside. And the way he reacted. He knew what I'd done was wrong too.

But it was him done it, I say. You didn't have a thing to do with it.

I know it sounds crazy, she says. But it felt right. For me it felt right. I wanted it to happen.

She sits up and brushes her hair back with both hands, pulling it back tight. Her face has gone hard.

I'll never forgive myself, she says. Never. I can't look Carol Gibson in the face anymore. And her kids. If I see them in town I cross the street to avoid them. And she knows. Everyone knows.

I can smell Charlotte's hair, warm from the fire, the wet smell filling the room. It is fragrant like women's things. She breathes deeply.

Sometimes I just want to run away, she says. Just get out of this town. Away from it all. But that's not going to change anything, is it?

I get up and look out the window into the backyard and the muted colours of the day. The limbs of the camellia are lifting and hovering with the wind, the flowers already bloomed and died but still clinging stiff to the branches, tough, brown and dusty. The bottlebrush swarms. By the fence, pale grapefruit sway and the folds of the paperbark flap back and forth, its angry sprouts of foliage tossing. Unmown grass and dandelions are blown flat. Wind sweeps through the ivy. The sloughing bark of the ghost gum flutters, mottled pink and grey, its cracked edges scorched. Underneath, the new bark is white and smooth, winding ribs at the base of the trunk. Spit's old punching bag hangs from the bough, creaking on its frayed rope, the bag weathered, sunk and split, moulting stuffing. The birds flock to gather it in spring and have done so for many years.

In the afternoon I walk into town, looking for Brett Clayton. I just want to see his face. It remains dank and humid, the air thick, sullied, swimming in filth. The wind has died and all is still. Exhaust fumes hang. There is something strange and unreal about the day.

I find Brett Clayton at The Crown, sitting at a back table with his

mates. Uncollected jugs litter the table and those surrounding it.
The other drinkers sit away.

Spit joins me at the bar. He is looking gaunt, more so than usual.
He is unshaven, his eyes red-rimmed and bloodshot, his face grey.
He stinks.

You all on a bender or something? I ask him.

Spit shrugs.

They are loud at the table. Brett Clayton yells over to us.

Hey Spit, he says. That your old man?

Brett Clayton is leaning back on his chair, with one foot balanced
on the carpet, the other against the table. He is looking at us. His
eyes are glazed and staring. They are the glazed, staring eyes of a
violent drunk.

Yeah, Spit yells over his shoulder.

Brett Clayton turns to his mates.

Spit's old man, he says. Shacked up with my old lady.

His mates guffaw.

There is the sound of glass, the smell of beer. A grey cloud of
cigarette smoke rolls from the table. Behind the counter the
barmaid is drying pots with a tea towel. The other drinkers throw us
sideways glances and silent.

Hey Spit, Brett Clayton yells. Ask your old man if it's true love or
just a physical thing.

His mates laugh and drink.

Don't worry about Brett, Spit says to me.

When I leave it is me who is shaking.

The sun falls and shadows come. The air has lifted and it is fresh
and floats with cooking smells. Birds wheel after insects in the dusk
and daytime thins on the breeze. Men are home and few cars pass.

Far off across grainy spaces farmers whistle and call to their dogs, turning themselves home, weary, the grind of tractors.

Night and darkness and me and Charlotte are sitting. I haven't put the lights on. I am weary too, something about the day, and I can feel my age and my weakness, the sickness inside me, pains in my bones. Charlotte talks and there is only the glow of the fire flickering across her face, soft light and shadow, her face as though in movement, strange like in dreams, and my eyes strain to see her.

Brett and I went hitchhiking after we got married, she says. I suppose it was our honeymoon, not much of a honeymoon, but that was all we had. We'd been staying at his cousin's place in Melbourne, but we didn't have anywhere to live, back then. My family weren't talking to me, not after everything that had happened, and Brett didn't want to stay with his father. His father was still alive then, but he was already sick, and Brett hadn't had much to do with him for a long time already. So we went hitchhiking, to Surfers Paradise, that was our plan, but we never made it there, just to Sydney, and we had no money so it was all pretty miserable really, the whole thing, not much of a honeymoon, but that was our honeymoon, that was it.

We hitched with truck drivers mostly, semi-trailers. We'd go to the rest stops, where the semis were parked, and the drivers would be sleeping or resting and most of them would give you a lift. Some of them were friendly, others hardly talked to you at all, but I suppose they wanted the company, or it was just the thing to do. Brett said there was no point trying to thumb a lift. He'd done a lot of hitchhiking before, so he knew the ropes.

Anyway, we'd got a ride, somewhere. It was night and I'd lost track of where we were, but it was somewhere on the way to Sydney, and the driver was this young guy, Brett's age. Most of the drivers were these fat middle-aged men who didn't talk much, even the friendly ones, so I would have remembered this guy anyway. He had long hair and tatts, he was a lot like Brett really, and I thought at first that was good, that maybe they'd get along, maybe he'd take us all the way to Sydney, which he said he would when we first got in.

But for some reason, I don't know why, after we got moving, I think maybe because of Brett, maybe he didn't trust him, or he just wanted to scare us, or he was showing off, the driver pulled out this big knife, and he didn't really threaten us with the knife, but he showed it to us and he said he could kill us if he wanted to. I don't know why. It was probably because of Brett, something about Brett. I mean, lots of people don't like the look of Brett, but I would have thought this guy would have been all right, because, as I said, he was sort of similar to Brett. But maybe that's why, maybe he didn't trust Brett because he knew what he was like, because he was like him.

Anyway, after he put away the knife he was friendly and quite chatty, compared to the other drivers anyway, but Brett was furious about the whole thing with the knife. I could tell at the time and I was worried Brett was going to do something, and he did say afterwards that he would have decked the guy if he hadn't been driving, and I suppose Brett was right to be angry. I mean, even if the guy was just trying to scare us, just letting us know not to try anything, it was still over the top.

I don't know where it was exactly, but eventually we pulled up at a rest stop. It was in the middle of nowhere anyway. So we all got out and Brett followed the guy into the toilets and I thought something was going to happen, but nothing did, well, Brett must have said something. I asked him afterwards, and he just said he'd had a quiet word with the guy, but whatever he said, the guy came outof the toilets and got straight into the truck and drove off. I don't know what Brett said, but we lost our ride anyway.

And it was late and you know those rest stops, just lines of trucks sitting there, occasionally one coming and going, but there's something strange about them, something a bit scary, or I found it all scary, out in the middle of nowhere, with no one about, just trucks sitting there with the lights off and the drivers asleep inside. And I thought we'd get a lift with someone else, but Brett was still angry and he said he'd had it with truck drivers.

So we decided to camp out, or Brett decided. I wasn't too happy, because I didn't know where we were and, like I said, the place scared me. Also it was freezing. It must have been winter, now that I remember it. I remember when we got to Sydney it was raining the whole time. It wasn't raining that night, the sky was clear, but it was icy cold, cold and there was frost in the morning. I would rather have got another lift, but it wasn't a good idea with Brett in that mood.

We had a tent, at least. Brett's cousin had lent us his tent and some other gear, and we went away from the truck stop to find somewhere to camp and I just remember how dark it was and going through a lot of scrub. It was pitch black down where we were, you couldn't see anything except the stars, and it got even harder to see when we got away from the truck stop. I really didn't know where we were or where we were going and I got all scratched up from the scrub and wet as well because everything was covered in dew. And I started to get really frightened. I mean, I was just a kid, and I'd never done anything like this before but I suppose I trusted Brett because he had. I thought he knew what he was doing, really he didn't, but anyway, I was just a kid, I didn't know anything. But I thought Brett did.

So we kept walking through the scrub until it started to thin out and then we were walking through paddocks, I suppose. I don't know whether we were on someone's property or where it was, but we were a long way from the truck stop by then. You could still hear the trucks coming and going and the sound of the brakes, but you couldn't see much, just lights in the distance. And eventually we came to the top of a hill and we saw this fire down below and we thought it was probably other hitchhikers camping out, like us.

Anyway, Brett told me to wait while he checked it out. I suppose he did used to look after me like that. So I waited while he went down. The fire was sort of hidden in a ditch, we hadn't seen it at all until we got to the top of this hill, and I stood there in the cold, and I could hear Brett's voice and another voice, and I waited for such a long time, absolutely frozen, just waiting and waiting. I was nearly in tears by the time Brett came back. And he said it was all right, they were cool. And I thought it would be young people, like us, but it wasn't.

What it was, there was this couple, I suppose you would call them a couple. But it really wasn't what I expected. I thought they'd be backpackers or something, other hitchhikers, but young people, like I said. I was sort of happy about it, for the company, until I saw these people, who it was, this man, this awful man, and this young girl.

The man, this man was really, you know when there's just something wrong? When you can just feel there's something wrong, like a gut feeling? Well, this man, there was something very wrong about him. He was probably in his fifties, older maybe, but rough, really rough. I mean he had no teeth and this long beard and his face was sort of tough and sunburnt, you could tell he lived outdoors. And he had some problem with his back, he was hunched over when he walked, or even when he was sitting, and when he talked to you he had to bend his neck to look up at you. I just remember these eyes looking up at me all the time. And he acted nice enough, but that sort of made things seem worse, I mean, he was acting nice, but overdoing it, like he was hiding something, or guilty about something, which he was, I mean, that was obvious. Like I said, I could tell straight away there was something wrong about the whole thing. I could just tell.

And the man had these tattoos on his fingers, like from cards, a deck of cards, aces, spades, diamonds, clubs, on the fingers of both hands, red and black. But they weren't proper tattoos, they were sort of messy and uneven. Brett said afterwards that they were prison tatts, he said in prison they'd cut their skin with razor blades and they'd do the tatts with pen ink or oven grease. I didn't know at the time, but I wasn't surprised when Brett said the man had been in prison. I didn't trust him from the start, and he scared me, and, like I said, I was already scared being alone in that place, out in the middle of nowhere, but this was so much worse, because even though the man was short and bent over, he looked strong, really strong. And I knew Brett could handle himself, but this man could have done anything to us out there, and I wondered why Brett was so relaxed and I just remember thinking, Brett better not go off and leave me here, with them.

So they had this camp set up around the fire and they must have been there for ages, I mean, they lived there, they weren't camping out, they were living there, it was obvious they were living in this ditch and there was all this junk lying around, old car seats around the fire and a fridge sitting on its side and styrofoam eskies and dirty mattresses, piles of sheets and rags and old clothes, just rubbish, most of it. And there was a tarpaulin set up on sticks, near the fire.

133

But it was the girl, that's what really creeped me out, this old man and this young girl, and I didn't really see her until we'd sat down by the fire, on the car seats. She was just sitting there, not saying anything. She didn't say a single thing, the whole time, not one word. And she was retarded or something. You could tell by her face, she just sort of looked wrong, in the face. And the whole time she was looking at me, staring at me. When I first sat down I smiled at her, but she didn't react at all, she just kept staring. She was holding a kitten, and she just sat there stroking the kitten, staring at me, the whole time. And she was really young, just a kid, or maybe a teenager, it was hard to tell, but too young, definitely too young to be with this man, living out in the middle of nowhere. She just shouldn't have been there. Especially not with this awful, awful man. It was ghastly. The whole thing was just horrible.

And Brett and the man kept on talking and passing around this plastic bottle. I don't know what was in it, meths, I think. I nearly threw up, but Brett drank it. The girl didn't, the man didn't even offer it to her. She just kept sitting there, staring at me, stroking this kitten. And then for some reason she got up and came over to me and held out the kitten, not saying anything, just holding it out, like a child does, for me to pat it, and I started to stroke it and, I couldn't see it properly, but it felt odd. The kitten. It was stiff and cold and I suppose I could feel it but I kept stroking it and it took me a while to realise that it was dead. And I looked at it more closely and I saw that its face was sort of frozen, like a mask, and it had no eyes, just these black holes, where the eyes should have been. It was dead, a corpse, and it must have been dead for a long time.

But the worst part of it was, after Brett and the man had finished the bottle of meths, or whatever it was, the man said he was going to turn in, and he said goodnight to us, shook Brett's hand, he was still being polite, and he went under the tarp, and the girl followed him, went under the tarp with him. So we put our tent up near the fire. I wouldn't even talk to Brett. And not because I was angry at him, I was too upset to be angry. I just didn't want to talk to him. And even though I was exhausted, I knew I wasn't going to be able to sleep. Brett did, he dropped off straight away. But I just lay there in the dark and the cold and after a while the man and the girl started having sex. And you could hear him talking to her and making noises, but she didn't say anything, or make any noise, you couldn't hear her at all. It was like she wasn't even there. So he kept grunting away, going at it, and after a while I did hear her, very quiet. She was making these sounds. And I realised that she was meowing, like a cat, and sort of purring, making the noises a cat makes. And the meowing got louder and louder. My God it was horrible. It was just unbearable. And I just lay there, in the freezing cold. Having to listen to it.

Charlotte stops talking. Her face swims in the light. She is looking into the fire.

I don't know why I just thought of that, she says. I'd completely forgotten about it. I don't know why I thought of that just now.

After Charlotte turns in I get my old shotgun from out the hall cupboard and clean it at the kitchen table. I find a box of shells in the garage. I load the gun and put it under my bed and then I change into my pyjamas and go to sleep.

THURSDAY I wake from broken dreams and Charlotte's voice. All night in my dreams and half asleep, Charlotte's voice, and I dreamt she was there in the room, talking from out the darkness. I get up, exhausted, my pyjamas soaked in sweat. Dawn breaks and the song of magpies. I shiver as I dress.

What did Boss say? I ask Roy.

Roy shrugs his shoulders. He's left the motor running.

Not much, he says. Didn't say nothing.

Yeah? I say.

Not as far as I heard, said Roy.

So nothing, I say.

Roy shakes his head. He winds up the window and leaves.

I sit in the living room and watch the sun rise over the trees. There is movement in Charlotte's room and then the bathroom. She is in there for some time.

I remember I left the shotgun cocked and I go and get it from under my bed and unload it, putting the shells in my pocket. I stand the shotgun against the back of the wardrobe and wipe my hands on my jeans.

Charlotte comes out of the bathroom scented and made up, her hair done and colour on her cheeks. Her eyelashes are long and dark, her brows high and arched. She walks in carrying herself, her back straight, and sits down on the couch, her back straight still.

You look well, I say.

She is arranging Florrie's bathrobe.

I just woke up and I thought, bugger it, she says. I'm not going to let this destroy me.

She pats her pinned-up hair. Her straight back and arched eyebrows give her a proud look.

I've got to keep going, don't I, she says. Whatever happens.

Good for you, I say.

I owe it to myself, she says. I deserve better than this.

The dawn clears. The sun is full, the sky untroubled. Charlotte stands up and goes to the window. Cars and utes pass.

I watch her, the morning sun on her.

I make porridge for Charlotte. She eats at the kitchen table while I clean up. The mealy smell turns my stomach.

You know I've lost five kilos, Charlotte says. I've been trying to lose that for years. The one good thing I've got out of this whole bloody mess.

Oh yeah, I say.

I scrub the saucepan and the wooden spoon. The kitchen smells of starch and detergent, the sink water grey and swimming with globules. I nearly retch.

I'll probably just put it on again, she says.

That's what they say, isn't it.

I keep working on the saucepan.

So how come you never take that hat off? Charlotte says. You've got beautiful hair.

What? I say, my hand going to my hat. I look at Charlotte who is watching me, smiling.

Last night I woke up in the middle of the night and my heart was racing like crazy, she says. And I was breathing funny. It was like I couldn't breathe, like I was suffocating. I think it must have been a panic attack or something. Anyway, I was still half asleep, sort of confused. I'd been dreaming and I thought I was at home, I mean back at my parents' house, on the farm. When I finally woke up I was in your room. I didn't know your hair was so white.

I didn't hear you, I say. I would of thought I'd hear you come in.

It was all spread out around your head, she says. I never knew it was so white.

I put the clean things onto the dish rack and drain the sink. I sniff my hands and wash them and sniff them again.

You're blushing, says Charlotte.

Even old men got vanity, I say.

He didn't come back? Charlotte asks, looking out the back window.

Not that I saw.

We are in the lounge room. The gas fire is off today and I look at the cold waxy ceramic. Light splashes the room.

I'm just sick of it, says Charlotte. These games, these stupid games. Whatever it is he's playing at. My useless bloody dropkick of a husband. I'm just sick of it. I've had enough.

There is a sharp pain in the knuckle of one of my fingers. I rub it but the pain does not go.

I mean, I should be the angry one, says Charlotte. I'm the one who's been hard done by, aren't I? Not Brett. No matter what he thinks. I'm the one who should be, whatever he's doing, holding a grudge or whatever. It should be me. I should have stayed home, told him to pack his bags, told him to never come back. That's my right, isn't it? After what happened?

Of course it is, I say.

The police told me I should get a restraining order, she says. And I should have. But instead I go running off and hide, like it's all my fault. Which is how he sees it, I'm sure. Well, I know that's how he sees it. And I'm just playing into his hands, aren't I? I mean, running away, whatever I'm doing. I really don't know what I'm doing. I mean, you tell me. Why am I here? Can you tell me that? Why did I come here, of all places? It's ridiculous. No offence Smithy, but I don't even know you. I mean, I appreciate what you're doing for me, but really we don't know each other, do we? So what the hell am I doing here? Hiding out like this. I don't know what I'm doing.

Charlotte turns from the window and looks at me and turns back again, looking out at the fences and trees and the light striking the landscape, in places, in parts, here and there. There is still the smell of boiled oats and starch coming from the kitchen.

I suppose it just goes to show what sort of friends I have, she says. Why didn't I go to them, my friends, my so-called friends? I mean, what I wish I had, what I really need right now, especially now, is a proper friend. A woman. Someone I can actually talk to, especially now, with all this, with Brett, whatever it is that's going on. I need that. But I don't have anyone, a friend, a proper friend, I mean, obviously. Because I came here, didn't I?

Charlotte walks over to the couch and sits down. She fixes up the bathrobe, pulling it down over her legs, tightening the belt, smoothing it over her thighs. The glowing pools falling across the room tremble, receding with the rising sun.

Oh, well, bugger it, says Charlotte. It's my problem anyway. Why should I be lumping other people with my problems.

Charlotte paces the room. She looks at Florrie's crystal cake-stand, picks it up, turns it over, puts it back, looks at the family photo. She walks over to the glass cabinet with the wireless at one end, the framed print of the sea over it and crouches down, her arms folded. She looks at the Franklin Mint plates on stands and the silverware, the old photos in frames inlaid with pieces of mirror and mother-of-pearl, things of coloured glass and Florrie's collection of porcelain cats set out in a row.

I honestly don't know what I do with myself, she says. During the days. I sleep in. I watch TV. I have long baths. I do my nails, my hair, I put on make-up. I mean, not for any reason. There's no reason. I don't even leave the house. It's all just passing the time, just something to do. I mean, there's no actual reason. I've got no reason to do anything.

Charlotte stands up and stretches. She looks at the picture of the sea.

But I'll tell you this. When the day's over, somehow it makes me, not happy, something else. I mean, when I go to bed, it's like I've achieved something, even though all I've achieved is getting through it. That's all. Getting through the day. And it goes on and on, like that, every day. Days, weeks, months. Years. All these years. All this time.

Charlotte comes over and sits on the couch. She smooths down the bathrobe. Her eyes are dark.

It's like all this time I've been waiting for something to happen. And it's like I still am. Like things are going to get better and I'm just sitting it out. Counting down the days. But nothing's going to happen, is it. I mean, really. Not for me, anyway. I know that. Of course I know. But it's like somehow I can't help acting like it will, like something's going to happen and I don't even know what. It's just that I feel like something has to get better. Something has to change. And if I don't believe that. How else can I live with myself?

Outside the sound of insects. Things crackle in the heat.

I don't know, says Charlotte. I should probably just leave town. I should have done it while Brett was inside. Just left. Disappeared. It's just that I don't have the energy. I mean, I think about it all the time, and not only now, with Brett getting out and everything, but before then. All the time. But I don't. I don't leave. I couldn't face it. I just can't seem to face anything these days. And it's like that more and more. Sometimes I just can't be bothered. I go for days without having a shower, don't get dressed, don't do anything. I just sit there. All day. I mean, there doesn't seem to be any point.

She looks at me, her painted face, her high arched eyebrows.

You wouldn't understand, she says.

We sit there. The morning keeps on. The sun seems to pulse audibly, a distant scream. Charlotte puts her feet up on the couch and leans against the armrest, arranging the bathrobe again.

How do you do that? I ask Charlotte.

What? she asks.

I point to her hair and face.

Charlotte gives me a funny look.

What do you mean? she says.

I point again.

I don't know, she says. Pins. Make-up.

Women have to learn those things, I suppose.

Charlotte shrugs.

I suppose they do, she says.

And I do understand, Charlotte, I say. It's what made me used to start the day with a glass of brandy, waiting for the pubs to open.

So what did you do about it? she asks.

Me, I say. Work. Without work it would be an early grave for me. Would've been anyway.

Well, I've missed the boat there, she says.

Rubbish, I say. You're young. Healthy. No reason you can't work.

I've got no qualifications, no experience, she says. How am I going to find work.

There's always something, I say. Look at me. At my age.

It's different, she says. I can't just go and get a job at some checkout.

Why not, I say. There's no shame in that.

But there is, she murmurs. For me there is. I know there shouldn't be, but there is.

She is patting down her hair. She sees me watching and she stops.

Besides, she says. Think what people would say.

What does that matter? I say.

It matters, she says. I couldn't bear it. I couldn't face them. I know what they'd be thinking. I just couldn't.

The outside is like a faded photograph. Sunlight comes off guttering and tin roofs, slicing from gashes of peeled paint, piercing my vision, leaving burning spots long after I look away. There is no noise, no bickering of birds today, just the occasional cawing of a crow. The day is still.

So every day I ask Brett what he wants for his tea, says Charlotte. Because that's the one thing I do, at least, make tea for Brett. And he always says, whatever, you know. Whatever. I mean, he doesn't care and the thing is, I don't care either. It's not like that's my purpose in life, cooking Brett's tea, looking after Brett. That's not how my life should be. I mean, there's better things I could be doing, so many other things I could be doing.

But I cook for Brett every night anyway, and whatever Brett might say, he does expect me to. And then I sit and wait for him to come home, and whenever he comes home late or drunk or whatever, I start yelling at him and he acts like I'm this nagging housewife. You know, he hears me out, he apologises, but like it's nothing important to him, like he's just putting up with me, his nagging wife. And he never thinks that maybe it's not important to me either, maybe I don't want to be yelling at him and nagging him, maybe I don't care either, maybe I don't care any more than he does. But what I hate is that I actually do end up caring, because I make the effort. And I don't want to, but I do. And so this is what my life has been reduced to. Cooking for Brett, waiting for Brett to come home. I mean, does he think that's what I want? That this is all I want out of life?

And that's the thing. It's not what I want and it's not what he wants, so what are we doing? But that's how it is and, I don't know, it's like I can't get out of it. It's like neither of us can get out of it.

I remember there was this one time, years ago, I was cooking dinner for Brett, as usual. It was early, but I often cook early, I mean, what else do I have to do? I cook early and I heat it up whenever Brett comes home. So I was cooking. Chops, I remember. Chops in the grill. And for some reason I just turned off the stove and I went outside and sat on the kerb. It was like I was sleepwalking or something. And I couldn't get up, couldn't move. I just sat there. And I was sitting there thinking, I've got to go and cook those chops. But it all seemed too much. So I just stayed there.

Anyway, these kids were playing on the street, riding their bikes around me, watching me. And after a while they started throwing stones at me, yelling stuff, making fun of me. Like I was some mad person. And I didn't do anything, I just put up with it. Like a mad person would. But eventually this woman came along, I didn't know who she was. I still don't know who she was. I'd never seen her before and I haven't seen her since, thank God.

But she was nice. She was really nice. She came over and asked if I was all right, if there was anything wrong. I can't even remember whether I answered her. And she asked me if I knew where I was and I said no. But of course I knew where I was. I was sitting outside my own house, but for some reason I said no, that I didn't know where I was. And so she went off. She said she was coming back, I suppose she was probably going to get help of some sort, I don't know, the neighbours or the police. So I went back inside, because I didn't want someone I knew seeing me. I didn't want people hearing that I was sitting outside my own house saying I didn't know where I was, because they'd have known I was lying. But for a moment, just for that moment, it felt like a relief to say it, that I didn't know where I was, like I'd forgotten, like I had amnesia or something. I can't explain it properly, but I sort of wished it was true.

Charlotte keeps going over to the cabinet and looking at the porcelain cats.

Whose are these? she asks.

Florrie's, I say. I used to give them to her birthdays.

Charlotte crouches down to look into the cabinet, her hands on her knees.

You're a good man, Smithy, she says.

I didn't always remember, I say.

Charlotte opens the cabinet and starts taking the cats out, laying them across the green felt on the top. They are white with gold paws and gold around the eyes, sitting and stretching and lying and standing with their tails in the air. And I notice that their painted eyes are like Charlotte's painted eyes and today her face is somehow like a cat's face, something about it like a cat, her face perfect and proud and a cat's face never shows nothing and it has a pride and a strength because of it, because you can never tell what a cat is thinking.

Charlotte arranges and rearranges the cats. It is like a child playing. She puts them away again.

I wish you could have known Brett when he was younger, she says and stops.

God, listen to me, I'm like a one-track record.

Well you got to think these things through, don't you, I say. Better now than never.

You don't mind? she asks.

I'm here, aren't I? I say.

Charlotte is standing looking out the window, shielding her eyes.

Some days I find myself sitting at home trying to make myself remember, reminding myself what he used to be like. I just don't know whether it's there anymore. I honestly don't know.

A breeze stirs the leaves and twigs rap gently on the guttering. Charlotte looks up, listening to the scrape of metal. The breeze dies and crows call.

It's so strange, she says. It seems like it was such a short time ago, but really it was half a lifetime. Half of my life. Even so, it feels more real than things do now. It's like I've been asleep all these years, like nothing's changed, like I'm still back then and still the same, me and Brett and everything. And it's like I want to wake up but I can't. Now, I mean.

She listens for the breeze again but there is only the high sound of insects and sun.

Brett's always telling me I'm living in the past, she says. And I say, well at least it's better than living in the present. Better than living in the present with you.

But it's all over now, isn't it? I say.

Charlotte looks out the window, blinking. She rubs her eyes, a silhouette lost in the streaming sun.

Charlotte walks up and down the room.

Everything's so serious, isn't it, she says. So serious and miserable and boring. I mean, God forbid I actually ever have any fun, ever enjoy myself once in a while.

I look down at my jeans, sitting heavy on my legs. I can feel the bones through them and what's left of my muscles, shrunk and loose and smaller than what they once were, and I think of the skin gone white and powdery, pinched and folded, the thick purple lines like welts across my legs, and my arms too, where the muscles have wasted and the skin hangs. I try to remember when all that started to happen but I can't remember.

Well, you lie down with dogs you get up with fleas, Charlotte says.

Charlotte keeps pacing the room. She is restless and says so herself. I ask her if she wants to get some fresh air.

I wait while she gets dressed. It is nearly noon before we leave. We walk into town.

The sun is strong and hot and the streets are empty. We don't go in by the railway track and I realise that yesterday I didn't go in by the railway track either. Flies swarm in shady places. We pass houses.

Charlotte is wearing mustard-coloured slacks, tight like riding pants, a white singlet. She has made herself up again, even more

146

made up than before, her lips red and her hair the colour of syrup in the midday light. Walking beside her I realise how tall she is. She is taller than me.

Starting down the hill to the curve in the street and the railway bridge, we pass the high concrete wall of the old convent and girls' primary school. The buildings are overgrown with English ivy and wisteria, coiled tightly around green copper pipes to the high terracotta roofs and reaching out over the eaves and the walls and the footpath. Where the wall has cracked and fallen I look through the dark mass of ivy to hopscotch squares on the asphalt playground, the paint faded and peeling, rusted netball hoops.

The church is just across the road, built of orange brick with a concrete saint out front on the concrete paving, small cypress trees and recently laid buffalo grass around it, well watered, thick, green and mowed. Behind the church the land falls to sparse sloping paddocks, a few sheep, lone trees, and dried-out dams piled with swollen carcasses, the hides festering in dark and riddled patches, the sweet awful smell of death faint in the still hot air. And flat land and vines to the horizon.

We cut through the Rotary Club park, past the war memorial and start up Main Street, Prescott's caryard, the hardware shop, crumbling gold rush terraces, the whitewashed front of The Imperial with its iron lacework balcony and Parker's Workwear with rows of elastic-sided boots in the window, hanging wool jackets and jumpers, khaki pants, oilskins, rabbit-felt hats. Outside the post office, a eucalypt in bloom, sprays of pink on the new foliage, masses of hard, bare gumnuts behind. We go past the barber's shop and museum with its single chair of chrome and blond vinyl, the glass cases of rusted mining tools and pans, old photos and newspapers, spearheads and digging sticks, bayonets, clay pipes, mortar shells, a nugget. Joe McLaren is asleep behind the counter, his black cigarette-holder still stuck between his teeth, the cigarette dead and brown.

At the petrol station, two roan guard dogs lie chained on the concrete among crates of soft-drink bottles, their tongues out, brows twitching. They open their eyes and lift their heads to watch us pass. We are alone on the street. The buildings cast no shadows.

I stop outside the newsagent's to look at the headlines in their caged metal stands. Dot Slater is watching us from inside, eating Lions Club mints. I wave to her but she looks away. We stop outside Poachers.

You feel like a drink? I ask Charlotte.

God no, she says.

How about an ice-cream or something, I say. Hot day. Ice-cream, fizzy drink, something like that?

Charlotte is looking at the footpath.

I don't want to go into any of those places, she says.

Well, I'll go in, I don't mind, I say. You can wait outside.

We go over to the milk bar and takeaway.

You mind waiting outside? I ask.

Charlotte shrugs.

Where have you been hiding yourself then Smithy? asks Chris Johnson.

The ceiling fan is going inside the shop but it does nothing except move the air. Heat comes from the griddle and the vat of oil, the charcoal rotisserie under lights. Glen Johnson is wearing a singlet. He is a hairy man with long sideburns. Behind him there is a chalk-board with a list of things and prices. Old Big M and Chiko Roll posters are along the walls, girls in tiny bright bikinis. A video game.

I go over to the freezer and pick out an ice-cream for Charlotte.

148

Not a superstitious man then, ay Smithy, says Glen Johnson when I take the ice-cream to the counter.

What's that? I say.

Well, George Alister, he says. You must have heard about George Alister.

Yeah, that's right, isn't it, I say. I forgot about that. You here when it happened? I ask him.

I certainly was, he says. Happened right out there.

He nods towards the footpath where Charlotte is standing. She is standing with her arms folded and hunched over, staring at the ground, occasionally glancing up and down the street. She looks different seeing her through the window.

Like a begonia in an onion patch, says Chris Johnson. He is grinning at me.

What's that? I say.

Like a begonia in an onion patch, he says. You not know that saying?

Yeah, I know it, I say. I pay him and leave.

You all right? I ask Charlotte, handing her the ice-cream.

Can we just get off this street, she says.

I look back into the shop. Chris Johnson is watching us, still grinning. He winks at me.

Me and Charlotte go to the municipal gardens and I start walking along the path.

No, it's too hot, says Charlotte.

We sit on the grass under one of the big gums by the footpath.

I mean you'd think they'd at least plant some trees along it, says Charlotte, pointing at the path. It circles the thin grass. There are electric barbecues and children's swings and scrub and ironbarks at the far end.

I mean, who wants to go for a walk in this sun? says Charlotte. I mean, honestly.

She hasn't opened the ice-cream.

But that's typical of this town, isn't it, she says. They can't do anything properly. Everything's crap. And God forbid you have anything nice, nice clothes, anything. Because that's flash, isn't it. You wear anything nice and they call it flash and it's like an insult. You know, they have this nasty way of saying it. Flash. Isn't that flash? Aren't you looking flash? God forbid you have anything that's not utter crap, anything nice, anything flash. It's all so bloody petty, everyone around here. I'm sick of it.

She looks across the gardens drenched in full light, the grass gone pale and russet, studded with crab grass, piebald with worn patches of earth, clay and dust. The ironbarks are thick-crusted and furrowed, black as though scorched, burnt by the summer, the scrub brittle and spindly. The sky is an endless, unchanging blue.

God I hate this town, says Charlotte. I hate it so much.

You going to eat that? I ask.

I can't, says Charlotte. It's too hot. It's too hot for anything. I'm sorry Smithy. Do you want it?

She holds out the unopened ice-cream. I shake my head. Charlotte stands up.

Well, let's get back before it melts, she says. This was a bad idea. I'm sorry Smithy. It's my fault.

We walk back to the house and I put the ice-cream in the freezer.

Charlotte is sitting silent on the couch.

You got something on your mind? I ask. You want to talk about it?

No, I'm fine, says Charlotte.

Is it about Brett? I ask.

No, she says. It's not Brett. For once. It's not about Brett at all.

In the distance the school bell rings and the shouts of children. Patterns of light move slowly across the couch and the chairs and the carpet, creeping over surfaces, meeting, melding. Dust shows up on the coffee table. Heat hazes off the roof tiles. The bell rings again and the noise rises and is gone.

Charlotte sits, tracing unseen patterns on the bathrobe. Her hair has come loose, falling in places.

Cars and utes begin to pass, early knockoff from the abattoir, and I recognise the voices of men walking by. They have a jovial bark about them. Their work is over for the day and it is a Thursday, after all, payday, and on a Thursday men cannot help but start already, in a life measured in weekends. The room is cool despite the day.

I am standing in the kitchen drinking a glass of lemonade. From far off I can hear the clatter of hooves and the groan of iron-rimmed wheels on the bitumen. It comes closer, the hooves and the squeaking wheels and I go to the window to watch the Clydesdales and the carriage come along the road.

Lort Dory's son is at the reins and bearded men and well-dressed women are sitting up top, holding glasses of white wine and talking, looking over the houses to the old gold mines which Lort Dory's son is pointing out to them. As the carriage rattles past they fall against each other and spill their wine and laugh.

The Clydesdales glisten with sweat and snort and shake their manes as a cloud of flies hovers and settles on them. One of the men looks down and sees me at the window. He holds up his glass and I wave and then all of them are waving to me, smiling and calling out. Lort Dory's son looks over too and he grins and shakes his head.

A boy with a schoolbag is walking along the footpath on the other side of the street. He holds up a finger at the carriage and yells something I don't hear. The faces of the tourists drop and Lort Dory's son turns and glares at the boy. And the carriage goes but the boy stays standing there with his flushed and angry face and his finger held up, yelling after them and still holding up his finger and still angry and yelling even after they are long gone.

FRIDAY, SPIT doesn't show.

When me and Roy arrive we see Wallace alone out on the vines.

What's bloody Wallace up to? says Roy, rolling a cigarette.

I get out and walk up the row. Wallace is swinging a mattock and the thud sounds across the quiet of the morning.

You got some clumping? I ask him.

Yeah, he says.

He swings the mattock over his shoulder and brings it down into the clump. The vine shakes and the blade sticks in the wood. Wallace twists it around, trying to lever it off. I watch the vine.

Nah, you're going to crack it, I say.

Wallace swears and bends over to pull out the blade. He puts the mattock down next to the open tar tin and takes off his hat, wiping his forehead.

You hear what happened last night? he asks me.

No, I say.

Wallace takes off his glasses and blows on them, flicking wood-chips off the lenses.

Everyone's talking about it, he says.

He blows on his glasses again and wipes them on his singlet. We stand there looking at the clump.

What happened? I ask.

Someone smashed the cop shop window, says Wallace. Put a pig's head through it.

Jeez, I say.

Yeah, says Wallace, bloody pig's head.

He picks up the mattock and swings it. The blade sticks again and Wallace swears, pulling it out.

Copper's ropeable, he says.

I can imagine, I say.

Bloody pig's head through the glass, says Wallace. Gone right through. Whole thing come down.

He kicks the clump and the vine quivers.

Of course he knows who done it, says Wallace.

I thought cop shop windows were made of some special glass, I say.

You'd think so, says Wallace.

I thought they was meant to be bullet-proof, I say.

Maybe they are, says Wallace. Maybe they're bullet-proof, but they're not pig's-head-proof, are they? Who ever heard of that, anyway? Pig's head.

Wallace puts his glasses and his hat back on. He takes another swing and splices the clump through. He picks it up and throws it.

No witnesses of course, says Wallace. Even if there were, nobody's going to come forward, are they? Copper's made no friends in this town.

He takes the tar tin and brush and churns it up, smearing tar over the cut.

Besides, he says, no one wants to get on Brett Clayton's bad side, do they?

He glances at me and falls silent.

*

Boss comes up lunchtime.

Iris needs someone for the garden this afternoon, he says.

He clears his throat and looks down at the ground.

She asked if Smithy could do it, he says to Wallace. You think you can spare Smithy for an afternoon?

Wallace is bent over, cutting a vine.

If that's what Iris wants, he says. I wouldn't say no to Iris.

Boss chuckles and leans back on his heels.

None of us can, Wallace, he says.

After lunch I go up to the house and through the garden, looking for Iris. She is in the prize rose garden bare-headed, her grey hair tied in a bun. She has a pair of secateurs in her hand.

Off with their heads! she shouts when she sees me coming, waving her hands in the air.

What's that? I say.

I can't bear to do it myself, she says, handing me the secateurs.

I look at the roses.

What, I say, all of them?

The whole lot, she says. We've got black spot.

Iris brings me a wheelbarrow. I begin in the prize rose garden where the flowers bloom on tall stalks in different colours and tints and blushes. Native bees are all about me as I work, hopping from flower to flower, crawling inside. They waft and buzz, the secateurs click and the sound of falling roses.

I move on to the other roses, freestanding in their beds along the paths. The plump yellow buds, the red roses and the limp-petalled whites. They drop by my hand.

The roses stand in the full sun but the garden is cool. Dragonflies dart about the pond and the silver birches shine. Birds twitter and shuttle about in the shade.

I watch a honeyeater hover among the thin branches of a weeping tree, falling in small pink flowers. The bird feeds slowly from the flowers, hanging in the air, its wings lost to the eye. I cut the roses from the bushes along the front, massed in thick foliage. By the time I have finished the wheelbarrow is piled high.

I go and knock on the back door.

Where do you want them? I ask Iris.

Just throw them in the compost, she says.

But they're still good, I say.

I couldn't stand looking at them, Iris says. I just could not stand it.

I take the wheelbarrow out to the compost heap and stand there for a while, watching the cloud of vinegar flies swarming and crawling about the rotten and fast-drying pile. I go back to the house.

It seems a shame, I say to Iris.

Well, she says, that's how it is.

She looks at me.

What is it, Smithy? she asks.

It just seems a waste, is all.

Iris laughs.

What? she says. You want them? You, Smithy? Well, help yourself. Be my guest.

Inside the house she is still laughing.

I borrow some buckets and move the wheelbarrow under the shade of the Moreton Bay fig. I sort through the roses, taking out the best ones and carefully placing them in the buckets. I fill three buckets and carry them home.

There is a note from Charlotte on the kitchen table. She says she has gone to a friend's house and will be back later on. The note says please not to worry.

I get out Florrie's vases but I cannot use them, as I did not cut the roses with any length of stem. I put the vases away and take out glass bowls and oven dishes and baking trays. I fill them with water and float the roses on the top. Petals fall and drift among the flowers.

I place the containers on the coffee table and mantelpiece, in a row across the glass cabinet, and in the bathroom. I put a large bowl of red roses on the dresser in Charlotte's room. The house smells of roses.

I sit down and look at the clock. After a time I realise that I am waiting for Charlotte to come home. I take the bowls and dishes and trays and pour the roses out over the back fence. I go back into the house and rinse everything and set them on the drying rack. Then I sit in the living room, doing nothing. She doesn't return until late.

SATURDAY I am woken early by the roar of engines. I hear a plane take off. It circles high above the town. And then another.

Charlotte comes out of her room frowning. She squints in the light, her eyes tired. I watch her as she yawns.

What's all the racket? she asks me.

Looks like they're spraying after all, I say.

Charlotte falls onto the couch. She rubs her eyes.

Spraying what? she says.

Locusts, I say. The locust plague. They must be headed this way.

Charlotte stretches and lies down on the couch. She puts a cushion under her head and closes her eyes.

That's all we need, she says. They could have told us.

They did, I say. Government's been warning about it for ages.

Charlotte groans and puts the cushion over her face, squirming about and kicking against the armrest. The robe comes loose and falls, showing her bare legs.

Why today? she says. Why do they have to spray the locusts anyway?

What? I say. Because it's a plague, isn't it. Wipe out the crops, the vines, the fruit. I seen it once before. Even eat the grass, leaves off the trees, plants, flowers, just about everything. Like that, I say, snapping my fingers. Gone.

Locusts get here, I say. Be nothing left.

A government man comes to the door wearing a blue suit and a badge, carrying a clipboard. He is young and his hair is slicked back and stiff and he is sweating. He starts telling me about the locust spraying.

Yeah I know all about that, I say.

He hands me some leaflets and writes down my name. Sweat drips from his brow onto the clipboard and paper, spotting the page and making the blue ink pale.

So you would know that pregnant women and families with infants are being advised to leave the area, he says. Did you know about that?

Well, what, should we leave too? I ask.

No, that's not necessary, he says. It's perfectly safe. This is just a precautionary measure. But that is the advice we are giving.

He closes the clipboard and wipes his face.

And if you have any pets you might want to keep them in the house today, he says.

So it's not safe for animals, then, I say.

No, it's safe, he says. Again, this is just a precaution, you understand. It won't affect humans, animals. It's not anything to worry about.

He taps his pen on the clipboard, looking down the street.

But not safe for the locusts, I say.

No, says the man. Not for locusts.

I walk over to Spit's house to see what Belle is doing. People are out on the footpath with dogs on leashes, the dogs squatting on the nature strip. A man is at the side of his house shooing chooks into their coop and covering it with a tarpaulin. Cars pass quickly, and, despite all the people about and the rush and activity and the thunder of planes above us, there is something still and quiet about the place. I pass fresh dog turds and clouds of flies erupt and scatter. A woman stands in her front yard, calling for her cat.

All around the town hall and spilling onto the footpaths there are winemakers and farmers, standing in groups and talking, nodding and looking up at the planes and the sky. They are in grey suits and old sports jackets, brilliantined hair and faces like leather. Government men move among them in their blue suits and badges and clipboards. I see Charlotte's father by the footpath. He doesn't see me and I walk into the crowd before he does. On the other side of the town hall, Boss is talking to a group of vignerons. I go over to him.

Well, Smithy, says Boss. Hail-fellow-well-met. So what do you think of all this locust business, then? This government spraying?

It's meant to be safe, isn't it? I say.

The other men snort and mutter.

According to the government, it's meant to be safe, says Boss. He looks at me with his grin.

There is talk all around, the whole crowd, the dry, slow talk of men who own land and work it. They agree with each other and argue with the government men, raising their voices and talking over them, answering their own questions and angry but not so angry that they do not laugh and talk amongst themselves, enjoying the day and the excitement of the day, of things happening, and there is something about the crowd of men, talking their lazy talk, something like a holiday.

160

You trust the government, Smithy? You believe what the government tells you? Boss asks me.

Government says one thing one day and another thing the next, says one of the men.

They all nod. The men are all of them like Boss, heavily built and powerful with long gazes and faces creased by the sun. They keep talking and looking up at the planes.

What's all this about? I ask Boss.

Meeting, says Boss. Usual useless government meeting.

That's right, say the men, nodding.

It's the wine, says Boss. What we want to know is how it's going to affect the grapes, with all this heavy spraying, this aerial spraying.

He watches one of the planes.

The government says it's going to be all right, but I don't know. I mean, what do you reckon? he says to the men. Didn't have much in the way of hard facts did they?

Well they had plenty to say, but not much of substance. That's my opinion, for what it's worth, says one of the men.

They were being a bit evasive, don't you think? says Boss. Would you say that? That they were being evasive? I mean, it seemed to me they were talking in circles. Seemed to be saying the same thing over and over again, didn't they?

The others agree.

Well, that's the government way, isn't it? That's where our taxes are going.

They pause to watch one of the planes pass overhead, its white fuselage moving across blue sky. The government planes are large and white and modern with twin propellers and they fly high up. Everyone stops to watch the plane and then the talk starts again.

The government already says the wine's toxic, Boss says to me.

161

They say it's toxic from the spraying we're doing already, the herbicides and fungicides. And, well, they tried to get it banned, didn't they? he says to the other men. A while back.

The men nod. Their heads are bare and pale skin circles the tops of their foreheads.

So what we want to know, says Boss, is if the wine's toxic from the spraying we already do, then what's this locust pesticide going to do to the grapes? That's all we want to know.

But the grapes are hardly out yet, I say.

Doesn't matter, says one of the men.

The farmers and vignerons talk, looking up at the sky or down at their toes, kicking their heels against the gutter, their arms folded. It is an open sky and full sun. Light comes off the chrome of parked cars. The town hall is behind us, an old building of red brick and terracotta, a ragged gumtree towering over it. Magpies fly over the building and the crowd, birdcalls and men's talk all together in the morning.

Boss looks around.

Well truth be told, he says. Well what I reckon is if what they're saying is right then we shouldn't be growing vines at all. No, he says to one of the men. Well you have to face facts, don't you? The government says the wine's toxic, but if we don't spray then we lose them, don't we?

Boss turns to me and grins. He folds his arms over his chest and rocks back on his heels.

I don't know Smithy, what do you reckon? Think we should chuck it all in? Maybe we should. What did they say? he says to the men. Not fit for human consumption, wasn't it?

That's right.

The men are all looking at a government man standing close by.

162

He is talking to a group of farmers. They are all talking at once, pointing fingers. The government man keeps opening his mouth to speak but he can't get a word in. He looks at his clipboard as the farmers talk at him. The tree casts a long shadow over the lawn and the crowd. Branches sway, leaves flutter and the shadow moves. Light dapples the crowd. Men standing in the sun shade their eyes with their hands.

But if we chuck it all in, do you think the government's going to compensate us? says Boss.

Not bloody likely, says one of the men.

I thought you would have known all this, Smithy, says Boss. I mean, it's your living too.

Grab that bloke when you can, says one of the men, nodding over at the government man, who is backing away from the other group.

One government department tries to ban it, another one sweeps it all under the carpet, says Boss. Doing too well off our taxes. Ever heard of the government turning down taxes?

Boss grins his gummy grin, his mouth open. He turns to the men. They shake their heads and look at the ground.

And the exports, says one of the men.

Well that's taxes too, isn't it, says Boss.

He turns to me again.

But this locust stuff, this aerial spraying. What we're worried about is it might be the straw that breaks the camel's back. I mean, we can't have people dropping dead on us, can we Smithy? Even the government doesn't want that.

One of the men scrapes his foot along the concrete.

Yeah, but since when's the government done anything for primary producers? he says.

Oh well, says Boss. If the vintage gets ruined they'll send in the social workers, won't they. You see, that's what they do, Smithy. Crops get ruined, farms go broke and the government sends in the social workers. Won't put a cent in to keep the farms going. Let the farms go broke and send the social workers in. That's the government solution.

Got to keep the university graduates happy, says one of the men. Got to keep them in beer and skittles.

That's right, says Boss and the men all nod.

At Spit's place there are cars up the drive and along the kerb. The door is open and a woman with a baby stands outside. The baby is crying and she is holding it to her, rocking it, talking to it quietly. The planes drum in the distance.

Belle around? I ask the woman.

The woman nods towards the door, still rocking the baby. I don't know her.

I go inside the house and into the living room. It is full of women and babies and toddlers running about. The room smells of talcum powder and nappies and milk. The women are all talking but they stop when they see me. The toddlers keep playing, piping away. The women look at me.

Belle is in the kitchen standing over cups on the counter, putting in tea bags. The electric kettle begins to boil. The women in the lounge room start talking again but in low voices and whispers.

I forgot he was the grandfather, I hear someone murmur.

Belle stops and listens to them but doesn't say anything.

I thought I'd come and check on you, I say to Belle. Make sure you were all right getting out of town.

Belle spoons sugar into the cups. Her back is turned to me.

We're car-pooling, she says. All the single mothers. And me, seeing I don't seem to have a husband at the moment.

You can still hear the plane engines in the distance. Belle is dressed in jeans and a blouse and sneakers.

Where are you going? I ask.

Melbourne, says Belle. Me and the kids are staying with my Aunty Prue.

She reaches up to a high shelf, grunting, and takes down an enamelled tray. She puts the cups on it.

How long you going for? I ask.

Just the night, Belle says. We'll be back tomorrow afternoon.

That's not much of a trip, I say. You should spend some time down there while you've got the chance. Take the kids to the zoo or something.

The kettle boils and clicks off. Belle pours water into the cups. The drone of the planes grows louder.

Some of the other girls work, she says.

Still, I say.

A plane passes over the town. Glasses tinkle. Belle looks up.

Well, I know where Spit is, if that's any consolation, I say. Or who he's with, anyway.

Belle snorts.

Everyone knows that, she says.

Do they?

Belle pushes past me to get the milk out of the fridge, saying something under her breath.

What's that? I say.

Belle has her back to me again, pouring milk into the cups. She shrugs and mutters again.

Getting himself into strife just because bloody Brett Clayton's pissed off with the world, she says.

How do you mean? I say.

I watch her with the tea.

You need any help there? I ask.

Belle shakes her head and puts the milk back in the fridge.

It's not my problem, she says. As if me and Spit didn't have enough on our plate without Brett Clayton getting involved.

Belle takes the tea bags out of the cups and puts them onto a plate. A plane comes over again and she swears.

So everyone knows, I say.

Pretty much, says Belle.

She picks up the tray and then puts it back down on the bench again. She counts the cups.

So what are they saying? I ask.

Belle looks into the lounge room and she looks at me.

Don't worry about it, she says.

Let me give you a hand with that, I say.

I'm right, Belle says. She picks up the tray again and starts to leave.

Well, what about you? I say.

What does that matter, says Belle. You're old enough to think for yourself.

Well you seem to have something to say.

Belle shifts the tray against her chest and the cups slide and clatter against one another. Tea spills over the edges. Planes roar overhead.

She's using you, Belle says.

Yeah? I say.

Belle starts to push past me. I stay standing where I am.

Why do you say that? I ask.

Because I know her, says Belle. I know what she's like.

Leaving the house I see Spit and Belle's older boy on the footpath, sitting on his plastic tricycle. He is looking up at the sky.

What you doing all the way out here, then? I ask him. Ay?

The boy points up.

Plane! he says.

That's right, I say. It is a plane isn't it.

He looks at me, still pointing up.

There! There! he says. Plane!

I can see it, I say.

He smiles and looks up at the sky and back at me. His eyes are opened up wide.

How about we get you back inside, I say. We don't want you getting run over, do we?

I start to pull the tricycle towards the door but he drags his feet on the footpath and starts to moan.

It's all right, I say. You know who I am, don't you? I'm your grandpa. You know how to say that? Grandpa?

The boy looks at me.

Grandpa, I say. Pointing to myself.

The boy looks at me, his brow furrowed as though he is in pain. Then he points at me.

Smithy! he says.

That's right, I say. Your Grandpa Smithy.

I try to move the tricycle again but the boy starts to cry.

No, he wails. No. Plane.

Well how about I take you round the back, I say. You can see the planes just as well from there.

The boy looks up at the sky, sniffing. He starts to cry again and then stops, watching the sky.

I point towards the back.

You can see the planes from there too, I say.

He looks at me and then seems to understand and begins walking the tricycle into the front yard. I take hold of the handles and help him along. He lifts his feet and I pull him around the back.

The lawn is overgrown, the grass well above my boots. Spent dandelions tower, thick-stemmed and taller than the boy. Dead brown fingers of ivy cling to the hardwood fence and wandering jew runs under the shed and in the far corners of the garden, thick in shaded places.

You wait here a minute, I say to the boy. I break a stick off a tree and walk through the grass, banging it on the ground and looking for the movement of snakes. There is a shovel lying flat and hidden in the grass, its dry shaft cracked, a plastic watering can and toys. I pull the boy out on his tricycle and point upwards.

See, you can look for the planes from here, I say.

I squat down on my heels, next to the boy. The boy is studying the sky. I take my clasp knife from my belt and start stripping the bark off the stick. We wait there.

The sun is hot and there is no breeze. The noise of the planes continues. The boy is intent on the sky, but now and then he looks over at me and points upwards and smiles, like the planes are some secret between us, something only the two of us know about or understand. I finish cutting the bark off the stick and I give it to the boy to play with. He looks at it and looks back up at the sky without taking it. I throw it away.

The boy starts to make excited noises. He looks at me, his eyes quick and wide, pointing and breathing fast. We watch as the plane comes into view.

Yeah, you like those planes, don't you? I say. Maybe you want to learn how to fly them one day. How you like that, ay? Flying people around the world. Seeing all sorts of places. That'd be an all right job now, wouldn't it?

The boy keeps his arm up, pointing as the plane moves slowly across the sky. His arm still raised, he rests his head against his shoulder and closes his eyes.

Going home the streets are empty, the shops closed up, locked up, people gone or in their houses, a feeling of the town deserted.

I check the windows and put a rolled-up towel against the front door. The planes are going out further now, over paddocks and vineyards, a dull, constant hum. Charlotte has showered and brushed her hair and sits there rosy. She is drinking a cup of coffee.

I sit down opposite her.

I saw your father in town, I say.

What? says Charlotte, looking up at me. No, my father doesn't go into town, he never goes into town.

Well, he was there today, I say. Plenty of farmers were. All the winemakers too.

Charlotte puts her hand over her brow and looks at the floor.

Christ, my father in town, she says. Why on earth?

She looks back up at me, her eyes alive.

But what if he ran into Brett? she says. It would be a disaster. I mean, with Brett acting like he is. And my father in town. I cannot believe this.

You didn't see Brett did you? she asks me. Please tell me you didn't see Brett.

No, I say. Didn't see him at all. Was in one of the pubs most likely.

Charlotte groans, sits bent over, covers her face.

I can't believe this. Why now? Why does my father decide to come into town now? I mean, what if he ran into Brett? As if things weren't bad enough. But are you sure? she asks me. Because my father never goes into town. Why pick today of all days? My God.

My God, says Charlotte. I cannot believe this.

We sit for a while. I watch a wolf-spider hop across the window-pane. There are no birds about today, not even crows, nothing. Charlotte sits up, leans back and looks at me.

You know, it's almost funny, she says. I mean, the timing is so bad it's almost funny. Perfect. Why shouldn't he see Brett now? Why not? I suppose my father couldn't think any worse of Brett, or me, so why not see him now. You know, he probably wouldn't even be surprised if he ran into him. It's what he expects, isn't it? Exactly what he expects. It's what he's always thought.

One of the planes comes into view through the back window, a white shining dot. I watch it move across the sky.

You know, says Charlotte, and I know this for a fact, but my father, well, both my parents, you know they drive all the way into Corowa rather than come into town, for shopping or whatever, petrol. Even just to get a carton of milk. Someone I know was in Corowa one time, and she saw my father pull up outside the milk bar, buy a carton of milk and then get back into the car and drive off. They drive all the way into Corowa rather than risk running into me. Or Brett. I mean, God forbid they see me, see their daughter. They'd rather go across the border, just to avoid me. Did you know that?

No, I didn't, I say.

And so my father comes in today, of all days, Charlotte says. I mean it, I should be laughing.

I stand at the back window, watching a plane, far away and high up. It turns and a thin, white wake follows it across the sky and out of view. The line hangs and bloats and begins to fall in streaks that drift and plump and come together to marble the sky and the sky turns white to all horizons and glows from within, pearl now and blooming, growing thick and heavy across the expanse. Paddocks and farmhouses and lone dead trees disappear, crops and vines, the razor-lines of fences. They grow faint and fade and are gone. The sun is behind the cloud, pale and orange and a halo around it, bleeding into the cloud, the cloud like wax, and the light spreads across it, spits radiance and traces the billowing. The cloud grows and forms and re-forms in mounds and hollows, plateaus, eddies, shaved lines and frayed, edges of brilliance, colours of stone. It is a strange body of a thing, moving, changing, changing as it moves, swelling out of itself in slow clustered fists, carbuncles and wispy tendrils, enormous in all directions and everything lost in it as it comes, earth and sky, everything.

Come and look at this, I say to Charlotte.

Charlotte gets off the couch and stands next to me by the back window and we watch the cloud roll into town.

My God, says Charlotte.

I wonder where Brett is, says Charlotte.

A fall in light like dusk and the light strange, the copper sun veiled, smouldering, barely there. Something like a light rain falls, but not rain, and it hisses and spits as it hits the roof tiles and corrugated iron, the guttering and concrete. Steam bursts upwards, twisting and dispersing and hovering, forming a low smoky cover, cascading from the eaves. Drops splatter against the windows, making dirty white streaks and spots. Leaves flutter, struck and stained. A smell like burning rubber. It begins suddenly, stops suddenly and the cloud is upon us.

Charlotte is looking out the window.

So, what now? she says. What does this mean? Do we have to stay inside now?

Looks like it, doesn't it, I say.

Well for how long? she says. I mean, all day? How long does this all last?

Why? I say. You planning on going somewhere?

No, says Charlotte. Of course I wasn't planning on going anywhere.

She starts pacing the room.

It's just I can't stand being cooped up like this, she says.

She paces some more and sits down.

I feel like I've been stuck here forever.

Outside the fog is thick, the light dim. Everything has closed in and it is like there is nothing else, nothing but me and Charlotte sitting in this room, trapped within blind spaces, the world stolen by the fog and all that is left is this room, this house, me and Charlotte alone.

The pain in my finger has spread and the rheumatism is upon me. I have a fever. I look at my hand and it is red and swollen. It has gone numb and my arm numb too and it prickles all along when I shake it. My knees ache, everything aches, all the joints and bones in my body. My insides bubble and swell and feel fit to burst. I feel my age and my weakness and I think to myself, you were right old man, you were right and it is what you said all along. You stop and it comes and you knew one day it would all come down on you and here it is, nothing but a broken body and a wandering mind because you stopped, old man, and you should have known that when you stop it all stops with you, and this body has been coming apart for some time now but not stopped yet, not stopped quite yet but still going like shaking machinery works on in a rattling way, shaking but held together, slumping this way and that, spitting bolts and rivets, but held together by the movement, by the very movement itself, that's the thing, against all common thought, and it must have been long ago and forgotten but now I remember it. It was like life, some desperate life, some dogged will in that machine kept it going, kept it together in movement and against the very laws of nature was what it was because I remember men standing in wonderment, watching it heave its last, but only for a moment while the machine screamed and sparked, wheels and cogs racing, the spit pieces flying, but still going until a flick of a switch and the engine stops and slows and one great groan, the last, the very last, and it collapses in a heap of rusted metal, wheels and cogs and frame, all of it, a useless heap, a pile of scrap and I cannot remember for what or why or when, maybe as a child I saw it, and who knew that the memory would stick and that it would come back now and that now, not remembering when or where or why, just the tremor and movement in that dark shed and the collapse and groan and who knew that one day you would see yourself in that, like it was all arranged in time, you the same now, clattering along the same. But no, because I already knew and haven't I said it myself and said it so many times but nobody listens and nobody believes but here it is. I am broken, dried up, scrap, but for the movement, and this I know, I must keep on going, go until I drop, because to live like this, no, not like this, never like this, this waiting, this pain of mind and body worse than death itself.

Charlotte is reading from a women's magazine she must of got from somewhere. She leaves the room and comes back with a small zippered bag and takes out tiny flat boxes and a tiny bottle, a black pencil and a shiny little tool. She arranges them on the coffee table and opens up a round clasped mirror and stands it in front of her. Then she flips through the magazine and starts reading again.

I watch as she pulls down her bottom eyelid with her finger and draws a black line along the rim with the pencil and then the same along the top, one eye and then the other, looking into the mirror all the time. She colours her eyelids green and silver and brushes it all together and up to her eyebrows, silver and green, then smooths it with a cotton bud in quick small strokes, everything done in quick small strokes, drawing and smoothing and brushing over and over again. She squeezes her eyes near shut and opens them to look in the mirror, she does everything looking into the mirror, turning her head and looking from side to side and askew. And she darkens her eyebrows and brushes them as well and takes the little tool and clamps her eyelashes with it, clamping and unclamping and then brushes the eyelashes upwards until they are thick and black and long and high and then the bottom ones, brushing down. She goes to it again with the cotton buds and the brush and looks long at the mirror from all angles and holds it up and does things over again.

Charlotte looks at me.

It's supposed to make my eyes look bigger and brighter, she says. What do you think, Smithy? Do my eyes look bigger and brighter?

I look at Charlotte's eyes. She opens them wide for me to see. Charlotte laughs and looks back at herself in the mirror.

I sit looking out at the backyard, watching the slow-moving plumes of fog, the fog thinner now, like mist, the mist of a winter's morning. Trees and roofs and fences seem far off, everything seems far off.

The sun breaks through the clouds, their edges craggy as slate and bright as embers. Shafts of light slice through the hanging poison and fade and reappear, filtering through the weaving mist, but not like mist now, not in the light, because it does not lift with the sun but moves about illuminated, not mist now but something nearly solid and real.

Muted light pulses latticed through the windows and casts its brief movement across the room. I watch the play of light and shadow and look about the room with its armchairs and couch, green and faintly checked with orange to match the orange carpet, the patterned curtains and scrim, the mantelpiece of coloured rocks and the mirror above, Florrie's crystal cake-stand, the display cabinet with its things, the picture of the sea.

And the room the same, always been the same, never changed, not from the beginning, and a sudden feeling comes over me as though I am seeing it for the first time, the familiar unfamiliar and vague recollections of bustling noisy presences, voices, but faded now. And I think how it is at this time of life, at the end of life, that it is now I sit in this room as though for the first time and for the first time I feel the stillness and the silence, those long-time presences gone and even after all the long years it is only now I realise that they are gone for good. And even with the girl sitting close by me, the room and the house feel empty and it is only now, for the first time and after all these years, it is only now I know that I am alone, this room, this house, but not just that, more than that, gone, everything, all of it, it is all gone.

I look back out the window at the overcast sky, the dampened sun, the poison swimming like oil and the backyard shrouded and strange, everything become strange.

*

Things pass through my mind, things of childhood and forgotten but always there somehow, at the edges of my mind they were always there. Iron things, heavy latched doors and shutters, kerosene tins, canvas waterbags, sacks and harnesses, hessian sacks and trace chains, greenhide ropes, plaster saints among dry yellowed books, tin baths we used as boats in the floods but only bathed in once, yokes and swingle trees, the tamped earth floors and wooden bunk beds, straw mattresses, coarse and prickly sheets, we slept in dirt as we lived in it, dirt and dust, my childhood. And I remember the tins of jam and boxes of salt, tea, the single tiny bottle of vanilla essence, cod-liver oil, the jar of humbugs, things with coloured labels and names and pictures that we would look at in quiet fascination, things from far-off places. I once tamed a cockatiel.

And I remember the cats, half wild, that scattered and spat and milled about at feeding time, waiting for the sisters to put out scraps, darting up and speeding away with tails in the air, the patterns of their coats, tabbies and brindles and ginger cats, their coats clean and they were the only things. And I remember we loved the kittens, sprung forth in litters and I suppose it was in spring, some time of the year that only the cats knew, for there were no seasons, just the dry and the wet, and we spent many hours trying to catch those kittens, crawling under the foundations and into the wood pile, setting up traps, but they were slippery fellows and vicious, and I remember the sisters scolding us as they tended to our arms and hands with their filigree red lines and beads of blood, the sting of iodine and I don't think we ever caught a single one.

Metal objects. A silver candelabra with twisting arms and two matching candlesticks, a chalice, finely worked incense burners, a crucifix bursting in all directions, more a star than a cross, and other holy, nameless things. Copper oil lamps, a coffee pot, a silver tray, all taken down once a year and dusted and washed and the silver and copper polished and we would watch as the dun objects turned to shining, radiant things and they were as though from another world.

And I remember the wild blacks came in hard times, dark and gaunt and near to naked, their long thin legs and squat bodies, and faces like horrors from dreams, carrying their children, flanked by dog packs, and they would set up camp against the stone walls and demand flour and sugar which the sisters doled out for them every morning, for they feared them. And they would huddle in the shade of the buildings and we would watch them go about their ways, campfires smouldering day and night, the women laughing as they cornered a cat and beat it with their yam-sticks, then skinned and cooked it with damper and lizards and grubs and us boys standing at a safe distance to look at their clubs and spears and thick raised patterns of scars and at the women, but them giving us barely a glance, although their dogs stood and snarled, showing their teeth, and they went about their ways until it was heard about and men came with guns and drove them back into the desert.

Always with an eye on the meat locker, always starving, us boys, and I remember jutting ribs and the constant gnawing in my belly and we would sneak into the larder to inspect its changing contents, mutton quarters, skinned rabbits, wild goat, beef when times were good, wallaby when times were tough and sometimes a rooster killed and its twitching body wrapped in cloth, hung out and bled out, the meat brought in with the other supplies, sacks of flour and oats, potatoes and onions, tea, sugarbags and hay bales, brought in by a worn-out man in a worn-out truck that was little more than a chassis.

And in the mornings cracking the ice in the enamelled wash

177

basin, the precious spring water shared among us, the flannel stiff. And on those frozen desert mornings we would run out, shoeless, shivering things to fight over fresh cow pats and I remember the pleasure of sinking my bare numb feet into the warm and steaming dung.

And Sister Margaret and her fancy chook, I remember, fancy chook the other sisters called it, Margaret's fancy chook, so proud of her fancy chook, a black silky hen, feathers gleaming, touch of green, a small bird and she loved her fancy chook, brought it back from some trip she made, her mother's funeral I think it was, none of the sisters allowed to buy things for themselves, they had a word for it, some church word, but Sister Margaret brought her fancy chook and I remember her saying they were good layers, the silkies, saying it to the other nuns but blushing and she loved that fancy chook and it never laid a thing and died in two days from the heat, and the other chooks, big solid squabbling things, stout, reminded me of the sisters, colour of the earth whatever colour they were, or had been, pecked out the eyes and the feathers and gashed the flesh before Sister Margaret gathered the bald and bloody thing in her arms and buried it, lashed two sticks together in a cross and planted it over the grave, and the other sisters laughed and they told the story often over the long dining table, to laugh at her again, and I remember them telling it, cackling away, Sister Margaret and her fancy chook and Sister Margaret blushing, and I realise now that she was scarcely more than a child.

And the man and his truck brought bare-rooted fruit trees and we dug holes and planted them and they withered and died. Small chalky pumpkins grew in a tangle with sour melons and that was all.

And we would play wild games, mostly of our own invention, running around like mad things, chasing and tackling each other and wrestling in the dust, kicking the melons about until they split and fell to pieces. And cricket with a piece of timber for a bat, war with sticks for rifles, clods of dirt for artillery, knucklebones and other games without name. And the flies would swarm us, cover us, crawl inside our ears and noses and mouths and I remember boys stopping in their stride to cough and they would cough out flies. And there were snatches of rhyme and we would recite the Lord's Prayer with dirty words and if the sisters ever heard us they would beat us with a length of spent leather until we wailed or the strap broke.

And we were all of us covered in chilblains and our skin blistered and split and itching with scab-mites and lice and the bites of insects, the sisters burning off ticks and lancing boils with a hot needle. And the measles went around and whooping cough and all childhood diseases, and it seemed there was never a time wasn't one of us laid up with something or nursing a broken bone or a festering and flyblown wound, and sometimes a boy with consumption or lockjaw and the doctor would come and take him away to some hospital and the sisters made us pray for his soul when news came he had died.

And the visits of the dog stiffener during his journeys through the desert, his large black Mexican hat with red tassels, larrikin boots and gold teeth, and he would show us his rifle and revolver and the scars and tattoos about his body and the bottle of strychnine he used to poison the waterholes, and he would say with a grin, and not just dogs either. And I discovered what he meant when I was older and had learned to walk the desert and knew the rocks and trees and tracks, and one day I came across such a waterhole, deep within rocks and not such a pool as I imagined but little more than wet sand, a dirty water seeping through to the surface and, yes, not just dogs, but birds and lizards, rat-kangaroos and wallabies and wild blacks, all strewn around the place, the bodies of man and animal bloated and ripe and food for ants and flies.

And I remember scrabbling about the place, exploring the old mission buildings of rough hewn stone, others of cracked pisé, flaking whitewash, leaking silt, some hollows deep, and we would dig into them with sticks and makeshift tools, as though expecting some discovery but only finding more of the dry hard stuff. The rarely used chapel with its crude altar table and benches and dry font, the old bullocks' stables, the empty stonewall pigsty and the deep claggy old quarry with its piles of rough rocks and cool inside where we would sit and make stories and take shelter from the sun.

The mad old Trappist, emaciated and long-haired, beard to his stomach, he lived in one of the outer sheds and rarely left it, and we would peer into the place and watch him as he wrote, great piles of paper all about the place, and when I got older they would send me with his meals and he would jabber at me in strange words which the sisters told me was Spanish but I heard in it also the voices of the blacks and occasionally he could be seen tending the pumpkins or waiting for the truck which brought his ink and paper also, and sometimes he disappeared into the desert for weeks at a time and returned sunburnt and ragged and sometimes painted in ochres, and you could hear him coming talking from far off because the man never stopped talking or writing in that old bark shed, and when he died the sisters took his sheaves of paper and used them for tinder and waited for a priest until the body stank, and when the priest arrived he gave him rites and buried him, digging the hole himself, and the sisters told us he was one of twelve who had left their monastery in Spain to come over the sea and trek through the desert with bullock-teams and drays and had quarried the stone and built this place as a mission for the blacks and had made no converts and had died here and he was the last.

And I remember the sisters' china, carefully placed on the high shelves and never used, for we ate and drank only from enamelled plates and mugs, worn through to black tin, but the china displayed all the same with its flower-patterned pieces, the matching tea-set, the enormous tureen, bowls, a gravy boat and a large jug showing a woman and a bearded man flanked by columns, wearing long loose robes which fell in folds. And the row of painted plates along a shelf with scenes of men in frock coats and tall hats, arm in arm with women in gowns, girls in flowing white dresses chasing butterflies through lush gardens, cobblestone streets with ruddy fat men and carts full of fruit and shop windows laden with meats and bread and all other things I did not know, snow-covered landscapes, lakes of ice with the same such men and women in their coloured clothing, scarves and hats and bonnets and fur-lined coats and long dresses, skates on their feet and all in motion, laughing and throwing snowballs and falling on the ice, red-coated men on horses with a pack of hounds and a fox running before them through shady woods of broad-leaved trees, all pictures in bright paint and wreathed in gold and gold about the edges of the plates too. And I wondered at these pictures of things that I had never seen and never thought I would see and never did see.

And I remember once a grim-faced man came in a car and drove me and Sister Bernard across the dusty roads to a black encampment, and the blacks lying about in the shade of their shanties and the man called them out and they came and sat before us on the ground and Sister Bernard had me sing for them, conducting me as I sang. And afterwards a man in a sack suit came before the assembly and I watched as he stood just as I had stood, taking on all the appearance of a young boy, chest out, head up, and his face become innocent as a cherub and he began to sing too, in a high falsetto and another man put his coat over his head and waved his hands about, his smile the smile of Sister Bernard's, and the blacks all laughed and the grim-faced man grew angry and shouted at them and struck the singing man with the back of his hand and Sister Bernard pulled me away and it was only then I realised they were laughing at us.

Lined up with our bowls in the great hall, waiting for watery porridge for breakfast and watery soup for tea, lucky sometimes for a chunk of bread, the sisters doling it out of a great iron pot and there was only one, breakfast, tea, every meal come from that black steaming pot. And stopping to look for a clump of oats, a chunk of meat on our way to the table and disappointed usually, and we sat and ate and licked our bowls and our stomachs gurgled. Treacle in the porridge on Sundays and that was close as we got to heaven and hope.

And the teams of stockmen would come in, hard-faced men with kangaroo-hide whips coiled over their shoulders and butcher's knives in their belts. And they would water their huge dusty horses from the bore pump and the sisters would line up the black boys and the men would pick out a few and strip them naked and squeeze their arms and legs and bark at them and give them a kick or a backhander to see if they would cry and the ones who cried they pushed back to the sisters. And the sisters would bring out the doctor's reports and any man among them who could read would read aloud to the others, who smoked and talked and looked at the naked piccanins all the while, their pale eyes made all the more pale by faces filthy as ours. And us whites and the half-castes would stand looking at the Chinaman cooks with their coolie hats and long braided queues that reached to their horses' flanks, and strange broad wizened faces with slits of eyes that watched us without acknowledgment or emotion, and sometimes one of us would hurl a rock at them when the sisters weren't watching. And the stockmen would talk and spit and empty out their pipes and hoist one or two of the piccanins onto the saddles of their great stomping, snorting horses and they would ride off and we would never see those boys again.

And I remember flocks of birds that blocked out the sun, turning day into night, lizards that came out in the cool of evening, running about in front of you and so thick on the ground that it seemed as though the ground itself was alive, the mouse plagues and frogs falling from the skies before the rains, plopping about the place and sitting surprised for a moment before hopping off, and then the rains coming down, water to your chest, the whole desert turned into a dirty sea and running in torrents, and after the rains the wildflowers, tiny things, the ground covered with them, every inch massed with bright colours, everywhere you turned and for as far as the eye could see, and they only lasted a day or two and then red desert again.

SUNDAY MORNING and the world is white, everything coated in residue and glistening in the sun, the lawn thick with powder.

It is like winter in other places.

I am still not feeling right and decide not to go into church. I get out my bible and try to read it, tracing my finger along the page, silently sounding out the words. I doze, I don't know for how long. When I wake it has clouded over again.

Charlotte is in her room with the door open. I look up at the mirror above the mantelpiece and in it I can see her reflection. Charlotte is brushing her hair and I watch. She parts her hair and leans to the side, brushing in slow, steady strokes. She brushes one side and then the other. She looks up into the mirror and sees me watching. She smiles at me.

SO IT all started with the Florence trip, says Charlotte, Brett, my father, everything. But I suppose there was a time before that and a time after, and I don't mean in weeks, months or years, but I mean in memory, and the time before soon forgotten and then the time after turned into now, and now I feel like I am at the end of things, but it has been like that for so long now and I remember at the start it seemed too dreadful, too dreadful to live and I didn't think I would live through it, because how can you live when there is nothing, no hope, no future and no emotion, not even sadness, and all good things in the past and lost to the past, and knowing they can never come back. But during that time before, not knowing, never knowing that, not then.

And so now at the end of things, and for a long time now, and as though stuck in time, waiting and watching life pass and everything pass me by and me falling apart, fading, growing older, and how could I live with that? I couldn't see how and I thought it would kill me because how could I possibly live like that, and knowing. But it is still at the end of things now, and the feeling that there is nothing and there will never be anything and that every day will only be as it is now and every day the same only worse because of time passing. And I remember I would lie as though dead, already dead, and I waited and I wanted to go out into the streets and shout, let people know, tell someone, because someone had to hear and see and care. But there was no one and there never will be anyone and nothing changed, and I feel as though a part of me has died and there is less of me now, that's true, no hope, no emotion, not even sadness, just getting through each day, and I don't expect the world to notice, not anymore, so I have learned that much.

And sometimes I think that it was because things changed too quickly for me or that I lived too much in too short a time, like I used it all up, because even then I knew something was wrong, I could see that, and everybody could see it at the time and they told me, of course they told me, and they talked about consequences, that I should think about the consequences, but it isn't consequences, it's nothing to do with that, what you do, how you end up. Because in the end nothing matters, not really, not in the end. It only matters to yourself and that's the thing, there's really no such thing as consequences, not in the end, it's just how things are and it doesn't matter why you are there because there's no going back, no changing things, so no, it was never about consequences, but it was that I never thought it would all be so brief, like I lived my whole life in that short time, not starting exactly with that Florence trip but with the time before and the time after, but brief, still so brief, such a short time, and now gone and at the end of things and only left in memory.

And I still remember taking the tram down to St Kilda beach and the hot air through the windows and the seats sticking and burning under my legs and looking outside as it all went past, and the light flashing through the trees and Brett beside me, Brett always beside me, because there were other times too, plenty of other times, after the first, but they all blend together for me now, all into that first time when it was like I had forgotten how to breathe but now I was breathing again and the feeling of a weight fallen from me and I was free, that feeling of freedom like I had never had, not before or since, and there were plenty of other times later, after it all, after it was all done.

And waiting for the tram outside Flinders Street station in the sun with the hot winds blowing and the grit of the city and the cars stopped at the lights and their engines running, the fumes of the cars hanging and you could smell them and see them in the heat. And businessmen in suits and sunglasses and old women in black, all of us waiting at the tram stop, the wind blowing the women's dresses about, waiting until the tram came and me and Brett would sit with our arms around each other, always together, as close as our bodies could get, together and kissing and sometimes we would kiss all the way.

And I had bought a green dress from an op-shop, a tiny tight summer dress, too small for me really, and I wore it every day, Brett touching me through the dress, and I wore a straw hat with a plastic orange sunflower on it and slipping off my sandals and swinging my legs and me and Brett all close and together and our bodies so close that they couldn't be closer and kissing and touching, and we would stay at the beach, lying in the sun until the sea was like a broken mirror, sunburnt and my hair stiff with salt, and we would take the tram back, tired but happy. And, yes, that was not the first time, those days came after, but even then, even back then it reminded me of that first time, and the tram and the beach and the sea were always memories of that first time, and they were the memories of that feeling, of being free, suddenly free.

And so yes, I was happy and I still think about it and if that was my big mistake, if that was the big mistake that changed everything, if it was that, the tram and the beach and the sea and Brett with me, always with me and beside me and my freedom, if that was the mistake then how could I have known? How could I have known when it felt like that? But I was so young, Smithy. I was too young, and how can you know, at that age. How can you know that this is the mistake, the mistake of your life, or that anything is right or wrong, when you don't know anything, when you're too young to know.

You meet someone and you fall in love, or you think you fall in love, because what could you possibly know about love or people or how things are or how they're going to be, when you're sixteen? You don't know a thing when you're sixteen. Everything's so confused and how can you know, how can you possibly know what you're doing or what's real, except love feels real, back then it felt real and you think, just because you're in love, you think you know this person. But of course I didn't know him and how could I have known him, but I thought I did, I thought I knew everything about him.

And I thought he knew me, that he knew me and understood me, everything about me and my thoughts and hopes and everything, as though his were the same, as though it was the same for both of us and maybe that's what love is, but there's no truth to it. It's not real. None of it is real. It was only me, me thinking that the two of us were the same. But really I wasn't even thinking of him at all. It was as though he wasn't even there, as though I had made him up and maybe it was the same for him with me, but it was because of that, because I felt like that and because he felt like that and because we were in love, because we were, even if it wasn't real, and I know that now, that none of it was true or real, but it was because of that I gave him my life.

So I gave him my life, myself, everything, and all because I was so young and because I didn't know, because it felt like that time would go on forever, but it didn't, not for long, hardly any time at all. And first the feeling gone and then the years and somewhere down the track changing, growing up, but still with this person, and somewhere along the way realising I didn't know him at all and I never did know him, because how could I have known him back then, sixteen, almost still a child, of course I didn't know him and even less than now, because even now I can't say I know him, no not at all, because now he's even more of a stranger than he seemed back then. But I had never felt he was a stranger then, even though he was, completely, and so I never knew him. Not then. Not now. Not ever. I'll never know him, my husband, and he'll never know me and that's the sad fact of it all. So, yes, it was all wrong then. It was a mistake, it was the great mistake, the one mistake in my life that changed everything, ruined everything, so, yes, they were right, all of them were right. I was wrong and they were right. But it's all too late now.

But even so, even now, even all these years later I still tell myself that there must be a reason, some reason we're still together and have been together all these years, and I say, well there must be something, there has to be, because this is the man I fell in love with and so there must be something between us, something there, something that was there at the start and must still be there. And I try to find it, try to think what it was, try to remember it, that feeling, and to find it again, to find it and to make myself believe that it's still there, that there's still something between us, because how can I bear the thought that maybe all of it, all these years, that they were some kind of accident, all because of a mistake I made when I was young and too young to know any better, too young to know anything at all. And so now I live with it and I am tired and broken and I just keep on going because there's nothing else to do, because there's nothing else I can do, no choices, not any more, now, at the end of things.

And sometimes I think back and then I think about now and I wonder if people still wait for the tram at Flinders Street station, in the sun and the hot winds and the grit of the city and do the trams still run to St Kilda beach, and do people still lie there until the sea glitters, and do they still have that feeling, going home, tired but happy. And I think, but how? How can it still all keep going? How can it all keep going on without me?

And so, yes, it all started because of the Florence trip, but there was a time before and a time after, and before it was school, the boarding house, and girls and their games, one day friends and the next thing tears and then friends again and someone else in tears and I was the worst of them, I really was, a spoilt little bitch, we all were, me and my friends, nasty, horrible, spoilt little bitches. And we knew exactly what we were, exactly what we were like, and we did whatever we wanted, treated people however we wanted, the other girls, guys we knew, even the teachers. And there was this boy Julian, who was in love with me, and I treated him worst of all.

And there were no repercussions, nothing. We just got away with it and we knew we would, I mean, we never thought we wouldn't, never. We acted like we were these perfect little princesses and that's how people saw us, people looked up to us and they liked us, they actually liked us, no matter how badly we acted, no matter how we treated them, and it was like the worse we were the more they liked us, the more they looked up to us, and not just the other girls, but teachers, parents, everyone. And so we just kept on and nobody told us it was wrong, that we were acting badly, and when I think back, about how we were, me and my friends, I always think that it was like we weren't real, we weren't real people.

Because it would be things like I'd break a nail or I'd get a pimple and it was like the worst thing in the world. I remember spending a whole night crying because I'd dyed my hair and it hadn't come out right, so I was up all night in tears and all my friends stayed up with me, and other girls too, because no matter how I treated them, no matter how horrible I was, they still wanted to be friends with me, and so they all stayed up, comforting me. Like it was the worst thing in the world. But the thing is, that's how it felt. And the way I was then, it really was the worst thing in the world for me, because I'd seen nothing of life, real life, how real people live, so it felt as bad to me then as anything, anything that's happening now or anything that has happened since, because that's how I was back then, not real, not a real person, not at all. Because that school, that boarding house and the people there, the girls, their families, boys we knew, all people with money, it was a different world and they didn't know and they won't ever know. I mean what life's like. Not like most people know it, not like you know it, or I know it, now, ordinary people. But I can't help thinking, and I think I'm right about this, that it was the reason my parents sent me to that school. Because they wanted me to be part of it, part of that world. It was because that didn't want me to end up like I have.

And I know we were only girls but that doesn't matter because if that made a difference then why would I still remember like I do? Why would I still feel so bad about the things I did back then and how I was? Because I do. I feel it like it happened yesterday, only then I didn't care and it's only now I care and it's more than that I care, it's like a knife in my heart, when I remember. And I think of it so much now, more than I did back then. I don't think I thought of it at all back then, and I would like to think I'm different now, that I've changed, that I'm not that person. I would like to think I'm a different person now, a better person. But sometimes I think that, despite everything, despite all these years and being stuck in this town and everything that's happened, when I'm really honest with myself, I think, well I know that I haven't really changed that much, deep down I haven't. I mean, some things have changed and I have changed in some ways, and I know everything seems so different now and on the surface things are very different, I mean, they couldn't be more different, when I think of that school and me and my friends and so many years ago and just a girl and now me, here, with Brett and stuck in this town. But maybe that's all just on the surface because I'm still spoilt, in my own way, and I might not be so nasty, such a bitch, but I wouldn't know, because I don't have the chance to see what I'm like now, how I'd act with people, I have so little to do with people anymore, and so things may have changed and my problems are so different now and everything has gone to pieces, but I still think there is something about the way I am, something the same as back then.

I mean, I still do whatever I want. I do what I want when I want and it's like I said, I do nothing all day. I sleep in, I sit around, watch TV, do nothing. But maybe it's because I don't have to do anything, not because I can't, maybe just because I don't want to, because I still only do what I want to do, same as always. I mean, I've only ever done things when I want to, when I feel like it, and never because I have to, it's always been like that for me, except now I don't do anything at all and I know I said I hate it and I do hate it, I really do hate it, watching time pass, doing nothing, but it's because I can't be bothered, because I don't have to answer to anyone, not now. I don't have to answer to anyone at all.

And I'm always blaming my mother and father for not wanting to have anything to do with me anymore, but truth be told, I suppose I wouldn't want them around, when it comes down to it. Because I do think my mother would be prepared to reconcile with me, now at least. My father, he's a different story. But I think if I were to make an effort, to make some effort with them, I think even my father would come around, he'd probably come around eventually, if I really did try to make things work. And don't think I haven't thought of it because I have and I do, all the time, and it wouldn't be easy, but all of it with my parents, a lot of it's on my part, well it's all me, really, to be honest. I blame them but it's always been because of me, from the start it's been because of me, because of what I did and the way I did it and I think that's why it's still there, the problem. It was the way I did it.

But the thing is I haven't made an effort, have I? I've never made an effort, with them, never even tried. But I don't think I really want to, I just don't think I want them back in my life. Not now, not the way things are now, not when I've become what I am and maybe it's because I'm ashamed, or too proud, because I know everything they said was right, back when it all happened, and everything that's happened since has been just like they told me, exactly what they said would happen, and so they were right and I never listened. I did the opposite, I went against everything they said and I knew it, at the time, I knew I was throwing it all in their faces. And so they were right, in the end, and still right, after all this time and maybe I just don't want to admit that, at least not to them.

And besides, I couldn't bear them seeing how I live now. I mean, my mother, I know exactly what she'd say. My God, she'd throw a fit. I can just see her, going around the house, telling me off for every little thing, nagging me. I mean, if she ever saw the state of the place, the way Brett just comes and goes or hangs around in the garage drinking and me doing nothing, not even trying to make things better. I know exactly what she'd say.

But my father, he'd be different. I mean, when I was younger my mother was at my throat all the time, but my father was the opposite, he was always trying to help, trying to understand. And he tried to help as much as he could, but the thing is, I hated that even more, and I know this sounds terrible, but I blame him for how I was then and I blame him for how I am now as well, because it was my father who spoilt me, he always spoilt me, ever since I was little. And he was never anything but kind and patient with me and he'd always hear me out, whatever sort of stupid little problems I thought I had. I mean, I hated being a boarder and I hated that we lived on a farm because most of my friends were day girls and it seemed so unfair that they got to go home after school and I was still there at the boarding house, being watched over all the time, always told what to do, and then that I had to come home on the holidays, back to the farm, in the middle of nowhere when all my friends were still in the city and meeting up and going out and getting together with guys we knew, and I was stuck on this farm with my parents and nothing to do and I felt like I was missing out on everything.

And so that's when it all came out, when I was at home, during the holidays, and my father would listen to me when I carried on, chucked my little hissy fits. I mean, I thought it was all so unfair, I thought my life was so unfair back then, I thought I had it all so bad and so I'd carry on about it and my father would listen to me, all my stupid, petty whingeing and he did try to help, but he couldn't. When it came down to it there was nothing he could do, and I suppose that's why I used to take it all out on him. I blamed him for everything and he really did try to make things better for me, but he couldn't and I knew he couldn't so I just threw it all back in his face and it hurt him, I really used to hurt him.

And he was always trying to be kind and understanding, but I think now that maybe my mother was right after all, he did spoil me too much, and I think it was to make up for the fact that he couldn't change things because I think he must have known it too. But he did listen and he did understand, he knew how important it was for me to keep up with my friends at school, so he'd give me money for clothes and going out and stuff like that, whatever I wanted, whatever I asked for, he never said no to me. But for me it was never enough, and in a way it really wasn't, because I could never keep up with them, my friends, the day girls, because no matter how much my father gave me, they always had more and so I was always fighting just to keep up with them, to fit in, and back then that was the most important thing in the world to me. But I could never have what they had, I could never really keep up. And I blamed it all on my father and I still blame him, but it's for other reasons now, it's for the opposite reason.

Because back then I thought I could have everything, not do anything for it, work for it, I just expected it, expected it all to be just given to me, and I know it sounds like a horrible thing to say but I do think it was my father's fault and I still think that. Because he spoilt me, yes, but not just that, it was the things he was always telling me, that I had so much to look forward to in life, that I could do anything with my life, and I know he meant well but it wasn't true, none of it was true. I mean, you can't do anything you want, you can't have everything. I suppose that was what he wanted for me and I'm not saying he wasn't genuine, that he didn't mean what he said, because he did. But that doesn't make it true, does it?

But I believed those things, I really did, and how could I not believe him, when that's what you're told all your life, when you're growing up. And I know he wanted the best for me, but surely he must have known that things don't turn out like that and life isn't perfect, not for anyone. He must have known that. I mean, look at him and his life, stuck on that farm with my old bitch of a mother. Having to live with her every day. And so why would he assume that things would turn out so well for me, so much better for me, and not just better than his life, but better than anyone's life. Because no one has it that easy, the way my life was supposed to be, nobody has that. I mean, why should it all be so great for me? Just because I'm his daughter, because that's what he wanted for me. It's not what happens in life. It just doesn't happen. But the thing is that I still half believe it, or, no, I still believe it all, all of it, somewhere at the back of my mind it's still something I believe and something I expect out of life and so can you see, Smithy, that just makes everything harder for me. It just makes everything worse. I mean, when I think where I am now, and it is bad, my situation, that's still true, but even so, maybe I wouldn't be so unhappy if I didn't expect my life to be so much better, not just better than it is, but so much better. That everything should turn out perfectly, that I should have this perfect life. Because I still do, I still expect those things, everything my father said. Even now, it's what I expect, even though I know he was wrong and it's not going to happen and it doesn't happen to anyone, I still expect this perfect, wonderful life and I can't help it.

And so sometimes I think I can never be happy, not ever, no matter what happens. Not when I expect so much, was promised so much. But can you blame me? Because it's not my fault, it really isn't. And so it's no wonder, is it, that life's passed me by. That it's all too much for me. Because I was never prepared for it, and I'm still not and I never will be.

And maybe it's wrong of me to keep blaming my father, but I do. Because he never gave me any idea that things might go wrong in life, like they have, or even not so bad as they are, but just that life is always going to be a struggle and it's hard, it's hard for everyone. But at least I know that now, at least now I understand things better, I mean, how things really are, not like back then, when I was at school. At least I'm not like that anymore. And as I said, I'd like to think I'm a better person, because at least now, I mean after all these years, at least I do feel bad about it, about then, the way I was then and I really do. I wake up in the middle of the night remembering things I did or said and I just feel terrible. Because when I look back I can't believe I was that person. And I'm glad I'm not, not anymore.

So I suppose at least, at the very least, I've changed that much. I've changed enough to be able to see things differently, more clearly, and I suppose that it's only because of where I am now, now that I've been dragged through the mud, everything that's happened. I suppose now I'm looking at things from the other side. Like I've seen things from both sides. And I don't know how many people have that happen to them in their lives, but it has happened to me and maybe that's a good thing, maybe that's the one good thing that's come out of all this mess, out of my life, what's become of my life. And, I mean, for me, not for anyone else, just for me, to know, just to know it. Because now, with things like they are, I suppose at least I do think more about what I'm like as a person and I'm glad that I'm not like I was, that I have changed, I mean, just being able to see things differently, that's changed me, just in itself. And it's not like it's anything real, it's not going to have any actual effect on anything, how things are, but just for me, just something that I can look at and I can say, yes, at least I'm different now, at least I've changed, in myself. To have known what it's like, to have seen both sides.

And it's only now that I keep thinking about this guy Julian, who was in love with me, back then, when I was at school. And I don't know why I keep thinking about him. I'll be at home, and my mind wanders and I find myself thinking about Julian, about then and about now, what he might be doing now, what he would be like now. And I really don't know what it is that makes me think about him all the time, I mean, of all people. Because if I treated anyone badly when I was at school it was Julian. I suppose it's because he was in love with me, or thought he was, as much as you can be at that age, so I suppose that's it and maybe it's guilt, the reason I think about him now, and, yes, it is guilt, partly, because I do feel guilty, I feel terrible, the way I treated him. But I can't help thinking that maybe it's something more than that.

I mean, he was just one of the guys we used to hang around with, but he was different from the rest of them. He was quiet and shy and I was never interested in Julian, none of us were. He was sort of a joke to us, because he was different. I mean, it wasn't like that with the other guys. I liked them. I even went out with a few of them, but it was never all that serious. They just sort of came and went. I can't even remember most of them now. But Julian was always there, always around, hanging around me, but I never took any notice of him except when I got sick of it, of him being around all the time. When we all went out he was always there, even when I was with some other guy, he'd always be somewhere, close by, never saying anything but just standing somewhere, near me, watching me, and everyone knew it, about Julian having this thing for me, and I was horrible to him, really horrible. And I can't believe I could ever have treated anyone like that, but I did and I think I did it because I could, because I knew that he was in love with me, this sweet guy, this genuinely nice guy. Just because I could and that's the worst thing about it.

And all this just went on for years, for what seemed like years. Julian used to ring me at the boarding house and most of the time, when he rang, I just treated him the same way, the same as when we all went out, him and his friends, me and my friends. Either I wouldn't come to the phone at all or when I did I was a complete bitch to him, same as always. But there were other times, and I think it was mostly because I was bored, just bored, or because I didn't have anything better to do, those times I would actually talk to him, I mean, it was me who did all the talking, telling him all my problems, or what I thought were my problems, back then. And I remember sometimes he'd ring and I'd be in tears, usually over some guy I liked, some guy who'd treated me badly, and I'd tell him all about it, let it all pour out. So he sort of became my shoulder to cry on and I suppose in a way I eventually became fond of him, just because he was always there, and he was, he was always there for me.

The thing is, back then I took Julian for granted, just like I took everything for granted, I suppose. But now, well there are so few people out there like him, like Julian, people who will actually listen to you, care about you, be there for you. And I suppose it's because I've learned about people now, because they scare me, people scare me now. Everyone's out for themselves and they don't care about you, and they don't care if they hurt you or use you, as long as they get what they want, and it seems like everybody's struggling against each other all the time, everyone fighting for themselves, just looking out for themselves. And it terrifies me, because I'm not like that, I mean there's just no fight left in me anymore. I couldn't even fight for myself, even if my life depended on it, I just couldn't. But everyone else, it's like they'll do anything to get what they want and nobody thinks it's wrong, being like that, it's just the way it is, how the world works. And I always think that if I were left to fend for myself, I mean I just couldn't, I'd be destroyed. And I wouldn't even do anything to stop it. I hate to think about it, because I think, well, one day that might actually happen.

And it's only now that I know it's people like Julian who you should value in your life, make an effort to hang on to. It's just that I never thought about Julian as someone important in my life back then. I mean I never really ever thought about him at all. He was just there and I took him for granted, as though he'd always be there, or someone like him, someone who'd listen to me and care about me, really, genuinely care about me, and well, that shows how much I knew, doesn't it? I mean, here I am without anyone and I suppose that's why it's only now, nearly twenty years later, it's only now that I've started thinking about Julian and I think about him all the time and it's ridiculous, because that boy, that boy from twenty years ago, well he doesn't exist anymore. But sometimes I feel like he does, like somehow he's still around, still there, somewhere, like I could go and find him and he'd be the same and things would be like they were, except I would be different this time, this time I'd value him, as a friend, and I'd stay friends with him and I would. This time I really would.

And of course it's absurd even talking about it, even thinking about it, because it's impossible, because that time has passed, it was so long ago. It's just how I start thinking when my mind wanders. Not that I'm saying I was attracted to him or that I wish I'd gone out with him back then, or ended up with him now, or anything like that. I wouldn't even have thought of it. I mean, I know I didn't, because it was the opposite, at the time. It just never, ever would have happened. But the thing is, I know I wouldn't act any differently, even if I had my time over, and that's the shame of it all.

And now. Now he wouldn't be interested in me at all, would he? He wouldn't give me a second thought, not if he knew me now, knew what I was like now. He'd be the same to me as I was to him. Because he's probably got the perfect life now. I mean, he was smart, really smart, and he's probably got a good job now, in the city, probably married with kids, a house, the whole perfect package. And God knows what he thinks of me now, the way I treated him. I mean, he probably doesn't ever think about me at all, after all this time. I doubt it would even cross his mind, me, back then. But if he ever does think about me, he probably just remembers some horrible private school bitch. He probably hates me now, well, no, it's worse than that, I mean, he probably doesn't even care, even if he does remember me, he wouldn't care where I am or what's happened in my life or anything like that because he'd have moved on. He's moved on and I haven't. Obviously I haven't, have I?

Sometimes I imagine running into him, seeing Julian again, now, somewhere in the city probably, seeing him on the street, somewhere. And I'd be so ashamed. I'd hide. I'd run away. I couldn't bear it, him seeing me, seeing me now, seeing what I'm like now. Not that he'd probably even recognise me anyway. I mean, we were just kids. Twenty years ago. God.

But the thing is, Smithy, when I do think about that time, twenty years ago, and no matter what I say, I miss it, that time and being young, people liking me, wanting to be with me, wanting to know me, having people in my life. I do miss it, I really do and it's so painful, thinking back to those days. But I'm always thinking back. Because that time is more real to me than things are now, more real than the life I'm living. And it's not that I miss it because of friends or being popular or anything like that, it's not even because things were just better, it's not that at all. It's something else, I don't know, this feeling I had back then and, I don't know, maybe it was just being young, maybe that's all it was.

But back then it was like everything seemed so important. My life used to seem so important, as though what I did and what I was really mattered, really actually mattered, and not just to me, but to everyone, to the whole world. It felt like everyone noticed, that they noticed me and what I was doing, everything, all of it. And I had so much to say and I thought that they were important things, things that actually mattered and I thought that people were listening to me. And there was this feeling, it was like everything I said was louder, like everything I said could be heard and everything I did could be seen, like someone was always watching, watching and caring, and it felt like the whole world was listening and watching and caring. Like I actually mattered to the world.

So it wasn't who I was, or what I was, or what people thought of me, but it was something else, just this feeling, this feeling of things being important and all eyes upon me. And I remember that and I miss it, I miss it so much. Because it's like somewhere along the way everything went quiet. Everything became quieter, smaller. Like I'm smaller, less important, or, no, not important at all, not important to anyone except myself, because now I know that I'm the only one. I'm the only one who listens and watches and cares. About myself. There's no one but me.

And it was like I used to feel more. Because now I just don't feel things, not like I used to. I hardly feel anything at all anymore. And I don't just mean the good things, I mean things like feeling sad, feeling terribly, desperately sad and I remember feeling like that, but I never feel that way anymore, not even that, not anymore. And I don't know when it happened, but at some time it all stopped. I stopped feeling things. And it's not like I stopped caring, God knows

I still care, but it's the feelings that have stopped and gone away and I just don't think they'll come back again, not ever. So now it's just about keeping on going, getting by, day to day, without feeling, without a reason, without a need. And no hope, no future, nobody watching or listening or caring, nobody but me, only me. And it's like I'm standing outside myself, watching and thinking, so this is my life, so this is what's become of me, and there's nothing I can do except watch, as though it isn't even me anymore, as though I'm already gone and have been gone for a long time now, and what's left is something else, something empty and just getting through it all, day by day, empty inside, nothing inside me anymore, and I don't care if I ended up on the street, I don't care what happens to me now, to what's left of me now. I just want to feel things again.

But I suppose it's the same for everyone. And I suppose it's just about getting older, just me getting older. But even so, it seems unfair, doesn't it, that it all only lasts such a short time and then it's gone, and nobody ever told me about this, about what would happen. But it hurts, Smithy. It hurts so much to think that it's all gone now. That it will never come back. That I'll never feel that way again, the way I used to feel when I was young. The things I used to feel. I mean, I know I should just get over it, but I can't. I can't get over it, I can't move on. Like I said, obviously I haven't moved on. I'm still living back then, in the past, like Brett's always saying, and it's true, and so I suppose that's the problem, my problem. But I don't want to think about how things are now. And I don't know, maybe it's not just that I never moved on, but that I never grew up. I mean I don't know whether I'm sixteen or thirty-four. It's like I have to remind myself all the time that I'm in my thirties now, that I'm an adult, but I always forget and, sometimes when I'm reminded of it, when something happens that makes me realise, it comes as a shock. I hear about people, and they've done so much in their lives, and I always think, God, they're the same age as me. But they're so different, they're adults. And I'm not. I don't feel like an adult at all, or that I've had a life. It's like I'm still waiting for life to happen. I mean, when I think about things, when I'm on my own, thinking about myself, I still think about things as though I were still sixteen, still a teenager.

I mean, I'm still obsessed with how I look, what I wear, I'll find myself sitting at home, and I'll be thinking about clothes, and I can't stop thinking about them. Sometimes it's all I can think about, when I watch TV and I look at what the women are wearing, at the fashion, and I worry about it, I mean I can worry about it all day. Because I keep thinking about what I would wear if I were going somewhere, if I were invited somewhere. In the city, somewhere like that, somewhere nice. I think, what if one of my old friends rang me up and invited me out, and I know it's not going to happen, but I can't get the idea out of my head, and I worry and I get anxious, thinking about what I would wear and how I have nothing to wear. Sometimes I can't even sleep, thinking about it. And I imagine it, I imagine what would happen if I were invited out, and I see myself walking into a room and it's like I have to look, not just fashionable, not just fit in, but it's like I have to look stunning, better than everyone else.

And I know it's never going to happen, but for some reason I act like it might, no, like it will, like it definitely will. And so I panic, it just gets caught up in my mind and I suppose I sort of go crazy in a way, something goes crazy inside me. And what happens is, and it's like I can't stop it, or I don't try to stop it, because at least I know it will make things go away, all the worrying, the obsessing over clothes. What happens is I drive into Albury and I go on these shopping sprees. And I can blow the whole month's rent, easily, in one day. And when I go in, it's always with this picture in my mind, of me walking into this room and how I have to look, the clothes I have to have. And I buy expensive things, ridiculously expensive clothes, brand names, beautiful clothes that I can't afford, but I buy them anyway. Because I have to. It's just something I have to do. So I go and blow the whole month's rent, or more, on these clothes, clothes that I never wear and I never will wear and then I take them home and I hide them. I hide them from Brett and from myself too, because it just makes me sad, the whole thing, and I don't want to be reminded of it, all those beautiful clothes that I know I'll never wear. And then I go and blame Brett for there being no money, and I accuse him of spending it all on booze and guns and Brett has no idea where it all goes, but he can always come up with the money. Brett can always come up with money if he has to.

But the thing is, these shopping sprees, the clothes and the madness, the thing is that I need it. This idea that some old friend might ring me up, invite me out. It's like I'm expecting a phone call from twenty years ago, like I'm expecting a phone call from the past and that's the thing, that's the whole point. Because I've done nothing all these years. I mean they're wasted, gone, and that's why this is so important to me, this thing I imagine, this picture in my mind of walking into a room in my new clothes. And I do know it will never happen, but no matter how well I know that, I still can't shake the thought that maybe it might, somehow. I suppose it's that I want it, that I desperately want it. I wish someone would phone me up, ask me out. I want to go out, somewhere nice, somewhere proper. And I want to wear new clothes, beautiful clothes, and I want to look stunning. Because, with these clothes, it's like I can make myself something different from what I am, make myself look like how I feel I should be and should have been, all these years. How I was always meant to be. And if I could do that, walk into a room, wearing these clothes, it would be like I was starting over. And even if it all seems insane, somehow it makes sense to me as well, because I can't do anything about my real life, not about my life today, not about my life anytime. It's not something I can change, it's not something I can do anything about. But if I could just dress up, look the part, somewhere away from all this, then it's like the last twenty years never happened.

So it is crazy, it is insane, but it's the easiest thing and maybe it's the only thing, the only thing I can do. And I mean about everything. I can buy clothes. At least I can do that. And I know it's all completely crazy and insane, but what I'm doing, what I think I'm doing, it's like I'm buying my life back. So in the end it does make some sort of sense and it is important. In a way it's more important than anything.

So it all happened because of this Florence trip. And it was at the end of Year Ten when they told us about it, our Italian class going to Florence for a semester, and it wasn't like I really wanted to go to Florence in particular, it was just because all my friends were going and the idea of going overseas and getting a semester off. So it's not like Florence itself was important, I mean, I didn't even know anything about Florence or care, really. But I did want to go.

So I gave my father the forms when I came home for the summer holidays and then the next day he asked me to come into his study. And he started talking about the drought and these big warehouses full of wool that they couldn't sell and the price of wheat and I honestly didn't know what he was going on about, or why. I just didn't understand, because my father had never talked to me about money before, I mean his money, the problems with the farm. I had no idea, none. And he told me that he was borrowing every year, from the bank, just to keep the farm going. That every year he was getting further and further in debt.

But one thing he didn't tell me, and he didn't tell me this until much later, after everything with Brett, when we really, finally actually had it out, the last time I ever spoke to my father, what he didn't tell me was that he'd taken out a mortgage on the farm and it was to pay for my school fees. He really couldn't afford to send me to that school and for me to stay at the boarding house, but I had no idea about it then. I had no idea that he'd done that, mortgaged the farm, for me, just so I could go to that school. I didn't have a clue, I just took it all for granted. Because I thought we were rich, or well off at the very least. The idea that we might not be able to afford something had never really crossed my mind.

And so when I gave him the form for the Florence trip I just assumed, I never thought it would be a problem, I mean, my father had never said no to me before, not for anything. So, when I finally realised what he was saying, that he was saying I couldn't go on the trip to Florence, I mean, I just didn't understand. I didn't believe we couldn't afford it, I really didn't believe it. I thought we had all this money and my father was just being mean, stingy. My poor father. I just went off at him. I was horrible. I said the worst things to him. I can't remember exactly what I said, but I know, I remember the look on his face, I'll always remember that look on his face. It was like he was ashamed. Ashamed that he didn't have the money, that for the first time he couldn't give me something I had asked for, this one thing. It was like he'd failed me, just this look of absolute defeat.

So I was throwing this massive tantrum, crying and screaming, and then my mother came in, and of course she just made things worse. And I stormed out of the house. I just kept walking and walking and I didn't know where I was going and I didn't care. I must have walked for miles, I can't remember, but somehow I found myself in town and it didn't even feel like I'd walked all that way, but I was just in this absolute rage, this blind fury.

It must have been a Friday or a Saturday, because the pubs were open, even though it was dark by then, and I went into one of them, because my father hated pubs, and beer, and, I suppose, the sort of men who went there. He'd always warned me off going into pubs, so that's why I went in. Just to spite him. But as soon as I was inside, all these sleazy old men started coming up to me, offering to buy me drinks and I got scared.

And it was Brett who came to my rescue. He was sitting down at the other end of the bar, and he just walked over and told all the men to piss off and they did. And at the time, there was something about that, it seemed brave or noble or something, and I think it was then, already way back then, I think that's when I was first attracted to Brett.

Because people respected him, or that's how it seemed at the time, anyway. Of course now I know that it wasn't respect at all. It was because they were afraid of him. It was fear, not respect. But, I don't know, maybe I knew that even back then. I mean, I knew Brett's reputation, everyone did. And to be honest, that might have been what attracted me to Brett. That people were afraid of him. Maybe I liked it, and I'd like to say that wasn't the case, but to be honest, I think it was, I think it was that. And I'd like to say that I don't like it about him anymore, and it's a terrible thing to say, but when I'm with him, around town, I think I do like it, knowing it, that feeling. Seeing the way people act around him, knowing that they're afraid of him. That's not good, is it. But I can't help it. It's just how I am.

Anyway, after that, after he had got rid of all the old men, Brett stayed at the bar with me and he bought me a drink and talked to me and I was surprised, meeting him for the first time, talking to him. I mean, everything I knew about him, just from people talking, all the things I knew or thought I knew about Brett Clayton, all the stories, they just didn't seem to fit. He was friendly and laid back and he listened to me. He was nice, he seemed really nice. And then he offered to drive me home and I said, yes, and I thought, I just assumed that, well, something would happen, on the way home, and I remember thinking it would serve my father right if I ended up getting raped by Brett Clayton, because of him, because of my father. That it would all be his fault. I mean, I can't believe I would actually think a thing like that, but I remember it. That's exactly what I thought.

But Brett didn't try anything at all, and that surprised me too. He even offered to walk me to the door and I suppose that's when I realised that all the things people said about him, well, they were actually true, most of it was true, but even so, Brett was still so different from what I expected.

And so that's when it all started. I hardly talked to my father at all that summer, I was still so angry at him, and I started hanging around with Brett and his friends. I think at first it was mostly just to get back at my father, but then it was because I enjoyed it. I liked them and I especially liked Brett. Not that we were together or anything, not back then. I didn't even think Brett was interested in me, I mean, not in that way. I thought if he had been, then he would have tried something that night, that first night I met him at the pub. But he hadn't and he never did, not that summer. I still liked him, you know, although a lot of the other girls did as well, in the group. But it wasn't just because of Brett that I hung around with them. I sort of became part of the group. And I really remember that summer.

So I suppose that summer was in the middle of it all, when some things had changed, but before everything really changed. Even so, I suppose that was part of it, part of things changing already, for me, being with Brett and his friends, that summer. I was just really happy when I was with them, because with them I felt like I could be myself and it was such a relief. It was so different to being with my friends at school, I mean, with them I could never be myself, and I don't think I realised that until I got to know Brett and his friends. At school we were always trying to outdo each other, like we were in competition with each other all the time, always bitching about friends behind their backs, bitching about each other and then changing friends and someone would be on the outside and then it would all change again and it would be someone else, and we were just awful to each other, as bad as we were to any of the other girls, well, worse really, much worse, because we were meant to be friends. And it was exhausting, always trying to be better than everyone else, better than your own friends, worrying about what they might be saying behind your back. There was something wrong about it, just plain wrong. They weren't real friends, they weren't friends at all. But I don't think I'd realised that before.

Because with Brett's friends everything was so relaxed and it was all completely different and it was so nice, just being with them, going down to the river and sitting around talking, lying in the sun, going for a swim and everyone laid back and easygoing and no pressure, none at all. I never felt like I had to impress anyone, or be anything except myself and it was just nice and I had never been with people like that before. And I was happy. That summer I was happy.

But my parents, I mean, they acted like it was the end of the world, me hanging around with Brett and his friends. Like I'd gone completely off the rails. And I remember fighting with my mother constantly, all that summer. My mother kept saying I was throwing my life away, and even my father, I mean, I wasn't talking to my father, but he still suggested, through my mother, that I invite one of my school friends to come up and stay. And how could I explain, I didn't even try to explain, because I knew they would never understand.

And Brett's friends never treated me as any different from them, I mean, because of me going to a private school or because my family had a farm and money. And they'd listen to what I'd say. You know, they were interested in me, as a person. And I don't think I'd ever really had that before. And sure, it's true they weren't perfect. They smoked a lot of dope and drank a lot and they did get into a lot of strife, with the police and shop owners and other people in the town, you know, they could get a bit wild and start making trouble, just for the hell of it really, and they always talked back to people, in town, but that's because the people, you know what they're like, they'd say stuff, make comments, tell us off, when we were hanging around the fish and chip shop or on the steps of the bank. I mean, there was always someone who'd make some comment, tell us off for something small, something petty, especially older men, you know, RSL types, just because they were old and bitter and didn't like seeing us hanging around doing nothing, having fun. So Brett's friends would give them lip and then of course they got the police called on them, but really nobody had any real right to tell them off in the first place, because they weren't doing any harm, they were just hanging around, being teenagers.

And a lot of them had pretty tough lives already, growing up, and maybe that was part of it, maybe that made them more mature, you know, like it had made them grow up fast, and maybe that's why they looked out for each other like they did, because a lot of them had it really hard at home. I mean, some of the stories they told me, especially the girls, some of the things that had happened to them, with their fathers or their fathers' friends, uncles. I could hardly believe some of the things they told me, I mean, I'd never heard of things happening like that before.

And you'd think all that would have made them worse, and it's true a lot of them had problems, drugs and alcohol, and some of the guys could get really violent, and it has got worse for a lot of them since. I mean, some of them have ended up junkies or in prison, that sort of thing. But at the time, when I was listening to them, when they were telling me about themselves, I felt like I'd lived such a sheltered life and I suppose I had. And, I mean, I felt so lucky compared to them, but at the same time I felt like I didn't have any real experience of life, I mean, nothing real, nothing like the things they'd been through. I felt like I hadn't lived, like I hadn't lived at all.

And Brett never had it easy either. Not that he ever talked about it back then, but after, when we were together, when he told me about his life, and I'm not making any excuses for him, for what he's done or how he is, but he's never had it easy. And sometimes, when I think about it, it seems like he never really had a chance, not much of a chance anyway, and really it's no wonder he's turned out like he has, and that's not an excuse, it's just how things are.

I mean, when Brett was growing up his father was never around, so he was pretty much raised by his stepmother. And she had her own two boys and they were horrible to Brett all of them. His step-brothers bullied him, picked on him, and the stepmother, I don't know what her problem was, maybe it was something to do with his father coming and going all the time and everything, but it was Brett she took it out on and none of that was his fault. I mean she essentially kicked him out of the house. He used to sleep on a bed on the verandah, even in winter. I mean, can you imagine that? And he says that he was scared all the time, when he was a little boy, he was always scared of doing something wrong, because his stepmother would beat the hell out of him at any excuse. He says that sometimes he didn't even know what he'd done wrong, and now he thinks that maybe those times he hadn't actually done anything at all, that she was just taking things out on him. His father was the same too, when he was around. And Brett was only a little boy, for Christ's sake.

So yes, Brett had it hard too, growing up, but he knew it wasn't so bad, not compared to a lot of his friends, but it was this thing that happened to him when he was a teenager, before I knew him. And Brett says I'm the only person he ever told about it. I mean, I can't even bear to think about it, what he must have gone through and what it must have done to him. I don't know, sometimes I even wonder why he's not worse than he is.

He must have been about fifteen, sixteen and he'd gone down to the beach for New Year's Eve with his mates. They were drinking on the beach and Brett passed out and his mates went off and left him there on the beach, sort of as a joke. But when he came to, there was this group of men, and, I mean, even today it's hard to believe it actually happened. These men, they were holding him down, and one of them had a belt around Brett's neck and he was strangling him. They were trying to kill him. They were actually trying to kill him. And Brett says that while it was happening, while they were trying to strangle him, none of the men said anything, not to him, not to each other, and he says that was one of the strangest things about it, the silence. And the man who had the belt around his neck, who was trying to strangle him, this man's face was right up close to his and Brett says he had this really foul breath and he says he'll never forget that, the man's face and his breath. He still has nightmares about it, even now.

Anyway, so Brett blacked out and he says the next thing he remembers he was in a caravan park, in the shower block, lying on the floor with the shower running on him. And a man found him and he asked him what had happened but Brett says he couldn't speak, and it wasn't because he'd been choked, there was no actual damage to his throat, he just couldn't speak, couldn't say anything. He was in shock, I suppose. So this guy went and got help and someone called an ambulance and they took him to hospital.

But what Brett told me, the really strange thing about it all, what he said is that, for years after, he still had these problems talking to people. And, like I said, there was no actual injury to his neck or his voice box, it was something else, but it was something that happened after those men did what they did, and Brett said it lasted for years after. He'd try to say something, but the words wouldn't come out right. And people, his mates, his father, people at school, used to make fun of him, because of the things he said, because everything always came out so strange, when he tried to talk. And he says that because of that he just stopped trying, he barely talked at all, not to anyone. The problem went away eventually, but still, Brett says it lasted such a long time that he thought it would never go away.

And Brett says that during that time, because he couldn't talk, or wouldn't talk, or when he did talk it came out wrong, he always got angry when he was around people. He says he'd never had a temper before, but it was because he was just so frustrated, not being able to talk and everything. And he started to get violent, lashing out at people. He'd get into fights all the time, at school, on the street, or he'd just beat people up, turn on them, and he says sometimes it was because they made fun of him, but most of the time there wasn't any reason at all, he just wanted to hurt them. He says it's something he still doesn't understand, but he really wanted to hurt people, hurt them really badly, and he didn't know why. He says it didn't actually have anything to do with the whole thing about not being able to talk properly, or because of people laughing at him when he tried to talk, or even because it made him angry all the time. It had nothing to do with that. He says it was a completely different thing, something else that happened to him after what those men did. He just wanted to hurt people, really hurt them. And he did, he seriously injured some guys in those fights, he could get really vicious. And Brett says he knew that he was going too far, he knew that at the time, and he was scared that he'd actually kill someone one day, he was sort of scared of himself, what he might do. But he says it was like there was something inside him, making him do it. He just couldn't stop himself.

And everyone thinks that Brett got kicked out of school for punching out a teacher. I mean even I knew about it, before I ever met him or knew who he was. I'd just heard this story about some guy who got expelled for punching a teacher. But he never actually got expelled. The thing was, even before what happened to him on the beach, the teachers all thought Brett was a troublemaker anyway, which he probably was, but different, before that. He says he just had a smart mouth. He didn't get into fights and that sort of thing, not before. But afterwards, everything changed and things got so much worse, you know, getting into fights nearly every day and then the teachers used to get on his back because he never said anything in class, or when he did he said weird things and they thought he was being a smartarse, or on drugs. They used to search his locker for drugs because the teachers thought he was stoned all the time, because of the way he was in class, the things he said.

But there was this one teacher who gave him a particularly hard time, who was always on his back about something. A maths teacher. And Brett says he'd give him a hard time for nothing at all, he'd just pick on him. And so one day Brett was in the hall, at his locker, not doing anything, and this teacher came up and started abusing him, again for absolutely no reason at all. I mean, Brett thinks that it was the teacher who was the one with the real problems, more than him. So this teacher was right in his face, yelling at him, and Brett just punched him out. Dropped him. Brett says it was almost a reflex thing, he didn't even think about it, it just happened. So Brett took his stuff out of his locker and walked out of the school and never went back. People say they expelled him, but that never actually happened.

And I'm not making any excuses for him, Smithy. I mean, certainly not for the things he's done since. But I don't know. It's just that it's like some people, nothing bad ever happens to them, people like me, or how I used to be anyway. But other people, it's like bad things just keep happening to them, nothing ever goes right. And I've always known that about Brett and, I suppose, well, I've always had this sympathy for him and I suppose that's why I find it so easy to overlook his faults, forgive him for things. And maybe that's not the right thing to do, maybe it just ends up dragging me down as well, and maybe I should be more selfish, but that's just how I am. I'm just saying that Brett hasn't had it easy, he's never had it easy.

So anyway, that summer and being with Brett's friends, like I said, I didn't think Brett was particularly interested in me, except as a friend, but that didn't matter because I was just happy, being with them, being one of them. But I still liked Brett a lot and I wasn't the only one, as I said, a lot of the girls liked Brett. I mean, I could tell, and I know I was right because he told me about it later, when we were first together. You know, that time at the start, when you tell each other everything. But I could already see it, during that summer. They all looked up to Brett back then, the whole group, and I suppose it was partly because of his reputation, because nobody would ever mess with Brett, nobody in the whole town, same as now, I suppose. I suppose that's one thing that hasn't changed. But it wasn't just that, it was more than that, it was because of him, the way he was back then. Because he was just so different, not like now, quiet and laid back and funny, he could be really funny. And confident too. It was like he had everything worked out, like nothing could faze him, and it didn't, nothing ever did, and the more I got to know him, the more I was attracted to him. I mean, I think I started to fall in love with him back then, well, I know I did, before I knew he had any interest in me whatsoever. I was just too shy to let him know.

And when I look back on it I always think how much he's changed and it's sad really, that he's gone from that to how he is now, that he's become like he is now. But I suppose things haven't gone right for him either, same as for me and, I don't know, I can only feel sad, because it's hard to think he's even the same person now. So I suppose we're not so different in that way, I mean, how I thought everything was going to turn out so well for me, just assumed it, and I suppose Brett, well, as different as he was from me, I think he thought the same, about himself and his own life. And if you'd known him then, the way he was then, that's how it seemed. He just seemed like the sort of person things were going to go well for, just like me.

So there were plenty of other girls who were after Brett and they weren't as shy as me about it, and when it happened, when it all happened, with us, I mean I really couldn't believe that he'd chosen me. But he'd been with a lot of the other girls already, he told me about it, later, when we were together. He'd slept with most of them at one time or another, over the years, back before I knew him, but the thing is he'd never actually gone out with any of them. It was just sex. He told me he hadn't been interested in relationships at all, not before he met me.

That's what he told me anyway, in the early days. Brett and I used to lie in bed all night, talking, can you believe it? I mean we hardly say a word to each other anymore, except when we fight, or I'm nagging him and I suppose that's what starts the fights, usually. And there's times when he goes silent, like for weeks, he can go for weeks on end, barely saying a word to me. What's for tea, or things like that, but nothing else, and I try to talk to him and he just answers in grunts or a few words, or just ignores me, like he doesn't even care, well probably he doesn't.

But back in the early days we'd lie in bed and sometimes we'd lie together in bed all night and all day, talking, making love, sleeping. It was probably our best time together. And sometimes we'd stay in bed for days on end. And it was Brett who said it, he said it was like we were on a desert island, just the two of us, and there was nobody else, just us, alone together, and that's exactly how it felt, like we were on a desert island, and that's what I wanted, what both of us wanted back then, just the two of us and nobody else, just me and Brett, and it was like the rest of the world wasn't even there, didn't even exist anymore, for us.

And Brett used to say that he never thought he'd meet someone he wanted to be with, to only be with one person, until he met me.

And he said that before he met me, he never thought he'd want to be with someone for the rest of his life, that he couldn't imagine it before, before me. He told me that he'd fallen in love with me the moment he saw me, which was sweet and I believed him and I don't know, maybe it was true, maybe he was just saying it because that's what you're meant to say, isn't it. Because I said the same thing to him and it wasn't really true. I mean, I was attracted to Brett from the start, but not in love, not straight away, like I told him I was, and really I don't believe that happens to anyone. But maybe it was true, for him, maybe he was in love with me from the start, or thought he was. Maybe he still is in love with me, despite the way he acts, despite everything that's happened and the way we are now. I mean he's still with me, isn't he. Even now, he's still hanging around, after everything that's happened. So it's possible, I suppose it is possible.

But truth be told I can't help feeling that maybe Brett thinks he made a mistake as well, same as me, about us, about all of it. Maybe he really shouldn't have ever been with anyone, like he said, maybe he was right and that's why things haven't worked out, or one of the reasons anyway. And I know I haven't been a good wife to him and really when I think about it I was probably the worst choice for Brett. I mean, if he'd chosen one of those town girls, you know, who didn't expect much, just to be with him, probably one of them would have been a better match. They would probably put up with everything, never complain, and be happy just being a housewife for him. Not like me, because I'll never be like that. That would never be enough. Not for me.

And I know I blame Brett, but it's because I'm unhappy, because I feel like I've missed out on life. And I blame Brett, but really I blame myself for marrying him in the first place, it's just that most of the time I forget that, that it's my fault and I think it's all his fault, that he's made everything go wrong, and so I blame him, I take it all out on him. I mean, I get so angry, even over the smallest things, and sometimes I just can't stand the sight of him, I can't bear having him around. It's like I hate him and that's how I feel, like I absolutely hate him and I think I really do sometimes, and he must know that. I mean I actually say it to his face, I tell him I hate him, when we argue, when my blood's up, and I mean it. I do hate him, at those times. And so I say it and I take it back later, most of the time, but he must know it, that I do actually mean it, that when I say that I hate him it's how I really do feel.

And maybe that's why he goes silent like he does. It's the same way my father used to go silent when my mother was nagging him or criticising him and I suppose I do the same to Brett. I do exactly the same thing, really. Well they say you turn out like your parents, don't they? So maybe I'm just like my mother, and God that's a terrible thought. I always used to say to myself, promise myself, ever since I was little, that I would never turn out like my mother, the way she treated my father. I mean I suppose she was miserable too, same as me, and she couldn't admit that she was unhappy, but the way she used to talk, it was like she was perfect, like everything she did or said was right and everyone else was in the wrong. And my father, it was like he was always in the wrong, all the time, every-thing he did. Every little thing. And that's a lot like me, now. I'm the same, the way I am with Brett. And maybe I was terrified I would turn out like my mother because I knew that I would, because maybe I have.

And maybe I hurt Brett far more than I think I do. It's just the way he ignores me, it doesn't seem like I'm even getting through to him, and then the more he ignores me the worse I get, but maybe I do hurt him, only he doesn't want to show it, maybe that's why he never says anything. But I never think of that at the time. It's only since he's been in prison, I suppose I've had time to think, because these things, what I'm saying, they're all things I've only really started thinking about recently, and it's the first time I've wondered, well, maybe it's me who's the problem, or partly me, as much as Brett, rather than how I've always been before, thinking it's his fault, blaming it all on him, everything, everything that's gone wrong, everything that's wrong in my life.

So now I wonder whether Brett regrets marrying me, whether he thinks he's the one who made the mistake. But before all this, having this time on my own, I really never thought about what Brett might be thinking, that he would think anything like that, probably because he never says anything, because it's always me, always me doing the talking and always me telling him how unhappy I am, how miserable I am with him, with my life. And blaming it all on him. And I can go on and on and I never give a thought to what Brett might be thinking, that he might be thinking the same thing as me. That he made a mistake and that it's me making him miserable, and I suppose the way he acts now, acting like I'm not even there sometimes, staying away from the house with his mates or drinking in the pubs by himself, just hardly ever around, maybe that means it's true, maybe it's all true and maybe it is me.

I mean Brett has his faults, he's got plenty of faults, but it's not like I've ever done anything to support him, to try and make things better for him, or easier on him. I've just expected him to do the right thing by me and look after me, and it's true he's always let me down, but is that really his fault in the end? I mean, I expected more, but he didn't know that, he never knew that. I suppose I assume he sees things like I do, that he wants more, like I do, but maybe he doesn't and maybe he never did, maybe this is all he wanted, just being together with me. So perhaps he just doesn't understand, I mean why I'm always going on at him, why I'm so unhappy all the time, why I blame him for everything. Perhaps he just doesn't understand what he's done that's so wrong. What he's done to make me hate him so much.

But the sad thing is, I mean, even after I've had this time to think it all through, the sad thing is that I can't see anything changing. It all seems too late. The damage is already done and I can't fix it and Brett can't fix it. It's just how it is and there's nothing we can do about it. There's nothing anyone can do.

And those things he used to say in the early days, at the start. It was sweet and romantic and maybe he was only saying what he thought he was meant to say, but of course I didn't think of that at the time, I didn't know it's what everyone says when you're like that, starting out, in love, or think you're in love, and so I believed it, I believed it all and it made me feel so special and I used to ask him, why me? Why did he pick me, when there were all those other girls? What was so special about me?

And he used to say it was because of who I was, because I was me and because I was different from those other girls. And he told me he'd never met anyone like me before. And at the time it made me feel so special and so close to him and it was so nice, just me and Brett in bed together and him saying those things and I had never felt like that before, not ever. It all seemed so romantic at the time, like it should have, I suppose, how it's meant to be, whether it's real or not.

And the thing is, I think he did actually mean it, what he said. About why he chose me and that it was because of who I was and because I was different and that he'd never met anyone like me before. I think that was all true. But when I think about it now, I think that maybe it's not quite how it seems, how Brett meant it. Because the thing is, I actually was different from those other girls, those town girls, and Brett probably hadn't met anyone like me before, but it was because he never had a chance to. I mean, you know, my family, me, where I went to school, the way I was brought up. And because I had nice clothes and I looked after myself, my hair, my skin, watched my weight. Some of those girls were pretty, but they just didn't look after themselves. They lived off takeaway food and they drank and smoked, they didn't know how to put on make-up properly and they were sort of rough too, the way they spoke and acted. So in the end, I think it was all of that, all of those things, and I see it so clearly now. I mean I didn't at the time, not at all. I only saw my faults back then and that I was shy compared to the other girls, and less confident and less experienced. Like I said, I felt like I didn't know anything about life, not compared to them. But I think that for Brett it was all true what he said, because I really wasn't like anyone he'd met before. I just never thought of myself in that way. But for Brett, I think I can see why now.

So there was a time before and there was a time after that, and that summer was in the middle of it all and it was a happy time for me, and in the time after, when Brett and I were first married and living at his cousin's place in Melbourne, that time, it was more than a happy time, something more, the time we were in love, both of us, so much in love and past and future, none of it mattered, it was just then, that time, being together, that was all that mattered.

And Brett and I would lie in bed all day or we would go down to St Kilda beach and it was like we couldn't be apart, couldn't bear to be apart, not for a moment, always together, and everything we did we did together, and so we lay in bed and talked and made love and everything was new for me, it was a whole new world and a whole new life and I was only sixteen and had only known home and the boarding house and now suddenly that was all in the past, and it all felt so wonderful and unexpected, that this was my life now and I was married and a woman and free, free to do anything, and everything had changed and I couldn't believe that this was my life now, and I thought that this was how my life was always going to be.

So we'd go to the beach or we'd explore the city together, go into the shops and just look at things and I'd try on clothes and make-up and perfume and Brett enjoyed being with me, doing those things, and he'd tell me what he thought of the clothes and smell the perfumes on my arm and it was the same for him as it was for me, a whole new life, getting away from this town and being together and in love and free, because it was freedom for him too, it was the same. It was the same for both of us.

And we'd sit at cafés and drink coffee or wine, there was this cheap Italian wine we used to like that came in a bottle with gold wire around it, and we'd buy a bottle of wine and sit at a table outside the café and stay there all afternoon talking and I felt so grown up and sophisticated and Brett would smoke and make comments about the people walking past and make me laugh, and we'd talk all the time, we'd never stop talking and I can't even remember what we talked about, but we had so much to say back then.

Then at night, sharing the same bed, having Brett in bed next to me all night, every night, my husband. And it was only a single bed so we were always close and wrapped around each other and I felt we were so much together and I was so much in love and I had never thought or imagined anything like that time or what it was like to be in love and I couldn't believe that Brett was in love with me, that someone could want me and want me so much to be with me all the time and forever and I couldn't believe it was happening to me and I never thought it would end and there was this feeling I had, as though anything, everything was possible. Like everything was possible for me and for us, like anything could happen, like we could do anything we wanted and it would all keep on going, on and on. That it would all go on forever.

And I don't know what happened to that. But somewhere, somehow, it all went away, slowly, but not so slowly, because it didn't last long, that time, not long at all, and the feeling went, and the joy and the freedom and the newness of it all, and so it's all gone now, it all went a long time ago, and just a memory now. But there was a time, there was, and it just seemed to fade into nothing, but there was a time and, despite everything, I do have that and I wouldn't change it, if I had my time over, I wouldn't change it for the world. So at least I have that. I'll always have that.

But now, what can I say about now, because I hardly ever think about now and about what's happened since, and there's no story, just days going by, everything so much the same that I can't remember one day from another, over all these years, every day the same but getting older and tired and falling apart, between me and Brett, and inside me too. Older and tired and fading and everything quieter and the feelings gone and like some part of me died inside and still dying, day by day, less and less of me, just the days and getting by, getting through it, going on and both of us unhappy but nothing we can do about it, nothing. So all gone, at the end of things and at the end of things for so long now, and I just wait, feeling nothing, not caring anymore, just waiting for it all to end.

So it hasn't been easy, none of it has been easy. I could never say that. And I don't try, not anymore, I've stopped trying, just let it happen, let it all happen as though I'm not even there. It all just happens to me and I feel like I'm watching my life, watching it pass but not living it anymore, never actually living it.

And it was Brett who was supposed to be the strong one and I thought he was, and at the start maybe, but only at the very start, and now it's like he's weaker than me and I know how it seems, but really he's so weak, he's only just hanging on and so it's me who's become the strong one and Brett just runs away from it all and I'm the one who knows and who suffers with the knowing. Because Brett doesn't want to know, but I do, I have to and so I'm the one who suffers. I suffer for the both of us.

And I know that there are plenty of people worse off, but I'm not them and they're not me and this is the only thing that's real to me, this is the only thing I know and certainly there are plenty worse off and there always will be, but this is my life and it's all I've got and it's all I know. So there are other people, yes, but I don't live their life and they don't live mine. So maybe I do feel sorry for myself, maybe I do feel hard done by, but I can't help it. How can I help it? And can you blame me? Can you blame me for that?

And I know I've dug my own grave. I know it's all my fault, that it's always been my fault, but how long are people going to keep taking it out on me? Because they make it so much harder, and it seems so unfair because it's all hard enough as it is without everyone watching you, talking behind your back, looking at you on the street, in the shops, and I know they're judging me, as if they know everything, everything about me and my life. But they don't know, they don't know a thing, not what it's been like for me, so why? Why do they make it worse? Why do they have to do that? And I know they say that I deserve this, that I deserve it all, that I brought it all on myself, but I know that, I know that already and

I'm the one who has to live with it because it's there all the time, it's always there for me, and, yes, it is my fault, and, yes, I'm the one who made the mistake, that one mistake of my life, the mistake that changed everything. But even so, I never chose this, I never chose any of it. Not this.

And now it doesn't matter what I do or what happens to me anymore. I'm just getting older and I can't bear the thought of it, I can't bear the thought of getting middle-aged, old. And I'm nearly there. I'm very nearly there. I can see it already. And it's terrifying for me. When you're a woman, when you have nothing, no money, no children, nothing. And nothing ahead, nothing to look forward to, nothing changing, and I'm always there alone, waiting, and nobody notices and nobody cares, no matter what happens, or how much I want things to be different, or how much pain I go through, there's nobody out there, nobody who can help, there's only me.

But despite it all, I do have hope, there is still hope and there has to be, because it's only hope that can keep me going now, hope that something will change, that something has to change. And I don't know what it is, or what will happen, or when it will happen, but I can't live without that, even if it isn't real, even if I know, deep down, that nothing can change, that nothing will change, will ever change. But somewhere there is hope and maybe it's crazy but it's only as crazy as everything else, because it's there, it's always there and I can't help it. I believe it because I have to believe it. So there is still hope and there has to be. There always has to be hope.

So the holidays ended and I went back to school. And it was all uniforms and assemblies and girls and teachers and classes and the boarding house, but everything seemed different. And it was different because of me, because I was a different person, because

I'd changed. Because that summer had changed me. It was all me.

And school and everything, the same routine as always, but I felt like I wasn't there, like I wasn't actually there at all, as though I was watching it from somewhere else, like I was looking at everything through glass, and I was on the outside, looking in. Nothing seemed real to me and it must have shown, because first it was my friends who turned against me, asking why I was acting so strangely and then starting to get nasty, teasing me, making fun of me, starting rumours about me, just like we used to do to the other girls, only it was me now. Suddenly I'd become like one of those other girls, and I was alone. And so I lost all my friends, and I had been friends with them for years, but I lost them so quickly, because of how I was now, because I had changed. But I didn't care, even though once upon a time, I mean, even a few months before, that would have been the worst thing in the world for me. But I really didn't care, it made no difference to me, not at all. They were just a bunch of stuck-up, horrible little schoolgirls and they didn't mean anything to me anymore.

And then it was the teachers, and at first they were kind, asking me whether I was all right, if anything was wrong, if something had happened to me over the summer. And I suppose something had happened, but how could I explain that to them, what had happened. I mean, I didn't even really know myself. But that's not the sort of thing they meant anyway. And then, later on, they started giving me a hard time, saying I had developed a bad attitude. They kept saying I had to change my attitude. I was even called into the headmistress's office and given a talking to, and she told me I had to change my attitude as well, but I didn't even know what that meant, I didn't understand what any of them were talking about. It was as though they were speaking a different language. Like that school was somewhere foreign, something I didn't understand. I just didn't understand anything anymore.

And so, yes, I didn't care about my friends turning on me and I didn't care about the teachers telling me off either, but I did feel alone, I felt so alone. Because even with all the people around me it was like I was trapped inside my own head, completely cut off from it all, and I got sad. And I mean really, terribly sad. I used to cry myself to sleep every night, and during the day too. I'd lock myself in the toilets and just cry. And I didn't know why I was feeling like that, or what was happening to me, or why. And there were days when I barely had the energy to get out of bed, to get dressed, to walk to class. It was like there was this huge weight on me.

And then one Saturday, in the middle of the semester, the boarding-house mistress told me I had a visitor and it was Brett. And seeing Brett in that place, that school. It was like suddenly everything melted away, fell into the background. And all I could see was Brett standing there in his old jeans and singlet, not even trying to hide his tatts, and there were girls all around whispering and putting their heads out of doorways to look at him and then giggling inside their rooms. And Brett standing there with this weird expression and I realised that he was trying to keep a straight face, that he was trying not to laugh. And I don't know how he did it, but he got permission to take me out for the day. And I really still don't know how, because they were so strict about that sort of thing. But he managed it anyway. Like I said, Brett used to have this confidence, this charisma, and I don't know how he did it, but he did.

And walking out of that school with Brett, through the boarding house, out through the grounds and past all the girls. With Brett. It just didn't seem real. I couldn't believe it was happening. I mean it was just so strange and everything seemed so out of place, it was like something that happens in a dream. It just didn't make sense to me. It all happened so suddenly, I don't even remember feeling happy about it. I don't know what I felt. It was like I was in a daze, walking out of that school, walking out with Brett.

So we went to the tram stop, with Brett laughing all the way, about the school and about seeing me there in the boarding house and the look he said I had on my face when I saw him. And we took the tram down to St Kilda beach. And it was one of those old trams and the hot air was blowing through the windows and the seats sticking and burning under my legs and I remember looking outside, watching everything go past, and the light flashing through the trees and Brett beside me, and I felt this enormous sense of freedom. Like I was suddenly myself again, like the weight I had been under for all those months just fell off, just went away. And everything else too, the sadness, the feeling of being outside everything, all the bad things just seemed to wash off me, being there with Brett, with him on that tram. And it was like I had forgotten how to breathe but now I was breathing again.

And so Brett suggested we have fish and chips on the beach and when we got there I saw that he had brought this picnic blanket, this old tartan picnic blanket. And until then I thought he had come to Melbourne to visit his cousin, because he had said he was staying there, and I thought he had just dropped in on the off-chance. Just because I was someone he happened to know who was in the city. But when he brought out the blanket, I realised that he had planned the whole thing, that he had come down for me, to see me, and I realised that he must have been thinking about me all that time. All that time since the end of the holidays. That he had been thinking about me and that he had come down for me, just for me.

And we lay on the beach all afternoon, not even talking much, but I felt so relaxed, because Brett was relaxed, just like he'd been during the summer, by the river, exactly the same, only there was nobody else around now, no other friends, no group, just me and Brett. And I wondered if that was why he'd come down to the city, because he knew it would be just the two of us. And it was then I understood what was happening. He never said anything, but I understood. Why he was there, there with me.

So we just lay there in the sun, hardly talking at all, and I remember Brett leaning up on one elbow and looking over at me, and him saying, so how's things? And I said, fine, and he said, well that's good then, and he rolled over on his back again, with his arm over his face and that's how we were, all afternoon. And we lay there and we watched the sunset, and the sea like a broken mirror, glittering and silver, and it was long past my curfew, but I already knew. Some time during that afternoon I had already decided. Not that I actually thought about it, but I knew and it just seemed to happen, and it seemed right. It just seemed so right, all of it. I knew that I wasn't going back to school, not that day and not ever. I knew I wasn't ever going back.

So Brett and I went to his cousin's house and I rang my mother because I knew the school would have rung already. And I told her everything. I just told her. And I don't think she knew what to say because she didn't say anything except to ask me to phone back the next day, to let her know I was all right. And so I called the next day and she put my father on the phone. And there was this strain in his voice. He was trying not to let me hear it, but there was this strain, and the way he talked, it was slow and strange and desperate. He was almost pleading with me. And he said that he had talked with the headmistress and told her that there had been some problems at home and that it had all been his fault, that he had been under a lot of stress because of the drought. And he told me that the head-mistress had agreed to let me back into the school on probation. And then my father said that he'd been looking into the money situation and he thought he could manage to pay for the Florence trip after all. And I just laughed. Because I didn't care about any of that anymore. Because I was with Brett now. Because everything had changed.

I shouldn't have laughed, Charlotte says.

MONDAY AND Spit shows.

Me and Wallace are sitting up back of the ute, putting an edge on the shovels.

Win anything on the races? Wallace asks me.

Nope, I say.

Win anything on the lottery?

No, I did not.

Wallace oils the blade. We are at Harris's close to town and cars pass, the smell of their exhaust wafting across the vines in the fresh morning air.

Well it's all been happening around here, says Wallace.

It certainly has, I say.

Locust spraying Saturday, says Wallace. Brett Clayton's mob gone wild.

Wallace squints to look at me.

You heard about that? Wallace asks me. Brett Clayton and his mob?

Yeah, I say. I heard about it.

Did a number on those kids, Wallace says. You hear about that? University students home for the holidays. Farmers' kids. Bashed them with axe handles. Friday night. Got them after they come out

Imperial. Just turned off Main Street. Jumped them there. Bashed them with axe handles, fence posts. Bashed them good and proper.

Yeah, I heard, I say.

Two of them in hospital, Wallace says. One with concussion, other one with busted ribs, busted spleen.

He counts it off on his fingers.

Wouldn't say who done it though, he says. But they would of known. For sure they would of known.

Wallace shakes his head.

They was scared is why, he says. Scared of the consequences.

I spit into the dirt.

And Saturday night, says Wallace. Saturday night they go and shoot up the town. Think they're in the wild west or something.

Yep, I say.

Whole bloody town shot up. Saw it myself. Sunday morning. Yesterday morning. All the shop windows blown out. Glass everywhere. Old Joe McLaren sitting in the barber's chair, head in his hands, display cases smashed up. All them old artefacts ruined, on the floor. I mean, that's history, that is. Local history. Garage dogs dead. Mechanic hosing down the blood. All blood and glass down the gutters. I never seen nothing like it.

Wallace shakes his head.

Jesus, he says. He starts working on his shovel. We watch the cars pass. One of them slows and stops and Bill Sparrow puts his head out the window and calls out. Wallace slides off the tray and goes over to talk to him. They talk for a while.

Hope they throw away the key, I hear Bill Sparrow say.

Wallace comes back and Bill Sparrow honks his horn and waves.

Get to work you lazy bastards, he yells.

He drives off.

Wallace sits back down with a grunt and picks up his shovel and stone.

I'll tell you what though, he says. There was plenty of men ready to string them up right there and then. Not just from round here either. Half the bloody RSL come down from Corowa with the Mayor. Mayor come to look at the war memorial. You hear about that? You hear what they did to the war memorial?

Shot the statue, didn't they? I say.

Shot off the head, says Wallace. Clean off. Digger's head. Now that's what they call sacrilege. Far as RSL's concerned, anyway. Lucky copper got them first, is what I reckon. Lucky they got them in the divvy vans quick as they did. You hear about that? Had to bring in divvy vans far as bloody Albury to take them off. Had them in lock-ups all over the place.

I heard they walked right through the town, I say. I heard nobody did nothing.

Well it took everyone by surprise, didn't it, says Wallace. You would've thought they'd have kept their heads down, wouldn't you? Shoot up the town Saturday night, come in for a drink Sunday morning. Nobody expected that. Bloody nerve of it all. Explains why the pubs were the only things they didn't shoot up.

Wallace runs his stone hard against the blade.

I mean, who do they think they are? he says. Driving up and down Main Street firing shotguns out the windows. Bloody cowboys. Bloody cowboys the lot of them.

He throws his shovel into the ground, takes a new one from the tray and leans it between his legs.

I never heard nothing like it, he says. It's a bloody disgrace. Disgrace for the town. Disgrace for all of us.

Wallace slides the shovel up and picks the dry dirt off the blade with his fingers, wiping his hand on his singlet. He gets up the oilcan.

I mean, you ever heard of anything like that? he asks me. You ever heard of anything like that happen before?

I shake my head.

Never, I say.

Wallace puts oil on the blade.

And you been around too, he says.

Wallace works on his shovel. I look at the sky.

You been up north, says Wallace. I mean, you might expect it there. Plenty of cowboys up north. But down here.

He shakes his head.

I thought we was meant to be the civilised ones, he says. Wine-making town.

Wallace jerks his finger from the blade, dropping the stone. He looks at the cut. Blood oozes out and Wallace sucks on it.

Well it just goes to show, says Wallace, finger in his mouth.

I look around for crows but there aren't any. The day is silent.

I once saw a copper shoot an aborigine out of a tree, I say. Up north.

What, dead? says Wallace. He looks at his finger and keeps sucking on it.

Nah, I say. Blackfeller was running down the street. All neked. I don't know why he was neked, but he goes and climbs up a tree. Right in the middle of town. Copper comes over and fires his gun into the air and he climbs down again. Whole town standing around watching, same as what it was like yesterday. It was a Saturday morning, small town. Everyone about.

Yeah, but that's a different thing altogether, says Wallace. That's the law.

Yeah, well, I say.

Wallace takes his finger out of his mouth and wipes it on his singlet. He reaches back for the bottle of meths and trickles some over the finger, shaking it dry. I finish my shovel and get another one.

Old feller, I say. Old blackfeller, white beard. He come down crying.

What'd he done? Wallace asks, sliding off the tray and looking around for his stone.

Don't know, I say. Caught drinking probably. That was the old days for you.

I knock the dirt off the shovel.

Tough justice back then, says Wallace.

I shrug.

Wasn't so long ago, really, I say. Old blackfeller come down bawling his eyes out. Completely neked. Copper shackled him right there, middle of town.

I reach over for the oilcan and smear oil across the blade. Wallace finds his stone and flips it in the air. He sits down, flipping the stone and catching it.

Not afraid of dealing it out up north, says Wallace. Could of used a copper like that down here yesterday.

He flips the stone and it bounces off his knuckles. He picks it up and gets back to work.

I sharpen the blade in long even strokes. Out in the yard the vines are bright with the residue of the locust spray, coating the leaves and the small hard bunches of new fruit, inlaying the bark. A kestrel passes overhead, its shadow flickering across broken surfaces.

Didn't use handcuffs on the blackfellers, I say. Used shackles and chains. Used to shackle them all up together with a long chain.

On the ankles too. All in a line, all shackled together.

Wallace laughs.

How'd you like to see them do that to Brett Clayton's mob, he says. March them up and down the street. Make them look at what they done. Make a spectacle of them.

Old feller comes down from the tree, I say. Crying, neked. Everyone standing around laughing. They was all laughing.

I plant my shovel.

Well, you break the law, says Wallace. Those days. Up north.

I look at Wallace. He is half black himself though nobody ever mentions it.

I take another shovel from the tray and knock off the dirt.

And you hear what the copper said when he went into Imperial? says Wallace. Catches Brett Clayton trying to jump the bar?

Yeah, I heard.

Has his holster unbuttoned, hand on his gun. Says, you just try me, Clayton. Just you give me an excuse.

I look closely at the shovel blade, feeling the thin juts of metal.

I heard different, I say.

Yeah? says Wallace, pausing. What you hear?

Pretty much the same thing, I say.

I take a pair of pliers out of the toolbox and start twisting off the jagged tips. A few break clean off and shoot into the air. Wallace swears and holds his hand over the side of his face. I wrench the others off, leaving the blade worse than it was before. I get out the chisel.

Well, it's all over now, says Wallace.

That's right, I say.

We can breathe easy now, says Wallace.

He plants his shovel and wipes his brow. I give the blade a good going-over and then put an edge on it with the stone. I show it to Wallace.

I don't know why you bother, he says.

We finish the shovels and sit up back of Wallace's ute. The boys come up the road. Wallace looks at his watch.

On time for bloody once, he says. He looks at his watch again. Just about on time.

The boys come up and pull shovels out of the dirt. Wallace watches them.

You two sober yet? he asks.

The boys grin.

Course, says the talker. Wasn't even hungover.

Don't bullshit me, says Wallace. You're hungover all right.

Not me, says the boy. First thing I got up, nicked one of my dad's longnecks. Drunk it. Don't feel a thing.

He looks at Wallace, scratching his sunburnt nose.

Hair of the dog, ay? says Wallace.

What's that? says the boy.

Hair of the dog, says Wallace. Hair of the dog that bit you.

He looks at the boy.

You not heard that before?

No, says the boy.

Jeez, says Wallace, turning to me. What do they teach the young people these days?

I get up to stretch my legs and go and take a piss in the vines and come back.

You was drinking was you? I ask the boy.

We was all drinking yesterday, says Wallace, wiping his hands on a rag. Boys got pissed proper this time. Could barely walk out the pub straight.

Where were you drinking? I ask.

Crown, says Wallace. Crown Sunday. Time they learned what real drinking's all about.

You should have come, Smithy, says the quiet one. We started drinking in the morning. We drank all day.

He grins at me.

It's better, says the boy. Drinking days. Better than at night. We were drinking for hours.

Spit's car comes down the highway and makes a handbrake turn into the vineyard. The wheels scream and dirt churns. Dust comes up from the side of the car and settles on it. The engine revs and the wheels spin, grinding into the ground. The car bolts forward and brakes with a high metal whine. Spit gets out and slams the door. He comes up with a lit cigarette in his mouth, a long bent line of ash hanging off it. He starts pulling the shovels out of the dirt, inspecting the blades.

I thought you were in the lock-up, says Wallace.

I was, says Spit.

He goes through the shovels and picks one. The boys stand watching him, grinning.

What's youse two looking at, says Spit.

Spit leans against the side of Wallace's ute, his back to us. He drags on his cigarette until a burst of flame shoots through the filter. He flicks the blackened butt out into the vines.

You hear about George Alister? Wallace asks him.

Who's George Alister? says Spit.

Mate of Roy's, says Wallace. Was, anyway. Dropped dead. Middle of Main Street. Sunday before last. Heart attack.

Yeah? says Spit, looking out onto the vines.

Yeah, says Wallace. Dead before he hit the ground they reckon.

He looks at Spit.

And you know what his dog did? After George Alister carks it?

Dunno, says Spit. Ate him?

Wallace laughs.

Close, he says. Pretty close to it, he says. George Alister, right. He's eating an ice-cream. When he dies. Has his heart attack and hits the ground. Anyway, dog goes and nicks the ice-cream. George Alister lying there dead, dog nicks the bloody ice-cream.

Spit lights up another cigarette.

And you know what Smithy said when I told him? asks Wallace.

No I don't, says Spit, smoking. Pray tell me what Smithy said.

Smithy says, that's dogs for you.

Is that right, says Spit.

And do you know Nora Alister? Wallace asks.

Spit shrugs.

Yeah, well she was George Alister's wife. Widow now though.

Well she would be, wouldn't she.

So I say to Smithy, I say, George Alister was Roy's mate all right, but I reckon he'll be after the widow now. Have a go at the widow.

Spit leans his head back and blows smoke rings into the air.

And you know what Smithy says? He says, that's Roy for you.

Wallace chuckles, shaking his head.

That's dogs for you and that's Roy for you.

Spit looks out at the vines. He swears and throws his shovel. It flies in an arc and hits the wire and bounces and falls among the vines. He takes out another cigarette and lights it from the first one.

You got a mortgage to pay, Spit, I say.

Yeah well fuck that too, he says.

He looks over at the boys.

And how are you two retards? he says.

The boys grin.

Wallace took us drinking, one of them says.

Wallace's whipped, says Spit, turning away.

I still got the record, says Wallace. No one's beat me yet.

That's ancient history, says Spit. Nobody counts anymore.

Roy gets out of his ute, whistling for Lucy and stretching. He comes over and looks at the shovels. Lucy bounds up and sniffs at our feet and trots off along the rows.

So you scored with this bird yet? Spit asks Roy.

What bird? says Roy, looking over a blade.

Wallace said something about some bird, says Spit.

He's talking about Nora Alister, says Wallace.

Roy takes out another shovel.

Gone to flaming Perth, hasn't she, he says. Gone to live with her sister.

So pay her a visit, says Spit. Get a few roots. She'd be gagging for it out there.

I'm not driving to bloody Perth, says Roy. Takes bloody days to drive to bloody Perth.

Take a holiday, says Spit. Do some sightseeing.

Roy examines another blade and sticks the shovel back into the ground.

Nothing to see, he says. It's all desert, isn't it?

True enough, says Spit.

Roy picks a shovel and leans on it. Wallace opens the toolbox and hands out knives to the others.

Besides, the ute would never make it, Roy says, wiping his knife on his shorts.

So take the flash car.

I'm not bloody well taking the flash car out there, says Roy. It's all unsealed roads. Ruin the paintwork.

He pulls up his shovel and goes and stands against the ute, next to Spit.

Boss been asking about you, he says quietly.

Yeah? says Spit.

Yeah, but Smithy told him you was crook.

Spit looks over his shoulder at me, cigarette in his mouth.

Cheers Dad, he says.

Yeah, but he's bound to find out, isn't he, says Roy. Whole town knows about you lot. Everyone saw it.

So? says Spit.

So he can lay you off, can't he?

Spit flicks away the cigarette, still burning.

So what? says Spit. I'll go down the river. Get some decent fishing done for once. Rather be down the river than out here with you jokers.

Wallace looks at his watch and swears. He shows me the time. He slides off the ute and takes his shovel and mattock and puts one over each shoulder.

Righteo, he says, and we go into the vines.

I am already in bed when the doorbell rings. I get up and put on my dressing-gown and go to the door. Brett Clayton is standing there, his hands in his pockets. His face is skull-like, whiskered and grey, his eyes tired, hard, without expression.

She here? he asks.

She's here, I say.

He walks past me as if I wasn't there. As if I was nothing. I follow him on weak knees.

Brett Clayton stands in the lounge room, looking around with his back to me. His clothes hang off him. He smells of stale booze and cigarette smoke.

He barks Charlotte's name into the empty room.

I hear movement and Charlotte comes out, tightening the belt of Florrie's bathrobe.

So you coming home or not, he says to her.

Charlotte's hair is down, loose strands over her shoulders.

Just give me time to pack, she says.

Brett Clayton tilts his head.

And how long's that going to take you? he asks.

Not long, she says. A little while.

Well how long? he says.

I'll be as quick as I can, she says. Can't you just have the decency to wait?

Brett Clayton folds his arms, looking down.

How about I come and pick your stuff up tomorrow, he says. I'm dead on my feet here.

Well can I get dressed at least? Charlotte snaps. Or do you want me walking through town like this?

I'm not stopping you.

Charlotte goes into her room and I can hear her rushing about. Drawers open and shut. Brett Clayton stands stock-still and straight with his back to me, staring out the back window. He takes a soft-pack of cigarettes out of his shirt pocket, shakes out a cigarette and then lets it drop back in. He puts the pack back into his pocket.

The night murmurs.

Charlotte comes out dressed in jeans and a jumper, wearing sneakers.

All right? she says.

Brett Clayton turns and walks past me, not looking at me, saying nothing. Charlotte hurries after him. I follow them to the door. As she is leaving, Charlotte turns back quickly and gives me a small wave, mouthing goodbye. Silently. The way women do. I close the door behind them.

I go into Charlotte's room and begin gathering up her things. I fold her clothes and put them into her suitcase. In the bathroom I put her lipsticks and bottles and tiny cases of make-up into a small zippered bag. Pink and fragrant dust puffs out of the bag when I open it. It sticks to my dressing-gown and falls onto my slippers and onto the tiles. I put the bag into the suitcase with her lotions and shampoos. Her hairbrush is sitting by the sink. I pick it up and look at it. There are strands of her hair wrapped among the bristles, long and honey-coloured. For a moment I think of keeping the hairbrush. I put it into the suitcase.

Back in Charlotte's room which is not her room, not any longer, I look through the drawers and the wardrobe, making sure that nothing has been left behind. Florrie's bathrobe is lying spread over the bed. It smells of Charlotte. I fold it and pack it with her things. I close the suitcase and put it by the front door.

Going into the lounge room, I catch a glimpse of myself in the mirror over the mantelpiece, my ruined old face, my bare head, my white hair.

The room is silent and empty.

I go outside for a piss. It is a moonless night and cloud cover hides the stars. It is still and quiet and dark. I can't see a thing in front of me.

I go to bed and wake before dawn.

AND I remember the sisters and the wind, the black kids all in a row and the nuns' robes flapping, wrapping about them, their hands holding down wimples and fussing about the children's clothes, white shirts washed and pressed and stiff, bright in the sun and a strange thing to see in that place of sand and dust, and us lived so long in sully that it was deep to our pores. And we had never imagined such a thing as cleanliness, not until this day. So there was excitement among us. And while the nuns straightened collars and pulled at the grey starched shorts and smoothed the sharp seams, the piccanins could not help but all of them smile wide and they were restless, looking out into the distance, shifting about and beginning to wander until the nuns shoved them into place again, the children holding paper Empire Flags in their hands, the flags drawn in crayon, the red sand skewing about us. We were waiting for the wife of the Protector of Aboriginals.

And the wife of the Protector of Aboriginals arrived in a big black car, the driver in a khaki uniform, a large peaked hat and a face without expression, the kids all waving their flags as the car approached, the nuns rushing to the car, the driver opening the door, the sisters holding their hands together and bent over saying, oh no ma'am it will ruin your clothes, and the driver standing watching. And he shut the door and a window was wound down and Sister Bernard stood in front of the smiling children, conducting with her hands. And they sang God Save the Queen and Land of Hope and Glory and For She's a Jolly Good Fellow and clapping came from inside the car, the driver slumped back in his seat with his cap over his eyes and the wind growing stronger. And Sister Bernard went to the open window and talked to the woman inside and she turned and gestured to me and I stood on the footboard and looked into the car and I saw the wife of the Protector of Aboriginals.

And the wife of the Protector of Aboriginals was all in white, a satin sash around her waist, an embroidered blouse high in the collar and patterned with tiny beads of mother-of-pearl that glistened in the slanting light and there were all colours in their sheen. And her hair was soft and short and in waves, a golden colour, catching the sun, shining in the sun. And on the shaded seat next to her an ivory fan lay open, filigreed, and a hat swathed in tulle. And she wore lace gloves and I felt them as she took my raw and dirty hands in hers and she looked at me, smiling, and she was beautiful. And I had not expected her to be beautiful and I had never seen such things before. And her eyes looked into mine and I forgot why I was there, only her eyes, only the woman, and it seemed that she was looking right into me and her saying, he's shy, her eyes amused, Sister Bernard prodding me and I remembered and I sang and I sang to the woman and when I had finished she touched my face and she kissed me gently on the forehead and her hands stayed on my cheeks and still looking into my eyes, the whole time looking into my eyes. And I was looking into hers.

You're an angel, she said. A true angel.

So there was that. I can remember that.

And the driver turning and hard-faced under the peak of his cap, pointing across the desert saying, it looks like a dust storm is coming ma'am, the wife of the Protector of Aboriginals turning to look.

A dust storm? she said, the driver nodding.

If we leave now I think we can make it into town.

And the woman looked out at the red and dirty sky and the milky spread of the horizon, the disc of the sun dangerous, a smouldering, seething ember. And the sky above a restless grey, us in uncanny shadow like dusk, the wind heaving and twisting plumes borne from the earth and towering. And she looked back through the open window at the piccanins and a gust of sand splattered hard against the car, the metal sounding, the children's flags tearing about in the wind, the paper crackling.

And the wife of the Protector of Aboriginals took her hands from my face and she moved back into the dim of the car, the driver saying, we need to get into town before it hits or we're stuck here until it passes. They can last for days, ma'am. I've seen it before. And as the driver leaned over to wind up the window I looked at the woman one last time, the car starting with a roar and a belch of dark smoke, the wheels kicking up a hail of sand over the line of black children who coughed and rubbed their eyes and they waved their Empire Flags as the car jerked forward and onto the road. And they waved their flags as the car sped into the distance and they kept waving their flags until long after it was gone.

The sand coiling, the nuns moving frantically as the dust storm drew nearer, marching the piccanins off in double time, bolting the doors and closing the shutters and I felt a pull at my arm, the sister saying, the cow, bring in the cow. And I walked out towards the paddock and as the wind roared and as the dust swirled thick around me I was struck by sand and twigs and stones, stinging my face and my bare skin and eyes. And as I wandered blind in the angry ruddy gloom, the cow bell sounding its low and hollow noise somewhere in the raging distance, I could think only of the woman, only of her, and of her clothes and finery, her hair soft and gold in the sun, the fan and hat beside her and the feel of lace on my cheeks, the touch of her lips and her eyes looking into mine and her beauty, and at that moment I did not care, I did not care whether I lived or died.

And what I want to know is, was that wrong? Was it all wrong? Has it all been wrong from the start?

JEREMY CHAMBERS was born in 1974 and lives in Melbourne. *The Vintage and the Gleaning* was inspired by summers spent working as a vineyard labourer whilst at school and university.

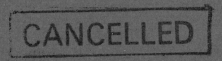